BLOOD SPORT

A BREED THRILLER

CAMERON CURTIS

INKUBATOR
BOOKS

Published by Inkubator Books
www.inkubatorbooks.com

Copyright © 2024 by Cameron Curtis

Cameron Curtis has asserted his right to be identified as the author of this work.

ISBN (eBook): 978-1-83756-405-7
ISBN (Paperback): 978-1-83756-406-4

BLOOD SPORT is a work of fiction. People, places, events, and situations are the product of the author's imagination. Any resemblance to actual persons, living or dead is entirely coincidental.

No part of this book may be reproduced, stored in any retrieval system, or transmitted by any means without the prior written permission of the publisher.

For that girl.

"War has no eyes."

-Swahili proverb

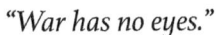

"We sleep soundly in our beds because rough men stand ready in the night to visit violence on those who would do us harm."

-Winston Churchill

1

SATURDAY, 1730 HRS, ST. CROIX – GUEST BUNGALOW

unters. The two men standing at the edge of the forest are Umbali. Shaved bald. Not one of them under six feet tall. Bare-chested, they wear plain trousers folded above their ankles or cut above their knees. Shoulders and biceps like those of professional athletes. Pectorals like panels of lacquered mahogany. They carry wooden lances with sharp metal tips. Leather scabbards are slung on straps looped over one shoulder and across the chest. Razor-sharp machetes.

I'm standing in the living room of our company-supplied bungalow, peering out of the window, the plain flowered curtain peeled back an inch. The Umbali are staring at the house, but it feels like they're staring at me.

My phone buzzes. It's Dan Mercer, CEO of Long Rifle Consultants. He's paying for this visit to Wambesa. Twenty thousand dollars a day, all expenses paid. My job is to evaluate security at a mine operated by Cobalt Resources Africa. A French company referred to by its acronym, COBRA.

"How's it coming, Breed?"

"It's not looking good. The French have their heads in the sand. The army has a company garrison where they need a battalion. The cobalt mine is protected by slack local security and two squads of French. At the top of the hill, French Village looks like a Parisian suburb overlooking an African slum. It's protected by local security and two more squads of French. St. Croix is buzzing with talk that Marien Tombaye has returned. The French ambassador is in denial. The way the townspeople look at us, I think the rumor's true."

Two more Umbali join their friends. Now four pairs of eyes are staring at me.

"Enwright doesn't agree with that assessment," Mercer tells me.

I glance at Nancy Enwright. Twenty-something, blond, bright-eyed Ivy Leaguer. Former Georgia Bureau of Investigation, now a Long Rifle associate. She's sitting on the sofa, her laptop open on the coffee table. Tapping away, working on our report. She's trading emails with Mercer, too.

"She says COBRA's security is adequate to the task," Mercer says.

I turn back to the window. My stomach is fluttering. "Is that for real or COBRA consumption?"

"Breed, let's not overreact. Keep the French mellow."

"Any mellower and they'll be comatose."

"Give Enwright room to write the first draft. She'll get the tone right. You can edit the details."

"Dan, I have to go."

I disconnect the call before Mercer can say anything else. Stab another key, wait for the phone to connect.

Drue Powell, head of security for the US consulate, answers. "What's up?"

"There are some big motherfuckers with eyes on us. Umbali. We need to circle up with the consul general."

"He just got back from the Presidential Palace. Spoke with President Mumbaye personally."

"What's the Big Kahuna say?"

"He says there is nothing to worry about. But when Consul General Wolfe left, he saw Mumbaye's aides emptying the wall safes. Stuffing suitcases full of cash. Like they were getting out of Dodge."

"Pick us up at the bungalow. Tell Wolfe to call the French ambassador. Have him alert the army."

"You think Tombaye is back?"

"Don't you?"

"Give me ten minutes."

"Do you have heat?"

"Some."

"Bring it."

I disconnect the call. Two more Umbali have joined the group. Six hunters are studying the bungalow. The sun is going down, and their hulking shapes are blending into the shadows. Their eyes are feral in the twilight.

The H&K Mark 23 feels solid under my waistband. Two spare magazines in my right hip pocket. An eight-inch Cold Steel OSS in its scabbard is velcroed upside down under my right jeans leg.

Somewhat comforting, but only somewhat. If six giants rush me at close quarters with spears and machetes, that Mark 23 won't stop them all.

I walk to the kitchen and lock the back door. Shove the dining table against it.

Enwright looks up from her writing. "What are you doing?"

"Getting ready for company."

The girl's confused. She's carrying a Glock 19 in a crossdraw holster. I have no idea how much it's worth. In a fight, she might shoot *me*.

The bungalow has two bedrooms. First, I look inside Enwright's, then mine. No way I can cover both bedroom windows from the living room. I close the bedroom doors. Block them with wing chairs dragged from the living room set.

"What company? Talk to me, Breed."

Like I have time to flap gums. I look left and right. The living room has one big window that overlooks St. Croix, and another that overlooks the forest. I part the front curtains an inch and peek out.

Two Umbali.

Where have the other four gone?

I call Powell. He speaks before I identify myself. "I'm on my way," he says.

"When you get here, leave the motor running. We'll come to you."

"That bad?"

"What's going on?" Enwright is on the edge of freaking out.

I address Powell. "It could be worse. Be ready for anything."

Powell is a hard guy, a former Navy SEAL. We never worked together in Afghanistan, knew each other by reputation. He's solid, doesn't need to have things spelled out. I disconnect, squeeze the phone into my pocket, draw the Mark 23.

There's a crash. An Umbali comes through the forest-side window. Breaks the glass with the butt of his spear, hacks the curtains aside with his machete. I raise the Mark 23 and shoot him three times in the chest. Tight group, I could cover it with a Kennedy half. He staggers under the hammer blows from .45-caliber hollow points. I fire a fourth round into his face and the slug punches him backward out of the house.

Enwright screams. Crash of breaking glass from inside her bedroom. An Umbali coming through her window.

Two Umbali burst through the kitchen door and sweep the dining table aside. Another smashes through Enwright's bedroom door and struggles to get over the wing chair.

I shoot the first man from the kitchen twice in the chest and twice in the face. He staggers back and falls against the man behind him. I pivot from the hips, shoot the man from the bedroom in the chest. He's staggered by the hit, but his momentum carries him into me. He swings his machete, right-handed. I cross my wrists and catch his descending forearm. The impact knocks our weapons from our grasp. Let me tell you, we were gripping them like they owed us money. That was the violence of the impact. The giant's momentum carries him into me and we both go down. With a crash, we collapse the coffee table. Enwright scrambles out of the way.

The Umbali's forearm is slippery. I'm overwhelmed by the stink of his body odor, a mix of rancid sweat and some kind of cloying sweet oil. I jerk the Cold Steel from my leg sheath and stab him in the side. Jerk the blade free, stab him a second time in the belly. Nonlethal wounds. I can't get the angle under his breastbone. Put my left hand on his face, shove his head back, stab him in the side of the neck.

Can't waste more time on this guy. I'm half on my back. The second Umbali from the kitchen pushes his friend's dead body aside. Cocks his arm, hurls his lance at me. I snatch Enwright's laptop from the wreckage of the coffee table, use it as a shield. The metal tip of the lance pierces the base of the laptop and punches through its keyboard. The weapon's lighter than I thought—one or two pounds. I cast the laptop and lance aside, pick up the Mark 23. Shoot the Umbali in the chest before he can draw his machete. One, two, three times. The rounds club him to the floor.

Roll to one side. The Umbali I stabbed jerks the Cold Steel from his neck. A fountain of blood spurts from the hole. I must have cut an artery. I squeeze the muzzle of the Mark 23 against his cheek, not hard enough to push the pistol out of battery. Pull the trigger. His head jerks and a hole blossoms in his face. Blood, brains and bits of skull splatter the sofa.

The Mark 23's slide locks back. I stagger to my feet. Drop the mag, reload, decock. There's a screech of tires outside. The black shadow of a vehicle is visible through the translucent curtain. Powell's rocked up in the consulate's four-door Impala.

Grab Enwright by the arm, jerk the front door open. Shove her toward the car, look left. The slum at the bottom of the hill is an endless field of shadowy structures. Scattered lights from kerosene lamps and candles. Barely half the dwellings, only those closest to St. Croix, have electricity. The forest's tree line is south of the slum, a hundred and fifty yards downhill. The sun's behind the line of trees, the sky pink with the sunset.

Two figures are running toward us with great loping strides, machetes slung, lances gripped in their right hands. I raise the Mark 23.

Powell steps from behind the wheel, an M4 carbine in his hands. "Get in the car."

I pull open the right rear passenger door. Push Enwright into the vehicle. Powell raises the M4 and opens fire. Two- and three-round bursts. One figure tumbles. The second hurls his lance with all his strength. The rear window deflects the steel tip. The lance caroms off the plexiglass and flies into the air, vibrating from the impact. The shaft lands on its butt in the driveway.

Powell shifts his aim and fires another double-tap. The Umbali staggers, sprawls in the dirt, and struggles to one knee. Powell fires again and the man crumples.

The Impala's an old car. Think it's been discontinued. The Wambesa consulate doesn't rate a big budget. I get in the front passenger seat, and Powell climbs in behind the wheel. He positions the M4 between his left leg and the door. Extra protection if a round should come through the metal. If he leaves the car, his weapon goes with him.

Powell glances at me. "You cut?"

The belly of my shirt is wet, black with blood. So are my right hand and forearm. "Not mine."

Both my Mark 23 and Cold Steel have textured, adhesive grips. A weapon can be hard to hold onto—bloody hands can make the grip as slippery as a wet bar of soap. That I didn't notice the blood meant the custom grips did their job.

More gunfire, a bit distant. I look up the hill toward French Village, the colonial-style enclave of the privileged French. Diplomatic officers from the French embassy. COBRA managers, engineers and their families. Businessmen. Muzzle flashes light up the hillside. Tombaye must be attacking the French army posted at the Village.

"The consul general wants us to pick up his wife," Powell says.

I jerk my chin toward French Village. "Up there?"

The SEAL nods.

"We can only save one of them."

The consul general has to be the priority. Powell grunts, throws the car into gear, and roars downhill toward St. Croix.

My heart is still pounding, but I can feel the adrenaline wearing off. I shove the Mark 23 under my waistband. What the hell possessed me to come to Wambesa?

2

TWO DAYS AGO - GEORGETOWN

Dan Mercer wore expensive business suits well. We sat together on the patio at Gilbert's, my favorite restaurant. It's halfway between Georgetown and Foggy Bottom, a long way from Afghanistan. Back then, Mercer and I had shared quarters at a forward operating base. Winters in the Hindu Kush froze our asses off. Huddled in sleeping bags to keep warm, we emerged from the cocoons only long enough to piss into empty whisky bottles. We lined them up on the floor under our bunks.

I preferred casual sport shirts, slacks and deck shoes. But I got it—Long Rifle Consultants' CEO needed to look the part. Especially if he was to navigate corporate boardrooms. Or mix and mingle at DC parties, nurturing his political ambitions.

"Are you good, Breed?"

Tracy, our waitress, gave me a generous smile. A rosy-cheeked Georgetown student, she wore a blue-and-white striped apron and tight white trousers. She's served me at Gilbert's for two years, joined me for an occasional romp.

"We're fine, Tracy."

Mercer watched the girl walk to the next table. Admired the sway of her hips. "Fifty thousand, plus expenses."

"What are you talking about?"

"Three days' work on-site, two days' travel."

"What's the work?"

The CEO adjusted the line of his tie. "Ever hear of Wambesa?"

"No."

"No reason you should have. It's a small country in central Africa. Four hundred miles north of the equator, just south of the Sahel. Fifty miles long east to west, forty wide. Scrubland in the north, mountainous and light canopy forest in the south. Wambesa is a former French colony. The French granted it independence in 1965, but maintained a presence. In exchange for independence, Wambesa signed treaties that allow the French to buy the country's natural resources at a quarter of the market price."

"Sounds like a great trade."

"It has been, for both sides. The population did not have much of an educated class. No professionals qualified to run a country. So the French gave them political independence and supplied the administrative and managerial class. Kept a French army garrison in-country, trained and supervised the police force."

"In short, nothing changed."

"They wore a fig leaf of democracy. Not all the middle class were happy with the arrangement, but they never caused real trouble."

Mercer sipped his wine. I took a pull of my beer. Waited for him to continue.

"One boy made a nuisance of himself. His name was

Marien Tombaye. A skinny, intellectual product of the middle class. His parents were shopkeepers. They sent him to Paris to study. Not the best school. He absorbed all kinds of newfangled notions of democracy. When he came back, he became a real shit-disturber. Agitated for the French to leave. He argued that if the people of Wambesa took over administrative and managerial posts, they might fail, but they would learn more quickly."

"Failing to success. It's been done."

"The boy organized demonstrations. He was arrested. The authorities held him for months. After his release, he crossed the border into Marawi, a neighboring country. There, he joined Boko Haram. He received military training and fought everywhere across the Sahel. He formed ties to al-Qaeda and was active across North Africa and the Middle East. That skinny look of his is deceptive. He built a reputation as a tough fighter and a charismatic leader."

Mercer shifted in his seat and leaned forward. "There have been rumors in Wambesa that Marien Tombaye intends to return."

"Any truth to them?"

"The French on the ground say no. Remy Bernard, the French ambassador, says everything is quiet in Wambesa. Management of COBRA's mining operation says the same."

"What do they mine?"

"Cobalt. It's necessary for the batteries that run electric vehicles. COBRA runs a huge open-pit mine in the north of the country, halfway between the airport and the capital. The management and engineers are French. French families and other expats live in a place called French Village. By all accounts, it's very nice. Built on a hill south of St. Croix. The

French army provides security. They're supported by local police."

"As far as I know, most of the cobalt on the planet is mined in the Congo."

"It is, but Wambesa easily yields enough to be economical. The Chinese own all the cobalt mines in the Congo. COBRA is one of the few operations in Africa owned by western interests. In any event, senior management in Paris is concerned. There have been a series of coups right across the Sahel."

"That business in Niger was particularly messy."

"Messy and embarrassing. The French have been kicked out of one country after another. COBRA head office in Paris is nervous. They want an independent assessment of security in Wambesa."

"And you want *me* to provide it."

"There's probably nothing to worry about. Tombaye is a rabble-rouser. It's unlikely he'll find a receptive audience. If he does, the French authorities will expel him. He's simply not a credible threat. You'll go over there and write a reassuring report."

"What if *I'm* not reassured?"

"Can you imagine one man returning after years of exile and starting a revolution?"

I looked across the crowded patio at Tracy. She met my gaze and smiled. I didn't need to go to Africa. Shacking up with Tracy for a long weekend would suit me fine.

"It depends," I told Mercer. "You and I have been trained to do exactly that."

Special Forces are trained to develop indigenous partner forces. Organize and train resistance movements, conduct asymmetrical warfare. Until I transferred to First Special

Forces Operational Detachment – Delta, unconventional warfare was my stock in trade. Mercer knew that. Maybe he was spending too much time away from the field.

I tried to imagine Dan Mercer running for Congress. Wondered what kind of a representative he would make.

"Yes," Mercer agreed. "But this is different."

"Is it?" I took a breath, made a decision. "Okay, I'll do it for twenty thousand a day."

"A hundred grand? That's nuts."

"No, it isn't. I don't like Africa."

"We seem to have settled on fifteen."

"No, twenty. I don't really need this right now."

"You're a pirate. Okay, come by the office tomorrow. We'll have your ticket ready."

We finished our drinks, paid the tab, and went our separate ways. I drove back to my apartment to pack.

If Mercer was willing to pay me a hundred thousand, Long Rifle was making a million.

I PACKED my duffel and one Samsonite case. It's the only legal way to get a firearm onto a plane. I unloaded my Mark 23 and placed it in a locked box. Three twelve-round magazines, a fifty-round box of .45-caliber hollow points, and my Cold Steel OSS went into a separate container. All the weapons were packed into the Samsonite luggage. I would check everything at the front desk. No muss, no fuss.

My phone buzzed, the caller ID flashed.

Anya Stein. Early thirties, the youngest assistant director in the CIA. Attractive and elegant, she was a Harvard grad, a former FBI field agent, and a CIA field operative. Stein came from money. Her grandfather gifted the Stein Center to Harvard. Her father is a private equity king on Wall Street.

Stein took calculated risks with her career. Accepted missions with CIA Ground Branch that had high payoffs but were potentially career-limiting. She pulled them off and advanced quickly. She was politically adept, but more than willing to do the dirty work. I can vouch for that. I do a lot of work for her department, and I've seen her in action. Over the years, we've become friends. I'm cautious about using that word to describe our relationship. There's an attraction between us that we recognize but have never acted on.

"What's up, Stein?"

"I need a date."

"For God's sake, Stein. Find some rich Harvard boy to go out with."

"Not *that* kind of date. I'm going to a symposium in London. We're going to discuss how to win the Ukraine war."

"Hate to break it to you, Stein. The Ukraine war is all over but the crying."

"So what? Come with me. You were at the Battle of Debaltseve. You can ad-lib a speech, then we can escape and check out London. It'll be a blast."

"That's when it becomes *that* kind of date."

"Not exactly. Come on. Save me from terminal boredom."

A tempting offer. "When?"

"Tomorrow night. We'll go for a long weekend."

I sat down on my bed. "I would, but I can't. Long Rifle is sending me to Africa."

"Africa? Whatever for?"

"To assess security at a French cobalt mine. Explain to

the board in Paris why one skinny nationalist can't take it over."

"Can't he?"

"I won't know till I get there."

"I'll double whatever Dan Mercer is paying you."

Now *that* was a bit much for an hour talk to a bunch of losers. "I can't, Stein. Mercer and I shook on it."

"Africa is a mess. The French are getting kicked out everyplace. Local politicians are telling European diplomats to fuck off, right to their faces."

"What do you know about a guy named Marien Tombaye?"

Stein hesitated. "He's heavy. Cut his teeth in Boko Haram. Joined al-Qaeda. He's fought everywhere. Highly respected, but they kicked him out."

"Why would they kick him out?"

"He's an independent thinker. He looks like a shrimp, but he's smart and charismatic. People started following him."

"Isn't that a good thing?"

"Not if he has his own agenda. He's Muslim, but he doesn't buy into their extreme ideology. The leadership figured he was using *them* instead of the other way around."

I didn't like where that was going. "What *was* his agenda?"

"He's a nationalist, Breed. He doesn't care much about religion one way or another."

Stein was telling me everything I didn't want to hear. I didn't want to ask her for help, not after I turned her down, but I needed to know. "*Is* he in Wambesa?"

For five full seconds, Stein hesitated. "Yes," she said at last. "Breed, there's no telling what might happen over there."

I laid back, stared at the ceiling. "What can happen in two days?"

Long Rifle Consultants' head office occupied a quiet, leafy corner of Falls Church. I parked my car, checked in at reception, and took an elevator to Mercer's office on the top floor.

"You look well rested," Mercer observed. He stood, picked up an envelope from his desk and handed it to me. "Here are your tickets. Your team flies out tonight."

My ears pricked. "You didn't say anything about a team."

"It's a small team. You're team lead."

I lowered myself into a chair in front of his desk. "You'd better tell me about it."

"Long Rifle is growing. We need to construct a portfolio of professionals with a wide range of skills."

Dan Mercer had let that two-thousand-dollar suit go to his head. He definitely had Congress on his mind.

"We're going to send an associate with you. She graduated Duke, and she's former Georgia Bureau of Investigation." Mercer leaned forward and activated an intercom. "Ask Enwright to come in."

The door opened and a pretty twenty-something stepped into the office. Shoulder-length blond hair and a conservative blue dress. Her skirt was cut three inches above the knee. A walking Colgate commercial.

"Breed, this is Nancy Enwright. She's going to tag along, help out any way she can."

"Nice to meet you." Enwright extended her hand. Her grip was firm and dry. She probably worked out an hour every day.

"Nancy, Breed is our top operator. You're lucky to be on his team. Learn all you can."

"I will, Dan. Breed, I'm looking forward to working with you."

Enwright's accent sounded too much like Scarlett O'Hara's for my taste. I don't remember what I said. Hoped it was more than a grunt.

"You two can meet at the airport," Mercer said. "Nancy, thanks for coming in."

The girl flashed her bright smile and closed the door behind her.

"How much field experience does she have?" I asked.

"Not a lot," Mercer admitted. "She has to get it somewhere. Breed, this is a milk run. Get her to write the first draft. She can do all the stuff you hate to do."

"We have to assume Marien Tombaye is in-country. What if something happens over there?"

"What if he is? What can one man do? Nothing's going to happen. You are there to calm down the French. That's all."

That weekend in London with Stein was starting to look pretty good.

"Just tell Enwright to stay out of the way."

3

SATURDAY, 1000 HRS - ARBOIS INTERNATIONAL AIRPORT

The arrival hall at Arbois airport was busy. The flight wasn't full, but there were enough passengers to keep things interesting. Mostly French mining company employees and their families. Aid workers. Doctors Without Borders. There was no luggage carousel. Enwright and I picked our checked baggage out of a pile that had been unceremoniously dumped into a corner of the hall.

My duffel was there, and my Samsonite case. The locks on the case had not been tampered with. Enwright had *two* Samsonite cases. We joined a line of passengers waiting to cross customs and immigration.

Dan Mercer had told me we'd be met. I wouldn't have to bribe my way through customs. We were conscious I'd be carrying a weapon into the country. Mercer had arranged for the consulate to deal with the customs officers before our arrival.

"Breed."

Former operators had a *look*. You could spot them a mile

away. Drue Powell was fit. Special operations is an athletic event. I tried to work out twice a day whether I was on a job or not. Physical training—PT—wasn't something you left behind. He wore a casual shirt with the sleeves rolled up to his elbows. His forearms were decorated with blue-black tats. The shirt was untucked—certainly concealed a pistol, appendix carry. Kühl tactical pants and Oakley desert boots. Finally, a bent-bill ball cap.

Apart from my choice of boot-cut Levi's, we were dressed alike.

I returned his wave, noting that he was meeting us on the wrong side of the customs desk.

Powell greeted me with a handshake. "Breed, I'm Drue Powell. Head of security at the consulate. I've heard a lot about you."

"I've heard a lot about *you*."

"It appears you've heard a lot about each other," Nancy Enwright said.

Powell gave her an amused look. Flashed a broad smile.

"This is Nancy Enwright," I said. "Works for Long Rifle. She's with me."

The SEAL took off his ball cap. Held it in both hands over his belt buckle with mock humility. "Pleased to make your acquaintance. I've liaised with Wambesa Customs and Immigration. Come with me."

Powell led the way past the lineup. Took us to a closed wooden gate. A Wambesa Customs and Immigration officer sat next to it. He wore a limp khaki uniform and a peaked cap with a red band. The man nodded to Powell and opened the gate for us.

Outside was a small parking lot. The sidewalk and driveway in front of the terminal was crammed with local merchants. Their wares were laid out on colorful mats spread on the ground. Women sat on aluminum cans, baskets of fruit and vegetables arrayed in front of them.

The consulate car, a black Impala, was parked close to the terminal. A Wambesa policeman in a khaki uniform stood next to it. Powell rolled up a couple of greenbacks and handed them to the cop. The man tipped his hat and walked away.

"Can't leave the car five minutes, it'll be stripped before you get back."

Powell opened the trunk and helped us load our bags. I stretched and looked around.

The terminal building was like other airport terminals, only smaller. There was a control tower at one end, overlooking the runway. Glassed-in, with a 360-degree view.

To the north, a flat savanna of shrubs stretched as far as the eye could see. All the way to the Sahel. The south was beautiful. I'd studied the terrain from the air as the plane descended. A green mountain range, covered by woodland forest, where the trees formed a light canopy. In the middle of the range towered a massive cone that looked like a volcano. From where we stood, I could see the entire north slope.

The north slope of the mountain was covered by dense woodland. As one's eye swept over the foothills toward the plains, the character of the savanna changed. The trees became less dense. Farther north, the savanna consisted of scattered trees and shrubs.

"Do you like Mount Wambesa?" Powell asked.

"Yes," I said. "Did they name the mountain after the country?"

"No. They named the country after the mountain."

The terrain all along the highway looked like more of the same. Scrubland to the north, forest to the south. I sucked a breath. The air smelled of heat and the sweet scent of fruit and vegetables. A bead of sweat crawled down my spine, settled at the small of my back. Soaked into the fabric of my shirt.

I got in the front passenger seat next to Powell. Enwright climbed in back.

Powell turned on the air conditioner and pulled onto the highway. An asphalt two-lane, laid down on flat ground, it stretched east and west. Traffic was light. Old, beat-up cars, flatbed trucks, and overloaded buses.

We passed a turnoff to the south with a large wooden billboard displaying an African landscape. Forest green letters announced:

MACHWEO

"Not many Americans in-country," Powell said. "About five miles down that road is Machweo, a safari ranch run by Troy Grady."

"Does he get much business?"

"Not yet. He's only just starting operations." Powell scratched his head. "You know, I think he might have had some inside information."

"How so?"

"He bought up the land before the international airport was constructed. Located the ranch at a commercially strategic spot. Built the ranch house at the same time as the airport."

The Impala hit a rut in the road that bounced us to the roof. Enwright grunted.

"We'll hit a concrete stretch soon," Powell promised. "Around the mine, and closer to St. Croix. I reckon they'll resurface the stretch to the airport soon enough. Don't know about the road to Machweo. They'll probably wait for Grady to pay for that."

I scanned the terrain with an infantryman's eye. The ground was flat, but deceptively so. Here and there, we crossed rickety wooden bridges. The bridges spanned wadis that ran north-south. I pointed the feature out to Powell.

"The northern half of the country is scrub and grassland," the SEAL said. "During rainy season, streams and rivers swell from the mountains to the south. These wadis turn into creeks. This time of year, the only two rivers worth mentioning are the Wambesa that runs through St. Croix, and the Lokola that runs between the airport and the Lokola border. Both wind their way northwest through the savanna, empty into Lake Chad."

"Are those *elephants*?" Enwright sounded like a child visiting the zoo.

I looked past Powell toward Mount Wambesa. The tree line was a mile away. There, a small herd of elephants was drifting slowly along the edge of the forest. The big bull was leading the way, followed by mothers and babies.

"That they are," Powell said. "Elephants are an endangered species. Most of the ones that remain are south of the equator, but we get a few here. The locals tell me there was a time elephants would wander into town."

"They seem brave." Enwright spoke barely above a whisper.

"They're looking for water," Powell said. "The bull knows where the watering hole is, in the forest. They can move more quickly in the open. They must be hot and thirsty."

"Will we see other wild animals?" Enwright sounded hopeful.

"There are lions about. They're territorial and curious. I've only glimpsed them. Out for a hike, heard them growl and cough. Seen them move in the high grass. There's a food chain. Jackals, hyenas. In the forest, you get a lot of monkeys and baboons. It's Africa, man."

There was a distinct bump as the Impala left the asphalt road and carried on over the smooth concrete highway. Fifteen miles on, we passed a traffic-light-controlled crossroads. Big signs in French announced that the COBRA mine was to the right, and the COBRA processing mill was to the left. There were two parallel roads that ran north-south. One was a concrete tarmac for light traffic. The other was a wide gravel track for heavy trucks.

Powell stopped at the light while a massive Caterpillar 793F mining truck crossed the highway. "The trucks carry ore from the mine to the processing mill. The final product is carried by train to the coast. East or west depends on shipping and the final destination."

I watched the Caterpillar rumble south. Waves of heat blurred the image of the forest. Mount Wambesa towered high above the landscape. "It's not that far away, is it?"

"No, it isn't. Five miles."

The light changed, and Powell continued toward town.

We approached another crossroads. Half a mile to the right was a group of wooden buildings surrounded by what looked like a chain-link fence. The sign next to the road read:

COMPAGNIE C
110 RÉGIMENT D'INFANTERIE

ARMÉE DE TERRE

"Are they up to strength?" I asked Powell.

"Yes. Four platoons, a hundred and thirty men. They have a tank destroyer platoon attached. Armor and a big gun are supposed to intimidate terrorists."

"Do they mount active sweeps?"

Powell shook his head. Gestured toward the forested flank of Mount Wambesa. "The French garrison is sized to protect the mine and French Village. That's it. It would take a significant national army to control that territory. An army Wambesa hasn't got."

"Neither do the French. I doubt they could deploy more than a brigade anywhere in the world at this point."

"And *we* would have to fly them out and back."

There was no traffic light at the crossroads. The highway continued straight west toward St. Croix. The southern road curved south-by-west, and Powell turned onto it.

"Where does *this* lead?"

"Up to French Village. That's the name of the suburb where all the expatriates live." Powell pointed to a low hill rising ahead of us. "The most privileged French live at the top. Corporate engineers and operations professionals live further down. My place is on the east side, halfway up. You guys share a guest bungalow on the north side, about the same level."

French Village was on a ridge that stretched north from Mount Wambesa. The cool green forest that covered the slope of the mountain folded around French Village.

We passed clean, freshly painted bungalows and two-story houses. Simple by western standards, but luxurious in Wambesa. There were gardens and flower beds. Green lawns and verandas. The French citizens of St. Croix lived comfortably.

Powell stopped in the driveway of a low bungalow. Popped the trunk and helped us carry our bags to the front door. The lawn was freshly mowed, the shrubbery neatly pruned. I stood at the threshold. Sniffed the fresh-cut grass, listened to the busy clicking of cicadas.

"It's a two-bedroom," he said. Fished in his pocket for keys and unlocked the front door. Set our luggage in the front sitting room, handed me the fob. Two keys on a single ring. One for me, another for Enwright.

The bungalow was simple, but it was clean and modern. There was a living room set. A sofa, coffee table and wing chairs. Floor lamps, side tables and table lamps. Paintings on the walls of African landscapes. The living room was an atrium leading to three chambers. There was a large kitchen that doubled as a dining area. To the left were two bedrooms, one bigger than the other. Each room had a box air conditioner set in a window, and a ceiling fan.

I was more interested in the layout of the town around us. I peeled one key off the ring and handed Enwright the fob. Stepped outside.

Looking uphill, I could see larger, more luxurious homes. Downhill, off to the north, I could see the compact community of St. Croix. It wasn't hard to see what looked like an administrative square, with business establishments and dwellings spreading out from the center.

Turning west, I could see a huge, sprawling mat of corrugated iron roofs covering metal and wooden walls. There wasn't a single piece of metal that wasn't being eaten by rust. Clotheslines were strung between the shanties, festooned with shabby clothing of every color of the rainbow. The slum extended to the west, toward the Marawi border.

The Wambesa River that Powell mentioned ran south to north. Born high on Mount Wambesa, it skirted French Village and ran past the slum and St. Croix. South of the slum, both sides of the river were crowded by forest. The tree line immediately below our bungalow was a hundred and fifty yards away.

"The Wambesa River is the life of St. Croix," Powell said. "St. Croix is downriver from the slum, where the river water is unsafe. It's way too polluted. Clean water from upriver to the slum is pumped into underground reservoirs that serve St. Croix and French Village."

"What's the plan?" I asked.

Powell checked his watch. "We're meeting the COBRA general manager after lunch. He'll take us out to see the mine."

"Let's go into town. I want to speak with the consul general."

"Don't you want to unpack?"

I shook my head. "Time for that later."

4

SATURDAY, 1200 HRS - ST. CROIX

Powell drove down the hill by a different road than the one we took from the French army camp.

"There are three roads that lead to French Village. The one we took on the way in, this one, and another on the southeast slope. This one runs by the Wambesa River."

When we got to the bottom of the hill, Powell turned right. We drove along the riverbank. It wasn't much of a river. Rocky banks, and a riverbed of smooth stones and sand. Water bubbled and splashed its way north. Laughing, half-naked children played in the water. Women washed clothing.

Fifty yards to the right, low on the slope of the hill, stood a whitewashed church. The structure sported a steeple and a cross that announced to all that over there stood a house of God. There were three smaller buildings next to it. I assumed one of them was the rectory.

Five minutes, and we left the slum behind and entered St. Croix. I supposed that, technically, the slum was part of St. Croix. There was no way I could reconcile the chaotic poverty of that slum with the organized streets of the town, or the Edwardian privilege of French Village.

Powell nosed the Impala into a public square. "This is the Vieux Carré."

I'd expected a bustling city. Instead, the streets were deserted, and it was only noon. The sun, directly overhead, shone bright on gray cobblestones. The square was devoid of shadows. A man looked at us furtively, hurried across the square.

The south side was occupied by a massive, three-story colonial structure surrounded by a stone wall. There was a front gate large enough for a car to pass, with a guardhouse. Khaki-clad Wambesa police armed with Belgian FAL rifles stood guard. They carried the weapons at sling arms.

"That's the Presidential Palace," Powell said.

The palace had a kind of decadent elegance. The architecture was grand—it would have been beautiful were it not so dilapidated.

Powell parked the car in front of a sturdy, two-story building on the west side of the square. A brass plate on the front wall proclaimed it to be the Consulate of the United States of America.

The SEAL pointed to another two-story building on the east side. "That's the Hôtel de Ville," he said. "The city hall."

Behind the city hall was another low building. Behind that was a tall metal tower four or five stories high. "They keep the radio and television stations next to city hall?"

"Small country," Powell said. "Centralized administration and communications."

A black, khaki-clad security guard came forward to meet us. Powell greeted him. "Watch the car, Edouard."

The man's eyes darted left and right. He was looking

everywhere except at Powell. "I cannot, Drue. I am going home."

"Home? It's only noon."

"I am not well."

The man hurried across the square and disappeared around the corner of a building. Enwright squinted after him. "That's odd."

"Come on."

Powell went to the front door of the consulate. The door handle was heavy bronze, on an ornate fleur-de-lys escutcheon. Mounted on the adjacent wall was a large combination lock—a keypad set into a sturdy plate. He stabbed four digits in quick succession. The deadbolt disengaged and Powell pulled the door open.

We stepped into a foyer. There was a central corridor with two offices on the left and two on the right. A heavy reception desk guarded the entrance. Behind it sat an equally heavy black woman in a floral print dress. She flashed a broad smile.

"Hi, Margot," Powell said. "Where's Consul General Wolfe?"

"Not here, Drue. He went to the La Salle."

"Where is everybody?" Powell asked. "Edouard went home early."

"I don't know," Margot said. "Annette did not come to work at all."

Powell led us back to the car, climbed behind the wheel. "The La Salle is the best hotel in St. Croix. It's on the other side of town, our favorite watering hole."

The town wasn't deserted, but traffic was light, and there were few people about. We drove a few minutes down the main street. The La Salle was as big as the Presidential

Palace, and every bit as run-down.

Powell parked in front, looked for a policeman or security guard to watch the vehicle. None were to be found.

"Fuck it." The SEAL was losing patience. "It's not my car."

He led us up the front steps of the hotel and pushed open the butterfly doors. We entered the lobby. There was no one at the front desk. To the left was another set of wooden doors with windows of frosted glass. "LA SALLE" was written across the glass in glittering gold letters.

I'd seen bigger, but the La Salle was a large bar. The malachite bartop was a good thirty feet long, though only about fifteen feet was backed by shelves of colored liquor. Ceiling fans rotated lazily. The air conditioners at the windows were off. The room was too big to chill economically.

There were five men in the bar. The bartender was an elderly black man. He wore black trousers, a white long-sleeved shirt, and a red bow tie. His hair and mustache were salted gray.

At a corner table, a man sat slumped over a bottle of whisky. He was about sixty, wearing a limp white dress shirt open at the collar. His gaze was focused on the far wall, but he was not in a stupor. Rather, he was concentrating with a supreme effort of will. I had no idea what he was focusing on.

The last three men sat at a circular table about ten feet from the bar. Close enough to refresh their drinks, far enough away to be private. Two men wore white suits. One had the frame and looks of Gary Cooper. The other was terribly average, with dark hair and a brush mustache. The third man was younger than the others. Clean-shaven, in tan trousers and a white dress shirt. He wore a tie, but the knot had been loosened, and his collar button was undone. The men were speaking earnestly, nursing gin and tonics.

Powell led us to their table and performed the necessary introductions. The Gary Cooper lookalike was Oren Wolfe, the US consul general. His mustached friend was Remy Bernard, the French ambassador. The younger man was Thierry Laurent, general manager of the COBRA mine.

All three men stood to greet Enwright. The French kissed her hand the way a lady's hand should be kissed—by touching their noses to the back, so as not to soil her skin with their lips. Not to be outdone, Enwright greeted them in perfect French. I wondered if her French carried a Southern plantation accent.

"We all know why you are here, Mr. Breed." Bernard offered us seats at their table. "Join us for a drink. Thierry will show you the mine this afternoon."

"Charles." Laurent signaled the bartender. "Please bring our guests whatever they want."

"The town seems rather quiet," I said. "Is it always like this?"

"It is Saturday," Bernard said. "The weekend is always so."

What the ambassador said was true of most cities, but by noon I'd expect more activity. "People seem rather tense. Did all your staff at the French embassy come to work this morning?"

Bernard loosened his collar with a pudgy index finger. "As a matter of fact, no. There may be an illness in the air."

Charles set a G&T on the table in front of Enwright. Pints of cold beer for myself and Powell.

"There must be." I looked Oren Wolfe in the eye. "One of

the American consulate staff didn't come in this morning, and their security guard has gone home early."

"Ha!" The man drinking in the corner slapped the palm of his hand flat against the table and turned to stare at us. It was an unfocused stare that seemed to take in our entire table with his peripheral vision. "Marien is back. Marien Tombaye."

Laurent snorted. "Don't be silly, Bröer."

"It's all over town," Bröer said. "Hell, it's all over the country."

The man's face was shiny with sweat. It was running down the side of his face and soaking his collar. It was hot in the room, but not that hot. His face was flushed from the alcohol. I could detect the distinctive scent of sweat and whisky in the air. That face had once been handsome—broad Teutonic face, with a long nose, blue eyes, and sensuous lips. Time, the blows of life, and alcohol had creased his features like a crumpled sheet of paper.

"How do you know he's back?" I asked.

"These people are ignorant and superstitious," Bernard said. "They have nothing better to do than exchange fanciful rumors."

Bröer seemed ready to hurl an insult at the ambassador, but I led him back to my question. "So, how can you be sure?" I asked again.

"These people aren't as ignorant as you think," Bröer said. "The women in the vegetable market sold him food."

"How many did you speak to?" Laurent's tone was challenging.

"All of them. You should do your own shopping, mate."

"Really! All of the women sold vegetables to one man? They will rot before he can eat them."

Bröer took a long pull of whisky.

I kept my tone gentle. "That's a lot of vegetables."

The man met my eyes, and for an instant he was perfectly lucid. "He had a lot of men."

In that heat, a cold hand clutched the back of my neck. Bröer's eyes lost focus again. He turned away and took another swig of whisky.

Bröer slammed the bottle down on the table. "White men *and* Umbali."

A vintage brass telephone was mounted on the wall behind the bar. It looked like it had been installed when the hotel was constructed. Charles plucked the handset from its cradle and dialed a number.

"What are Umbali?" I asked.

"A mountain tribe," Wolfe said. "Hunters."

Powell feigned insouciance. "Biggest motherfuckers you ever did see. Meanest rats in the shithouse."

I looked around the table. "It makes sense. Tombaye wouldn't come back alone if he wanted to cause trouble. He would bring men with him."

"You believe this?" Bernard's tone was incredulous. He gestured toward Bröer. "It's nothing more than gossip."

Powell looked at the consul general. "Sir, it's a data point. It could be significant."

"You old fool." Visibly angry, Laurent turned on Bröer. "These people tell you stories, and you embellish them."

Bröer slapped his palm against the table a second time. Turned on Laurent. "I embellish nothing! Marien is back, and we shall see who is the fool."

"Get out!" Laurent shook with rage. "Drunken sop. You peddle these stories, yet you cannot remember your own name."

Bröer got to his feet. It took an effort, and his left leg wobbled. "Damn you. You know who he's come for, don't you? All you bastard frogs. He won't throw you out of Wambesa. He'll roll you out. In coffins!"

Laurent shot to his feet and took a step toward Bröer so as to throw the man out himself. Bröer, every bit as angry, lurched toward him. His left leg gave way and he pitched forward. I stepped between the two men and caught him.

Bröer struggled against my grip. "Let me go!"

Motion on my right. From the direction of the door, a woman rushed me like a freight train. I raised my arm to ward her off.

"*Bâtard! Laissez-le partir!*"

I don't speak French, but the girl's voice told me everything I needed to know. That, and the impact as she stiff-armed me and shoved me off Bröer.

"Wait a minute, I was helping him."

"Get away!" The girl switched to English when she heard me speak. "You bastards. Grown men. You abuse one who cannot protect himself."

"Cecile." Charles sought to calm the girl down. "Mr. Breed speaks the truth. Mr. Bröer was going to fall, and Mr. Breed supported him."

The girl was clutching Bröer protectively. Stroking his shoulder like she might a cat. For his part, the man had retreated into his alcoholic fog. Breathing heavily, the girl and I stared at each other. I could hear her heart pounding, the blood singing in her veins.

Cecile was the most beautiful girl I'd ever seen. The most beautiful girl I'd ever see. Late twenties. Smooth, brown skin. Wavy black hair that curled where it fell to her shoulders. Hazel eyes, all pupil. A straight nose over a wide, sensuous mouth. I was stunned—in that moment, I knew her image would stay with me forever.

She hesitated. Her eyes, fixed on me, changed from anger to recognition. Then, from recognition, they changed to fear. She didn't like what she was feeling. She wanted out.

"Come with me, Rijk." Cecile tore her gaze away from mine. She put her arm around Bröer's shoulder and helped him from the bar.

"That is what happens when you give these blacks a little education." Laurent sniffed. "Ungrateful wretches."

"A diploma of specialized studies from Pierre and Marie Curie is more than a little, *mon ami*." Bernard's tone was dry.

I got up, went to the bar, and asked Charles for another beer. "Who was that woman?" I asked.

Charles poured my beer. "That was Dr. Cecile Abimbola," he said. "She operates the clinic at the base of French Village."

"At the base? I haven't seen anything that looks like a clinic."

"I understand your bungalow is on the north slope of the hill, sir. The clinic is at the bottom of the west slope. There is a mission there, also. The priest is Father Ducasse. He and Cecile make a good team. She cares for our bodies, he cares for our souls."

"Ah. I've seen the church. The clinic must be one of the buildings next to it." I switched back to my main topic of interest. "Dr. Abimbola is very protective of Rijk Bröer."

Charles accepted my payment and slipped the money into his till. "Cecile is a very special girl, sir. She cares for birds with broken wings."

"Bröer's a lucky man."

"So are you, sir." Charles smiled with the look of bartenders the world over who keep many secrets.

"You're a good man, Charles."

I drained my beer and returned to the group at the table.

Powell straightened in his chair. "Gentlemen, it might be a good idea to visit the mine."

Laurent composed himself. "I suppose it would. Let me call my car."

The COBRA manager spoke into his phone, laid it flat on the table. "Five minutes," he announced. "Who is coming?"

Wolfe and Bernard excused themselves. Laurent said, "The ambassador and consul general can ride with me. We'll let them off at the Vieux Carré."

We stepped outside into the midday heat. Laurent's vehicle, a black Range Rover Evoque, pulled up in front of the La Salle. We mounted the consulate Impala and followed the COBRA vehicle.

"That's the French embassy across the street from us," Powell said.

"What's that painted on the side?" I asked.

"It wasn't there an hour ago."

Someone had scrawled a message in black spray paint on the embassy wall. The graffiti, in foot-high letters, read:

MARIEN EST DE RETOUR

I twisted in my seat and looked at Enwright. "What does it say?"

"It says Marien has returned."

5

SATURDAY, 1400 HRS, COBRA – THE MINE

COBRA was a clump of low buildings, a mirage that rippled in waves of heat. Three Caterpillar trucks passed us going the other way, carrying ore to the processing plant. I'd seen the open-pit mine from the air. Viewed from above, the quarry was a hideous, amoebic wound torn into the earth.

French regular army manned the front gate. Two sentries in woodland camouflage, wearing red berets. They carried H&K 416s slung over their shoulders. Excellent weapons, reliable on full automatic. The French had adopted the 416s to replace their older FAMAS assault rifles. I never liked the FAMAS. The 416, on the other hand, had found a following in the US special operations community.

The soldiers closed the main gate behind our cars.

We dismounted in front of the administration building. Laurent pointed to the razor-wire fence. "The wire is new," he said. "It is meant to keep people out, not in. Workers on our rolls enter and leave through the gates. Illegals—women and children from the slums—come to steal. They used to come early and leave early, before our security force deployed. They would scrabble on the slopes, fill their sacks with cobalt."

COBRA security police drove pickup trucks in opposite directions around the perimeter.

"Can they steal enough like that to make a difference?" Enwright asked.

"In the Congo, twenty to thirty percent of the cobalt sold to the Chinese is purchased from illegals. Such theft is material. The Chinese have not taken this theft seriously because Chinese mines are vertically integrated. They are owned by the same companies that own the battery and automobile manufacturers. We are *not* vertically integrated. We cannot afford to tolerate theft."

A soldier stepped from the administrative building and approached. He didn't look old enough to shave. Blond and trim, he was dressed in a camouflage field uniform and beret. Too bad—I expected a *kepi blanc*. He wore the two black bars of a French lieutenant.

The boy carried a sidearm in a snapped-down holster. French army, it would be either a Glock 19 or a USP. I couldn't tell which. The lieutenant wouldn't clear it before a bad guy killed him.

"May I introduce Lieutenant Marcel Sauve," Laurent said. "This week, he commands our security detachment."

I shook Sauve's hand. "This week?"

"Yes." The lieutenant spoke like he was used to delivering rehearsed briefings. "We have a company in this country. Four rifle platoons. Each platoon provides security one week a month."

The kid couldn't have been a day over twenty-three. How did I come up with that figure? Left school at eighteen, college, a year's training. The French system wouldn't be exactly like ours, but all armies are close enough.

"Where's your platoon sergeant?" Meeting Sauve didn't tell me much about the French unit guarding the mine. Only that its officer was green. The real leader of the platoon would be its noncommissioned officer. The NCO would have more experience than Sauve, and *he* would have the pulse of the men.

"He is at French Village," Sauve said. "Half my platoon is here, and half on the hill."

"Are you full strength?"

"Yes. Thirty-two in all."

"You comfortable with that deployment?"

"Of course. There is nothing happening. The remainder of the company remains in camp with *Capitaine* Ferenc. Should trouble arise, we can be reinforced in minutes."

Great. Two squads at each location, and no unity of command.

"Come." Laurent raised his arm in an expansive gesture. "It is a short walk to the edge of the mine."

We followed the general manager across the parched field. I looked through the windows of an air-conditioned building as we passed. Inside, half a dozen French soldiers sat around a table. Smoking and playing cards.

Stick figures picked their way around the lip of the mine. As we got closer, I could see they were local blacks dressed in sweat-stained clothes. A roar of noise issued from the pit, growing steadily in volume as we approached. Close to the lip, I was able to discriminate different sounds. Male and female voices shouting. Hammers and pickaxes clinking against rock.

The stick figures climbed down into the pit. Our little group stopped at the edge, and I sucked a breath of hot, dusty air.

COBRA's mine was a crater at least two miles in diameter. A circle of hell. There must have been fifteen thousand human beings toiling in that pit. Crammed together, they scrabbled at the loose rock with their bare hands, picked the cobalt, and stuffed it into sacks. Some of the men hacked at the slope with picks, dislodging rock for others to sift for ore.

My eyes swept across the crater. Layered terraces divided the mine into different levels. If not for those terraces, the mine would be indistinguishable from a meteor strike.

"The mine is divided into twelve sectors like the points of a clock face," Laurent said. "Twelve o'clock is due north. Each sector has different levels. The levels are numbered—one for the surface, and the numbers increase the deeper one goes."

The workers swarmed over the mine like ants. That was what COBRA was—an inverted anthill. It was an ant *pit*.

"Deeper levels yield higher grades of ore," Laurent said. "Underground shafts yield the highest grades. Workers are paid more the deeper they work."

"How much are they paid?" Enwright asked.

"A dollar a day at the surface," Laurent said. "As much as five dollars for underground labor."

Workers carried sacks of ore to the surface on their backs. Each of those sacks must have weighed at least sixty pounds. Some were closer to a hundred. When they reached the top, the sacks were collected and their contents loaded into the Caterpillars.

"Are those children?" Nancy Enwright was aghast.

"Some, yes." Laurent frowned. "We try not to employ anyone too young because they cannot carry the load. Also, it takes a degree of physical strength to wield a pickaxe. The Chinese in the Congo do not care. They use the little ones to sift for cobalt and to fill the sacks for older children and adults to carry."

"That's horrible."

Enwright had good reason to be outraged.

"We are doing them a favor." Laurent further loosened his tie. "They beg us for work. Understand, some of these families are six months behind on their rent. They cannot pay for food, let alone rent, if their children do not work."

"Where do these people live?" I asked.

"In the town, west of St. Croix."

He meant the slum. "How do they get here?"

"They walk."

"Walk? It's six miles."

Laurent shrugged. "They wake up early."

The thought of walking two hours to work and two hours back appalled me. In Mexico, sweatshops provided buses to transport their slaves. The *maquiladoras* employed women, many underage. They assembled goods that satisfied America's consumer appetite. Enwright fumed.

A tremble shifted the earth beneath my feet. A cry rose up from the pit, and a siren sounded. Laurent looked exasperated. "*Merde*. It is a landslide."

The general manager spoke into his phone. Once the man on the other end had briefed him, he disconnected the call. "Landslide in Section 4-12. Below us and to the right. We cannot see it from here."

Laurent looked relieved that we couldn't see the accident.

A white van roared up and stopped at the lip of the crater. Rescue workers carrying shovels piled out of the vehicle and descended ladders into the pit.

"The landslide has covered a number of miners. Our rescue crews are digging them out."

Enwright looked toward the pit. "Women and children?"

I hoped she wouldn't try to go into the mine. She was upset enough.

"How many?" Powell asked.

"We don't know. It depends on how big the landslide was, and how many levels it affected."

"It can affect more than one?"

"Of course. If the landslide is small, it affects one level. If it is large and the upper level gives way, the weight of the rockfall can collapse a second and even a third level, each collapse bigger than the one above." Laurent caught himself as though he had said too much.

"How often do you get these slides?" I asked.

COBRA didn't arrange this accident for our benefit. If it *was* a coincidence, these slides *must* be frequent occurrences. Judging from the nature of the terrain, I wouldn't be surprised.

Laurent shrugged. "I do not have that data at my fingertips. Landslides on the surface are not so serious. We are generally able to save the victims. If an underground tunnel collapses, rescue is much more difficult."

The general manager's evasiveness convinced me I was right. These accidents were business as usual.

The landslides and exploitive work conditions were disturbing. "Do you have labor unrest?"

How happy could people be, watching family and friends being buried alive every day?

"No. I have said this before, Breed. The people beg for work. If we were not here, our people would starve."

"Do you believe him?" I asked Powell. Eyes focused on the road, the SEAL drove us back to our bungalow.

"It's not the whole story."

"What *is* the whole story?" Enwright's tone was demanding.

"It's obvious there are more landslides and cave-ins than Laurent lets on. How many? We can't tell without data. Why should he keep data? Why keep records that can raise questions down the road? It's a cash business. COBRA pays their workers cash for the loads they carry out. The company makes cash payments to the crippled and the families of the dead. I've heard a few things."

"Like what?"

"COBRA has an unofficial insurance program. If men are killed in an accident, Laurent pays cash to the families. Part of the cash comes from COBRA, part of the cash comes from reducing the day's payments to all the workers in the mine."

"For God's sake."

"He's right—the locals *need* the work. So they don't complain. What are they going to do, form a union? Let's be honest. If the odd worker or bereaved family member steps out of line, it's easy enough for COBRA to employ heavies to sort things out."

"I don't think this country has changed in a hundred and fifty years." Enwright's voice dripped bitterness.

I didn't disagree with Enwright, but my mission was to

evaluate security. I didn't like what I saw. "The army detachment isn't fit for purpose."

"I reckon they need at least a battalion to conduct active sweeps," Powell said. "A brigade would be better."

"France can't spare a brigade for Wambesa."

"Wait a minute." Enwright leaned forward in the back seat. "The adequacy of their force depends on the nature of the threat they face."

"Yes, it does," I said. "It's clear Tombaye's back, and we have intel that he is accompanied by white soldiers and Umbali."

"You believe Bröer? He's a drunk. That's not intel, it's a hallucination."

"*Somebody* graffitized the French embassy."

"Marien Tombaye's one man. We don't have evidence he has an army."

"I think it's prudent to prepare for the worst case."

Powell pulled up in front of our bungalow and let us out. "I'll see you tomorrow," he said. "If you need anything, you have my number."

"Where are you off to?"

"I'm going to check in with the consul general."

I unlocked the front door. Enwright and I went inside and carried our luggage to our rooms.

The first thing I did was unpack my Mark 23 and Cold Steel. I rolled up my right jeans leg and, hilt-down, velcroed the Cold Steel scabbard to the outside of my calf. Then I opened the lockbox and slapped a magazine into the Mark 23. I drew back the slide, charged the weapon, and decocked it. I opened the box of .45s and took out a single round. Dropped the mag and snicked the loose round into it. Finally, I seated the magazine firmly in the pistol's grip.

That gave me thirteen rounds in the pistol. I slipped it under my waistband and tugged my shirt down. Took the remaining two magazines and squeezed them into my hip pocket. Satisfied, I went back into the living room.

Enwright was already there, seated in the middle of the sofa. She had a laptop open on the coffee table and was tapping away.

I went to the front window and peered out. Swept the view of St. Croix to the north, the slum and river to the northwest, the forest immediately west of the hill. I wasn't comfortable. The situation in Wambesa stank to high heaven.

Stein had told me Marien Tombaye was in Wambesa, so that wasn't a surprise. More troubling was the tense atmosphere in St. Croix. It was obvious the townspeople were more aware of danger than the French. Bernard and Laurent weren't comfortable, but they didn't want to rock the boat. Oren Wolfe had the same attitude.

The only question was—when would Wambesa explode?

I turned away from the window. Enwright was wearing a paper-thin cotton cardigan open down the front. Under the left flap, she wore a Glock 17 in a cross-draw holster. The pistol grip was in full view.

"Keep that weapon out of sight," I said. "Do you know how to use it?"

"Of course."

"Ever shoot anybody with it?"

"No."

"Ever been shot at?"

"No."

Great. Pistols are the most dangerous firearms to be

around. Especially in the hands of the inexperienced. A rifle is three feet long, a Glock 19 is seven inches. Many idiots have no clue where their pistol is pointing. One year I remember, the US army suffered ninety-eight training fatalities. One guy got run over by a tank. Forty were killed by handguns. I had no idea how qualified Enwright was to carry a pistol. "I wish you'd leave it in your luggage."

"No."

6

SATURDAY, 1800 HRS - CROSSROADS

That's how I've come to be in Wambesa, having just killed four Umbali tribesmen who tried to retire me. Powell guides the Impala down the hill toward the slum. The rattle of gunfire from French Village grows in intensity.

"The consul general must hear that racket," Powell says.

"Has he served?"

"I don't think so." Powell reaches for his phone, stabs a speed dial. He holds the phone to his ear. After a minute, he gives up. "I'm getting voicemail. Wolfe must be calling in the cavalry."

"Bernard is calling the cavalry. The French army is right next door. I don't think the US will get us any help until this is over."

We pass the little white church. Next to it, the rectory. Next to that, the clinic. For the briefest moment, I think of my encounter with Cecile Abimbola.

Darkness comes quickly in Africa. Twilight doesn't linger as it does in Europe or America. They don't call it "the dark continent" for nothing. This is not a land of ambiguity. Good and evil are not abstractions. If the concepts are vague in your mind when you arrive, they will be concrete by the time you leave. My fingers stray to the butt of the Mark 23.

There's a roaring whoosh, followed by a shattering explosion. A fireball from behind the hill reaches for the sky.

Powell and I exchange glances. We both know the sound of an anti-tank rocket when we hear it. A second later, another whoosh, another explosion.

"That's the crossroads," Powell says.

"Let's see what's going on."

Enwright chokes. "Why aren't you going in the *other* direction?"

"We need to see what we're up against."

Powell speeds past the turnoff into St. Croix. Kills his headlights, races down the highway. In the distance, flames light up the sky. The sound of small-arms fire echoes from the flank of the hill.

The flames are shooting thirty feet high. The crossroads is barely a quarter of a mile away. Powell slows and pulls off the road, guides the Impala into a copse of trees. He opens the door, gets out, and reaches into the rear passenger compartment. On the floor, at Enwright's feet, is a load-bearing vest with six spare thirty-round magazines of five-five-six. They're velcroed in two vertical columns down the front. Powell shrugs on the vest and zips it to his sternum. Shoulders the M4.

I open the passenger door and get out. Poke my head in the back. "Wait here," I tell Enwright. "We won't be long."

Together, Powell and I run down the side of the highway. We stay off the tarmac, keeping as close as possible to the dusty trees at the foot of the hill. The flames and the volume of gunfire guide us. The closer we get to the battle, the brighter the flames and the louder the sound of gunshots.

When we're two hundred yards from the crossroads, I signal Powell to get down. Throw myself to the ground. Powell pitches onto his belly. He's a little bit further off the ground than I am because he's lying on a vest full of M4 magazines.

Directly ahead of us is a French AMX-10RC tank destroyer. The French like to call it a light tank, but that's a pretension. As far as I'm concerned, it's equivalent to one of our Stryker infantry carrier vehicles with a 105mm gun mounted on it. Neither is tracked. They run on wheels, which makes them armored cars. Excellent for cities, roads and firm ground. Terrible for off-road combat. The French gave a ton of them to the Ukrainians. All the wheeled vehicles bogged down in the mud of the Ukrainian steppes. They were cut to pieces by Russian drones and artillery.

The tank destroyer is burning fiercely. A terrible gash has been opened up in its side armor. The turret hatches are open, and flames are shooting through them like blowtorches. The blackened bodies of French tankers are propped in the hatches. They're standing upright in the rush of flames. Oily black smoke curls skyward from the engine compartment.

Behind the burning tank destroyer are four five-ton cargo trucks. The cargo beds are covered with olive drab canvas. The last truck in the column is engulfed in flames. The driver's cab has ceased to exist. The rocket struck the engine compartment, exploded, and immolated the driver and the man in the passenger seat.

A hundred yards away, to our right, a group of men are lighting up the column with automatic weapons fire. Two multipurpose machine guns with a distinctive noise. Russian 7.62mm PKMs. The other weapons are smaller. Not AK-47s. No one can mistake the sound of *that* rifle. These are 5.45mm AK-74s. Lighter ammunition, higher velocity, the kind that creates devastating wounds.

It's a line ambush, laid at the exact point the army column turned onto the highway to town. The support element knocked out the tank destroyer and the rearmost truck. The remaining vehicles were trapped in the middle. The PKMs lit up the trucks. Soldiers were sitting in two rows along the sides of the cargo beds. The half with their backs to the ambush were killed outright. The PKM bullets passed straight through the bodies of their first victims. Went on to kill or wound soldiers sitting on the other side.

The French are gamely returning fire. The troopers who survived the initial attack bailed out of the trucks and took cover behind the wheels and engine blocks of the remaining vehicles. Officers and NCOs bark commands. The men crawl into the ditch next to the road.

"No, no, no," Powell mutters.

The French are on the X. In an ambush, everyone who sits on the X dies. All the features in the kill zone have been pre-sighted. You have to get off the X.

I put my hand on Powell's arm. "Wait here."

Flat on my belly, I snake my way toward the firefight. I stay off the highway, move toward the line of the ambush. Tombaye's people know what they're doing.

Tombaye will have placed the support element in line, with the PKMs on either side. Next to those, he'll have security elements to prevent the escape of the targets from the kill zone. Prevent rescue by relief units. In the middle, he'll have placed his assault element.

I'm not looking to engage his assault element. His security element will be close to me, and I might be able to pick him off. From there, I can learn more.

Fifteen yards ahead of me, I see a shadowy figure kneeling behind a bush. Rifle to his shoulder, firing at the trucks. I change direction so as to come up behind him. Reach for my calf. Curse when I realize I dropped my Cold Steel at the bungalow. I draw my Mark 23 and approach the flank guard from behind.

Almost all the surviving French have taken cover in the ditch. It makes some sense, because soft-skin vehicles provide no cover unless you are behind an engine block or an axle. It's the wrong move, because they are still on the X, and every feature on the X has been pre-sighted.

There's a terrible series of explosions. Antipersonnel mines set to cover the ditch explode and send sprays of shrapnel into the bodies of the French. The screams of the wounded are bloodcurdling.

Tombaye makes his move. The men of the assault element rise from their positions and charge the trucks. The PKMs cease fire.

Now's my chance. I step forward, press the muzzle of the Mark 23 against the flank guard's head, and pull the trigger. A single shot, and he pitches onto what's left of his face. I shoot him again in the back of the head.

I look around. No one noticed the killing, they are too focused on the ambush. I decock my Mark 23 and shove it under my waistband. Relieve the dead man of his AK-74. Roll him over and pull off his load-bearing vest. Its pouches are loaded with six banana magazines and two hand grenades.

Not much left of his face. The two shots didn't exactly blow it off, but the exit wounds left gaping cavities. His left cheek is gone, the exit wound is a hole the size of a coffee mug. The explosive cavitation shoved his left eye aside, so it's staring forty-five degrees away from his right eye. The other bullet exited his mouth. The upper lip and teeth are mostly intact, but his lower lip, teeth and jaw are gone. It never ceases to amaze me how much a man's face is like a rubber Halloween mask. It's easily distorted by the force of objects blowing through it. A man's features are determined by the bone structure of his skull. Without that support, his face melts.

In the light of the flames, I pay attention. The man's features are important. He's not black. He looks North African. Tombaye recruited a cadre *before* he returned to Wambesa. Brought them with him. How many? I'd guess somewhere between thirty and fifty. From what I see here, closer to fifty.

The cadre and the remaining French are engaging at close quarters. It doesn't take a genius to figure out who's winning. I drag the corpse into the trees and conceal it as best I can.

Fall to my belly, cradle the AK-74 in my arms, crawl farther to the support element. This is what snipers do. The movies make people think that all snipers do is kill people from long distances with scoped rifles. We do that, but I'd say most of our job is intelligence gathering. Careful observation, note-taking, sneaking in and out to file a report. Much of our training consists of honing our memory and powers of observation.

Case in point. The next pair of cadre I encounter are a rocket team. They're armed with Kornet anti-tank guided missiles. This was the team that took out the tank destroyer. Those ATGMs are Russian. Just like the AK-74s.

I could kill these men, but that's not why I'm studying the ambush. I crawl another ten yards, come upon the first PKM team. Two men. The support element will be the same on the other side.

The volume of shooting has died down. I glance to my right and freeze.

Shadowy figures are standing in a long line, staring at the column of trucks. The roaring flames throw their features into ghastly relief. I shrink backward into the tree line and count the Umbali. There must be forty of them, in two straight rows. Every one of them over six feet, carrying four-foot lances and three-foot machetes slung in scabbards.

The Umbali stamp their feet in unison. They've assumed a military formation, and the stamping itself is martial. Tombaye didn't teach them that. The Umbali are hunters. Theirs is a martial culture. They march deliberately toward the column of trucks. Tombaye's cadre emerge and walk back toward their support element. Silently, I count them. Eight men in the support element, two in the security element, twenty in the assault element. A total of thirty cadre. I killed one.

A thin black man walks in the middle of the assault element. His eyeglasses are round, with metal frames. He walks with a measured step and an absolute certitude of intent. He's dressed like the others in battle fatigues. He carries a pistol in a holster, wears a load-bearing vest, and carries an AK-74.

That must be Marien Tombaye.

I continue to edge backward to Powell's position. The Umbali arrive at the column, draw their machetes, and move among the French. The screams of the wounded pierce the air. The long blades flash in the firelight. The Umbali hack at the wounded. At each upstroke, as the blades are pulled free and raised to strike again, droplets of blood glisten in the air.

Powell is waiting for me. "Let's go," I tell him.

We're far enough away from the massacre to rise to our feet. Hunched over, we run back to the Impala.

Enwright's voice is a hiss. "What kept you?"

Powell ignores her. We get in the car, and he starts the engine.

"Seventy men," I announce. "Tombaye and twenty-nine of his cadre. One man's dead. They might find him, they might not. If they do, they'll wonder where his weapons have gone. Arab in ethnicity, though not necessarily Islamic radicals. Forty Umbali. The tank destroyer and rearmost truck were taken out by Kornet ATGMs. The support element had two general-purpose PKMs. The rest are carrying AK-74s."

I examine the AK-74 I took from the dead man. "They're brand new. Clean, well cared for. The cadre have good weapons discipline. I swear there's still packing grease on this baby."

"Now that does bespeak of a good deal of money."

"Yes indeed," I said. "The cadre is well supplied, and Tombaye trained them well. Classic infantry tactics. That shouldn't be a surprise given the people who trained *him*."

Powell speeds toward St. Croix. Already, we hear gunfire in the town. Gunfire to match the gunfire coming from French Village. I wonder how many men Tombaye has in his cadre. Thirty at the crossroads. More at French Village, more in town, more than anyone imagined. Still, he couldn't sneak into the country with a hundred men. The cadre have to be near their limit.

That's why he's drawn on the Umbali.

"How big is the Umbali tribe?" I ask. "How many Umbali hunters could be working with Tombaye?"

"No one knows much about the Umbali," Powell says. "Could easily be a couple of hundred. Could be twice that."

"Tombaye's got enough to take Wambesa. The question is, can he hold it?"

"We have to find the consul general," Powell says. "The plan is to collect the Americans and take them to the French army barracks for protection."

I jerk my thumb back in the direction of the massacre.

"There's your French army."

7

SATURDAY, 1830 HRS, ST. CROIX – LA SALLE

London and Wambesa are separated by an hour. Wambesa clocks run ahead. When I call Stein, she's wrapping up the first day of the symposium and getting ready for dinner.

"Change your mind about London, Breed?"

"Yes. Stein, I need you to get me out of here."

"Hold on, tiger. Tell me what's up."

"Tombaye's in Wambesa, but he's not alone. He came prepared with minimum—I repeat—*minimum* thirty cadre. Well-trained, well-equipped. They went into the forest, south of St. Croix. It's mountainous. I don't know the exact nature of their relationship, but Tombaye's cadre is allied with the Umbali, a mountain tribe of hunters. Very big, very deadly."

"How well-trained, how well-armed?"

"It's not a shoestring operation. Tombaye's well financed. His weapons are Russian. His cadre just wiped out the French garrison. Well over a hundred men and a tank platoon. They snuffed the tank destroyer with a Kornet

ATGM. Wiped out the infantry with PKM machine guns and AK-74s. How well-trained? The ambush was textbook. Assault element, support element, security element. Flawlessly executed."

I've got my phone's volume cranked up. Stein's voice crackles from the speaker. "He's financed by the Russians. Wagner PMC is all over the Sahel."

"It would seem so." I wasn't about to agree too quickly. "Or someone who wants us to *think* he's financed by Russia."

"Oh, you are a cynic."

"Keeps me alive. Tombaye's people are already assaulting French Village and St. Croix. They held off to wipe out the army first."

A door slams. Stein's found a private office. She's firing up her laptop.

"I can't get a rescue force to you before tomorrow, midday."

"By then it will be too late. Everyone will be dead."

"Breed, you're unkillable. Take Powell and that bimbo into the bush. If Tombaye and his goons find you, God help them."

"I heard that." Enwright does outrage well.

"How do you know about Enwright?"

Stein pauses, lowers her voice. "Breed… I'm the CIA."

Oh, for God's sake. "Stein, nobody is unkillable. What about the French?"

"What about them? They misread the situation. Fuck the French."

"What about the Americans?"

"How many are there?"

"Half a dozen." Powell doesn't take his eyes from the road. Stein's voice is still carrying from the phone.

"Powell says half a dozen. We're looking for the consul general now."

"Do your best to round them up, then go into the bush. I'll send the cavalry."

Stein disconnects the call. I shove the phone back in my pocket.

"You should listen to the lady," Powell says. "Together, we can make it."

I shake my head. "Powell, why did you join up?"

We joined to fight for people who couldn't fight for themselves.

Powell is silent. Looks sideways at me. "Oh, fuck you."

Headlights off, the Impala crawls into St. Croix. Not the route we took this morning. Windows rolled down, we hear the sound of shots. There are shouts and screams. Night has fallen, and the streetlights are on. We drive down a side street and see flames engulfing buildings on the Vieux Carré.

Powell stops the car in a side street. The American consulate is a torch. The security police at the gate to the Presidential Palace lie crumpled in a lake of blood. They have been replaced by two of Tombaye's cadre. Another two cadre stand at the entrance to the Hôtel de Ville.

"I think we can assume President Mumbaye is either dead, captured, or long gone."

"Roger that." Powell jerks his chin toward activity in the square.

Ordinary townspeople are dragging men and women from the French embassy.

Two locals hold a well-dressed Frenchman between them, force him to his knees. Two more emerge from the embassy, laughing. One is carrying a tea kettle full of boiling water. One man grabs the Frenchman by the hair and jerks his head back. Pinches his nose until he has to open his mouth to breathe. The Frenchman thrashes in their grasp. The man with the kettle leans into him, forces the spout down his victim's throat and pours.

Enwright buries her face in her arms.

A woman screams. The mob discard the Frenchman, force her to her knees in his place. The men go back inside for more boiling water. The cadre guarding the public buildings stand and watch.

"Where do we find Wolfe?" I ask.

"He might have gone looking for his wife."

"At French Village? Not if he thought you were going."

"You're right. He's not the type for suicide missions."

The men return with another kettle of boiling water. The woman sobs, begs for mercy. The other French, held prisoner, try to run but are beaten down by the crowd.

Powell wants to get away from the scene as much as I do. "We can try the La Salle," he says. "It's on the other side of town."

"Let's do it."

The most direct route to the hotel is through the square. Powell backs up and swings around to give the Vieux Carré a wide berth. Menacing groups of locals stalk the back streets.

Powell approaches the front of the La Salle. It's dark except for the bar windows, which are dimly lit.

"Let's go around back."

It won't be long before those lights bring unwanted company. Powell guides the Impala the long way around. Parks facing the back door. We dismount, carrying our rifles.

"Get in front," Powell tells Enwright. "Keep the engine running. Be ready to bolt."

We stand on either side of the back door, and I test the handle. It's not locked, opens inward. I push it open, go inside, dig the right corner. Powell follows me, nut-to-butt, digs the left. We've entered the kitchen, and it's clear.

The lights are off. We can see by the light that filters in through the windows. I wish we had NODS—night optical devices.

I lead the way into the dining room, and we repeat the procedure. Clear.

Push into the hotel lobby. There's no one at the front counter. We turn right, go into the bar.

My second time in this place, and the La Salle feels familiar. Bernard and Wolfe are sitting at the same round table near the bar. They're working the phones. Bernard is arguing with whoever is on the other end of his call. He speaks loudly, as though volume will get him what he wants. Gestures with his free hand.

Wolfe is calmer. Calmer? No, he's defeated. He speaks into his mobile like an automaton.

There's no sign of Charles. Bröer has helped himself to a bottle of whisky from the bar and is sitting at the same corner table he occupied this afternoon.

"Let's go," I tell them. "St. Croix is burning up."

Bernard turns from his phone. "The army will be here soon."

"Your army's all dead," I tell him.

The French ambassador stares at me.

Wolfe looks up. "I can't reach my wife," he says. "We were speaking, and I could hear gunfire in the background. We were cut off."

"Tombaye's cadre is attacking French Village," I tell him.

Bernard disconnects his call. "What do you mean, the army is all dead?"

"Tombaye's cadre massacred them at the crossroads. He mounted a very efficient ambush."

"*Mon dieu.* That is why I could not reach them. I have called everyone else. No one knows what is happening."

I felt like telling the little Frenchman that was *his* job. "Marien Tombaye has returned. He's got a cadre of well-armed fighters. Brought them with him from outside the country. He's rounded out that force with a few hundred Umbali. To make matters worse, the local people have gone berserk and are killing all the French they can lay their hands on."

Powell searches for the switch, turns off the lights. Then he opens the curtains and looks out. Now the exterior is more brightly lit than the interior of the bar. The Presidential Palace and the La Salle occupy opposite ends of the main street, separated by half a mile. The American consulate is burning. On the other side of the square, the mob has set fire to the French embassy.

We can see what's going on outside, but people on the street can't see us.

"I've called State," Wolfe says. "They are liaising with the French."

"Can State send a rapid deployment force?" I ask.

The consul general shakes his head. "From where? We have some advisers in Burkina Faso. Elsewhere in the Sahel. A drone base in Niger, but no combat troops. Perhaps the French can mobilize from across the border."

"France has been withdrawing from Africa," Powell tells him. "Don't hold your breath."

Bernard's manner oscillates between fear, desperation

and anger. "This has happened before," he says. "In Oran, 1962. The bastards killed a hundred people we know about. Almost five hundred went missing. In Morocco, there was a Berber uprising, and a massacre at Oued Zem."

Wolfe looks exhausted. Puts his phone down on the table. "The Egyptians burned Cairo to the ground in 1952."

"We don't need history lessons," I tell him. "We need to get out of here. Do you have a list of Americans in the country?"

Wolfe looks annoyed. "There aren't many. Yourselves and Nancy Enwright. Troy Grady and his wife, Carol. Three COBRA engineers and my wife."

The annoyance in those Gary Cooper features changes to pain. Wolfe ages ten years in an instant.

"Where are they?"

"Enwright's with you. The Gradys are at Machweo. The engineers and my wife are at French Village." Wolfe flashes Powell an accusatory look. "I can't reach Grady, the engineers, or my wife."

Powell is holding his phone to his ear. He disconnects the call, squeezes the phone back in his pocket. "Grady's phone goes straight to voicemail."

"What are we going to do?" Bernard's voice is close to a wail.

"We'll gather the Americans we can and go into the bush," I say. "Evade Tombaye until we can be extracted."

"They'll find you," Bröer says.

I thought the drunk was comatose. He raises his face to me, struggles to achieve coherence. "The Umbali are trackers. They'll find you in the bush."

"We know something about the bush," Powell says.

"Not *this* bush." Bröer grunts. "No, there's another way. If you're lucky."

The man's eyes are shiny in the dark.

"What might *that* be?" I ask.

"COBRA has a De Havilland Dash-8 at the company strip," Bröer says. "Halfway between their processing plant and St. Croix. The pilots are at French Village. Find them, and you can *fly* out. If they haven't already left. In their place, I would."

"Tombaye's assaulting the Village," I tell him.

Bröer takes a monstrous gulp of whisky straight from the bottle.

"Tombaye's got a hit list," Powell says. "He's taken out the army, the Presidential Palace, and the Hôtel de Ville. He's attacking French Village. He's following a script called Coup d'Etat 101. That means he'll seal off the country."

Wolfe's head swings around with interest. "You think those pilots are on his list?"

"Count on it," I tell him. "They'd be on mine."

A thought wriggles like a worm in the back of my brain. I feel like I'm missing something, but I don't know what it is. I'm used to thinking fast under pressure, but much of that speed comes from seeing patterns. After years of experience, different situations share common elements. They present themselves in different ways, but certain features repeat themselves. Identifying patterns saves time.

There's something disturbing about Tombaye's target deck.

"What about the international airport at Arbois?" Powell asks.

"The COBRA pilots aren't qualified to fly jets," Bröer

says. "Besides, there's nothing there. That flight Breed came in on this morning is long gone."

"There's another flight coming in at 2300 hours," Wolfe says. "I was discussing it with Dan Mercer."

I frown. "How so?"

"I wanted to know which flight you were going to be on. We had to bribe customs to let you in without searching your bags."

"Tombaye isn't stupid." Bröer musters his last reserves of coherence. "He'll take Arbois to seal off Wambesa."

"Tombaye has limited resources," I say. "He doesn't have enough to hold all the key points. He has to prioritize."

"He doesn't need to hold the strip," Powell says. "He can crater it."

"Not if he plans to use it again."

A group of townspeople passes on the street outside. They look toward the hotel, but give no sign that they have seen us in the dark interior. They turn down the main street and head toward the Presidential Palace. The flames that consume the American consulate and French embassy reach high into the sky. They're spreading to other buildings. Which way is the wind blowing? The Hôtel de Ville and Presidential Palace are at risk.

Those people are moving with a sense of purpose.

"They're going to swarm the Village," I say. "The whole town's figured out what's going on. They want a piece of the French."

Hulking figures marshal at the Vieux Carré and trot toward us. Umbali.

"We have options," I say to Powell. "Let's see if we can find those pilots."

"They are billeted in a bungalow on the east side of French Village," Bernard says.

"Alright, let's move out."

I push Wolf toward the door, turn and take Bröer by the arm. He shrugs me off. "No, I'm staying."

"Do you know what they're doing to the French in Vieux Carré?"

"Spare me the details. I can guess."

Bröer staggers around the end of the bar. Squints at the shelves. The light of the flames at Vieux Carré flickers in the reflections from the glass bottles. The effect is hypnotic. He selects a full bottle and makes his way back to his table.

"Get out of here, Breed. Marien knows all about me. He'll let me go to hell in my own way."

Powell and Wolfe have gone. I rush Bernard out of the bar.

We cross the hotel lobby, step through the dining room and kitchen. I jerk open the back door. The black Impala is a shadow. The rear lot is dark—the bulk of the hotel blocks the light from Vieux Carré. Powell and Wolfe are getting into the back seat.

Enwright's face is pale above the steering wheel. I see her eyes widen. A whiff of body odor. I turn in time to catch a machete on the receiver of the AK-74. Butt-stroke the Umbali, knock him down. The impact of the AK-74's stock against the side of the giant's head sends vibrations through my arm. The left side of his face collapses. Bloody teeth explode from his mouth and rattle against the back wall of the hotel. I reverse the weapon and shoot him in the chest.

Umbali charge around the corner.

A second Umbali uses his lance as a thrusting weapon, stabs Bernard in the side. The French ambassador gasps.

There's a whoosh like air being let out of a balloon. He wears an astonished expression as the lance skewers his chest and penetrates a lung. The Umbali jerks the lance free. I raise the AK-74 to my shoulder and shoot him in the ear.

The Umbali drops where he stands. I run to the car, reach for the handle of the passenger door. My fingers touch it as a third Umbali jumps in front of the Impala. With a grunt, he hurls his lance. It smacks into the windshield, and misses Enwright's head by an inch.

Enwright floors the gas. Hand on the door handle, I swear under my breath, let go to keep from being dragged. The car rams the giant, lifts him off his feet, and crushes him against the back wall of the hotel.

Enwright reverses the car. Body mangled, the Umbali struggles to one knee and draws his machete. Again, Enwright floors the gas. The Impala leaps forward a second time. The Umbali's chest and head are crushed into the front grille.

The engine stalls. I rush to the passenger door, jerk it open, and climb into the car. Two feet of Umbali lance are sticking through the windshield between me and Enwright. More Umbali emerge from the back door of the hotel.

"Get us out of here."

Enwright starts the engine. Throws the car into reverse. The rear wheels smoke and the car leaps backward. The Umbali hurl lances at us, but they either miss or glance off the car's skin. The Umbali draw machetes and fall upon Bernard's motionless body. The blades descend again and again.

"Go," I say. "Go, go."

The Impala surges forward, and Enwright steers us through a side street. I look back at the Umbali and what remains of Bernard. In the dim light, there is little blood to be seen. So massive are the wounds, the ambassador's corpse bled out in seconds. Bernard's body looks like a carcass that has been sectioned by a professional butcher. The layers of skin, subcutaneous fat, muscle, bone and internal cavities have been sliced through so cleanly, the corpse could illustrate a medical textbook.

Umbali sprint after us and hurl lances that glance off the Impala. Powell twists around in the back seat and takes aim with his M4. Holds his fire.

We're heading south, parallel to the main street. We drive past the back of the burning US consulate. Once we've left it behind, I signal Enwright to turn into a side street and stop.

"Where are you going?" Powell asks.

"I want to check out the square," I tell him.

We need more intel.

I saw a dark side street two blocks before the burning consulate. Jog back, step into the shadows. More townspeople are flocking to French Village. When they've passed, I turn into the street and advance to Vieux Carré. I carry the AK-74 at high ready and stay close to the wall of the building. The sound of laughter and whooping carries from the square.

When I get to the square, I drop to one knee and lean against the side of the building. The cadre at the Presidential Palace and the Hôtel de Ville are still there. Two men at each of the gates. No Umbali.

The scene in the middle of the square is horrific. A dozen French men and women were dragged from the embassy before it was set alight. The man and woman we saw tortured with boiling water and ten others. None of the French are screaming anymore. But they're not dead.

Partially clothed bodies are strewn across the square. They're still moving. The crowd—locals—are pecking at them like vultures over carrion. Men and women are being raped on the hard stone surface. When the victims are too numb to react, they are poked with torches. A naked French man and woman are prodded to their feet and forced to run around the square for the amusement of the mob.

Four cadre. Is that all? I focus my attention on the Hôtel de Ville. The palace might be more luxurious, but the radio station, television station, and the communications equipment are at the Hôtel de Ville. I look down the main street and see Umbali jogging toward the square. They've returned from the La Salle.

When the Umbali reach the Vieux Carré, they march straight to the Hôtel de Ville. One of them steps forward and addresses the cadre at the gate. French has been spoken in Wambesa for a hundred and fifty years. Some of the Umbali would have picked it up. The cadre look North African. They, too, would speak French.

One of the cadre goes into the city hall. A moment later, he returns with a figure I know. Marien Tombaye. Tombaye strides to the Umbali and they greet each other. The Umbali presents an animated report. Stoic, Tombaye listens.

I take the AK-74 and select semiautomatic. I'm separated from the pair by about a hundred and ten yards. I slide the rear leaf sight to its hundred meters detent. Draw down. If I can get a clear shot at Tombaye, I can end this right now. A difficult escape, but worth it.

The fucking Umbali is half a head taller than Tombaye and half again as broad. Not only is Tombaye a shrimp, but he's covered by a hulk. I can't get a shot.

Tombaye and the Umbali finish their conversation. The

generalissimo turns on his heel and walks back into the building. I safety my weapon and withdraw along the side street. Ignore the spectacle in the square. The crowd will go all night, or as long as the French are breathing.

Back at the car, I take a minute to pull the lance out of the windshield. Get in next to Enwright and say, "Let's go."

"What did you find out?" Powell asks.

"Not much. Tombaye's HQ is the Hôtel de Ville. They took some time to look for Bernard and Consul General Wolf at the Vieux Carré. When Tombaye arrived after wiping out the army, his men gave him the news. He put his thinking cap on and sent the Umbali to check out the bar. Remember, Tombaye grew up in St. Croix. He knows where people hang out."

"He sent the Umbali after us."

"He didn't know we were there. He knew Bröer would be there, and he guessed the consul general and Ambassador Bernard *might* be."

"How did he know Bröer would be there?"

"They know each other. You heard Bröer back at La Salle. He said Tombaye knew him and would watch him go to hell in his own way."

"Damn. He did, didn't he?"

"Yes. Sometimes people tell you exactly what you need to know. If you will but listen."

We drive in silence. Listen to the crack of gunfire coming from French Village. Pass groups of townspeople converging on the hill. High up, muzzle flashes twinkle in the night.

"What's eating you, Breed?" Powell asks.

"Wambesa. St. Croix. This place has a story, and we don't know the half of it."

8

SATURDAY, 1900 HRS, ST. CROIX – FRENCH VILLAGE

Powell's hand-drawn map shines yellow under the light of my flashlight. We've pulled off the road again and have hidden ourselves in the forest. We've watched dozens of townspeople, men and women, swarm toward French Village.

The Impala is parked outside St. Croix, at the foot of the hill. I'm not about to drive up to the Village. The car is easy to spot, and men on foot have more freedom of movement.

"There are three main roads leading up and down the hill," Powell says. "We've driven over two of them today."

"Show me."

We huddle in the car. Enwright in the driver's seat, Powell behind her. I sit next to Enwright, and Wolfe sits behind me. I hold the paper between us, and Powell points to features with his ballpoint pen. He's drawn the map with contours to give me a sense of elevation. I doubt Wolfe and Enwright see the picture the way I see it, but Powell's good. To a man who can read contour maps, his sketch conveys the relative steepness of the different slopes.

"One road comes down the west side," he says. "We took that route at lunch, on our way to St. Croix. This other road descends the northeast slope. We used that road on our way from the airport and went back down when we scoped the ambush. You can see that route leads to the crossroads. The army barracks is directly north and St. Croix is a bit west."

That's clear. We're parked directly under the hill, between the two roads.

"Check this out." Powell leans forward. "The hill isn't really a hill. It's a raised spur that pinches off from that big mountain. In other words, there are two south slopes. One southwest, and the other southeast. There's a road that curls down the southeast slope. That road forks at the bottom of the hill. One branch leads east to the COBRA processing mill, and the other heads north to the highway."

I point to a set of tracks that Powell has drawn across the top of the paper. It is interrupted by the southern spur between the hill and the mountain. "Is this a railroad?"

"It is. COBRA ships its product out by train. You can see on the map where a tunnel has been blasted right through the rock of that spur."

"What do you suggest?"

"Tombaye sent the Umbali to kill Ambassador Bernard and Consul General Wolfe. They killed Bernard and watched us drive off with Wolfe. That means Tombaye knows he has a couple of armed men running around with the US consul general. We were last seen in St. Croix. He'll expect to find us on the north side. We should skirt the base of the hill and approach from the southeast. That way, we avoid both Tombaye *and* people going up to the Village."

"I know he has at least thirty cadre. It's hard to guess how many more than that he's got."

"No more than fifty," Powell says. "When he first arrived, it would have been very hard for him to take more into the forest. He would have to enter the country undetected. Not hard, with only a company of French army to worry about. But then he would have to *sustain* his force. Not so easy."

"Let's assume he has fifty. Ten in St. Croix, ten at French Village, ten at the mine, ten on the highway and ten floating."

"That makes Tombaye resource-constrained," Powell says. "He can spare ten men to look for us, but then he can't cover all the other points on his target deck."

"Okay, we follow your route. Where are the pilots?"

Powell points to a spot on the east side of the hill. It's on the same contour level as the bungalow I share with Enwright. "The pilots are there."

"That's perfect," I say. "It's not far from your route. What about the three American engineers?"

"I don't know," Powell says.

Not good. There won't be time to look for them.

Wolfe raises his eyes to mine. "Can you find my wife?"

"We'll try," I tell him, "but don't get your hopes up. Where's your house?"

The consul general points to a contour several levels higher than the pilots' bungalow. It's on the north side, overlooking St. Croix. Of course he would live in one of the choice properties in the Village.

"Fine." I turn off the flashlight, hand Powell his map. "Enwright, you wait here with the consul general. Lie low until we get back."

I put the flashlight back in the glove compartment and climb out of the car. Nod to Powell. The SEAL knows the ground. He should lead.

WE STEP THROUGH THE FOREST, just inside the tree line adjoining the road. Tombaye's cadre have had time to commandeer vehicles from the army barracks. They rocketed the tank destroyer and one five-ton truck. The other three trucks in the column were riddled with automatic weapons fire, but there is a good chance one or two were serviceable. There would be more unguarded at the barracks. It's likely Tombaye's cadre are driving around in captured army vehicles.

Powell turns south and starts to climb a gentle slope. I form an image of the map in my mind. Soon, we'll cross the road that leads from the highway to French Village. Two hundred yards farther up the hill, he drops to one knee and signals me to stop.

We've come to the road. The SEAL advances to the hardtop, waves me forward.

It's the same path we've driven twice today. There are bodies lying on the tarmac. Men in woodland camouflage. Shot dead, no weapons. Powell picks something from the asphalt surface, tosses me a red beret. How many? Three bodies within a hundred yards. Lieutenant Sauve told us he had two squads at French Village—sixteen men.

The sound of gunfire can still be heard echoing from the top of the hill, but the volume of fire has decreased. I'm not sure how the cadre organized their attack, but these three men must have been sent down to secure this approach. They were overrun. The rest of the French, led by Sauve's platoon sergeant, are still fighting it out farther along the slope.

I follow Powell across the road and into the forest on the

other side. I'm sweating in the heat. We're engulfed by the earthy smell of vegetation.

"The cadre overran those guys." Powell speaks in a low voice, barely above a whisper. "I doubt there's much fight left in the French. Tombaye's men will have set security on these roads."

"They drew the French into an engagement on the hill," I say. "Sauve or his sergeant called the barracks for help. *Capitaine* Ferenc mobilized his company and rolled right into an ambush."

"After they cleaned up the crossroads, Tombaye sent more men to the hill. He already had men in St. Croix."

"Let's go. I want to get up there while they're busy doing... whatever it is they're doing."

We plunge back into the forest, continue around the edge of the hill till we find the southeastern path. We stay inside the tree line and move up the slope.

Powell signals me to get down and drops to his belly. I flatten myself on the ground, crawl toward him.

We lie side by side, squinting uphill. I look for the danger that caught his attention. Thirty or forty yards away, three cadre are sitting in a shallow foxhole beside the road. They've dragged loose brush and branches around themselves. A bit of concealment. They're oriented to keep watch in both directions.

They're placed to block the escape of people from French Village, and block the arrival of relief troops from the base of the hill.

Under different circumstances, I'd bypass this roadblock. But with all the shooting going on in the Village, there's little chance that shots we fire will be noticed. Tombaye has a limited number of troops at his disposal. We can whittle down his force.

I raise my rifle and line up the cadre on the left. Signal Powell to take the men on the right. A match flares, and the rightmost cadre lights up a smoke.

Thirty yards, and our targets are exposed from the waist up. I take the safety off and squeeze the trigger. Powell fires a fraction of a second after I do. The man on the left jerks and falls backward. The man on the right is hit twice and slumps where he sits.

The third man throws himself down and fires in the direction of our muzzle flashes. Bullets snap through the brush over our heads. Whacking sounds as 5.45mm rounds bury themselves in tree trunks.

Powell and I both zero in on the third man. His rifle falls silent.

I get to my feet and cross the road. Approach the foxhole from one side while Powell approaches from the other. We hold our rifles on the motionless figures. I would not put it past them to play dead, and these men have grenades. There are two on the vest I'm wearing, taken from the flank guard at the ambush.

The first man I shot is on his knees, bent over backwards with his head on the ground. I hit him in the face and throat. The man Powell shot lies on his right side. Unblinking, the white of his left eye glistens. Powell relieves the corpse of two grenades.

I roll the man in the middle over with my boot. Our rounds went into the top of his shoulders and head. His eyes are shut and he looks dead—but might not be. I point the muzzle of my AK-74 at the bridge of his nose and pull the trigger. His face splits, and his head bounces on the dirt.

Now I'm sure.

You don't want to be killed by a ghost. You see an enemy soldier on the ground, think he's dead, and move on. Then the "corpse" gets up, because he's still alive, and frags your team or shoots you in the back. A team fights *through* an enemy position. If there's an enemy soldier on the ground, *everybody* in the unit puts rounds in that guy.

Powell and I fade back into the forest and hurry up the hill. We move fast without being careless. Don't want to collide with cadre running the other way.

The road snakes into multiple paths that split off left and right. We've come to a residential area. Houses have been set on fire. The air is filled with the crackle of flames amid the crash of people breaking into houses. There's whooping and jeering.

Amazing. Tombaye didn't cut the electricity to either St. Croix or French Village. Many houses are brightly lit. The generalissimo figures he'll need electric power after he takes over. Coup d'Etat 101. He wants to make a radio address.

We're running through Hades. The first house we pass is burning. Townspeople are looting the next one. They ignore us. Outdoors, wearing load-bearing vests and carrying rifles, they probably take us for cadre. We can't assume everyone will make the same mistake, but we're driven by the urgency of our mission. If an unlucky townsman raises the alarm, we'll kill him where he stands.

"The company bungalow is around the next turn," Powell says.

We're jogging north, and the path turns left, following the curve of the hill.

We run straight into a blast furnace. The bungalow is engulfed in flames. A hot wind, like the breath of a fire-breathing dragon, stops me in my tracks. Instinctively, I lift my arm to shield my face. Powell grimaces. Teeth bared, he struggles to get closer to the burning structure.

"Oh my God."

Dante couldn't describe what we're looking at. Two men have been crucified on either side of the front door. Wrists and ankles nailed to the wood in obscene St. Andrew's Crosses. The flames have burned hair and clothes away from their bodies. The oil and moisture in their skin has been vaporized, and subcutaneous fat is melting from striated muscle and blackened limbs. Soon, those limbs will crack and shrivel into grotesque stumps.

The heat and flames drive us back.

Powell coughs from the smoke. "Tombaye didn't do this."

"How do you know?"

"One of those guys was shot in the head," Powell says. "The cadre killed them, the townspeople burned their bodies."

"Sons of bitches."

We turn away from the sight. "Tombaye's men don't have a grudge," Powell says. "Like you said, they're North African, not from here. The pilots were on Tombaye's list, so the cadre killed them. It's the townspeople who got creative."

"Which way to the Wolfe house?"

"Up there."

Powell points to a group of houses at the top of the hill. A hundred yards above us.

"Let's go."

French Village is a comfortable suburb. Lots of space between the houses, well-tended lawns and gardens. Cement-surfaced paths snake among the structures, connecting them to the wider roads. Garages have Land Rovers, Mercedes and Citroëns parked in the drives.

We run up the path. Trip over more bodies. They're laid out at a junction between the path and a road leading from below. Eight French soldiers. Most have been shot, but there are shrapnel wounds among them. Whoever killed them dragged the bodies into a row along the side of the road.

Powell inspects the tarmac, picks up a handful of spent shell casings. Shows them to me.

"NATO 5.56mm and Russian 5.45mm," he says. "Why am I not surprised?"

"This road leads down to where we found the other dead French soldiers. They had a gun battle down below and lost three men. These guys dug in up here and tried to hold off Tombaye's cadre. They were overrun. That's eleven dead for sure, out of Sauve's two squads. Five men left."

Powell inspects the French soldiers' uniforms. He pokes a dead man's insignia with the muzzle of his M4. "Check this out."

The man's wearing the three stripes of a chief sergeant. This man was Lieutenant Sauve's platoon NCO, his second-in-command.

"If Sauve's not up here, we have five missing French army."

Townspeople are looting the houses. Some are trying to get the vehicles started. Others are carrying furniture and valuables outside. Two men are trying to fit a sofa through the front door of a two-story. Others have broken windows on the second floor and are throwing valuables out onto the lawn.

We make our way higher on the hill. The scene in the village is worse than that in the Vieux Carré. Men and women are being tortured and raped. Bloodcurdling screams pierce the air. A middle-aged Frenchman is being held down in front of his garage while a man punches holes in his knees and shins with an electric drill. Judging from the number of holes, they've been at it for a while.

I follow Powell through hell. Run past townspeople breaking some Frenchmen's bones with hammers, torturing others with pliers, nails and blowtorches.

Men are dousing another bungalow with kerosene. A match flares, and the house explodes into flames.

Wonder which house is Bernard's. Is Bernard married? Where's *his* family? What about Laurent?

A man and woman are carrying a child's rocking horse out of another house. A Frenchman and woman have bled out on the lawn. They look like they've been stabbed a hundred times each. Little bodies are lying on the driveway, their skulls crushed flat. My God, the kids.

The woman stealing the rocking horse is wearing a maid's uniform. She *worked* for that family. Probably lived with them. Cooked their supper, did their cleaning and laundry. First chance she got, she and her man murdered the parents, killed the kids, and now they're looting the place.

I raise the AK-74 and shoot the woman in the face. The man turns to me, mouth gaping. I shoot him in the chest.

That's for the kids.

Powell grabs me by the arm. "Breed! We don't have time for this."

I reckon not, but I feel better.

Eyes wet, I follow Powell. Let's find Wolfe's wife and get off this fucking hill.

We reach the summit. A crescent of mansions on the south side is in flames. There are no houses to the west. No one wants a view of the slum. The houses to the south have a view of the mountain, those to the east have a view of the mine, and those to the north have a view of St. Croix. The mansions on the north side are arranged in a crescent. Two- and three-story structures. None of them are on fire yet.

The center of the summit was a well-kept park. Townspeople have piled valuables from the houses into the middle. They've dragged men and women from the houses, and are doing unspeakable things to them. I focus on the mission and try to block out the horror.

Where are Tombaye's cadre? Where are the Umbali?

Powell runs to a two-story. The front door is open and he takes position on the right, waits for me to reach the porch.

My AK-74 is on a sling and I throw it behind me. Draw the Mark 23. I prefer the pistol for close quarters. I nod to Powell, and he goes in, digs the right corner. I follow right behind, dig the left. Empty.

We move fast, clear the ground floor. Living room, dining room, kitchen, library. The place has been looted, but there are no bodies.

Take a breath, go to the stairs. Looks like we're going to have to fight uphill. Fighting uphill sucks. We don't *want* to do it, but if Wolfe's wife is up there, we *have* to do it. Powell nods to me. I'm carrying the handgun, I'm number one in the stack.

I hate stairs. More than I hate corridors. Both are fatal funnels. One man can wipe out a squad caught in the middle of a corridor. Stairways add a vertical element that is more difficult to deal with.

Right here, at the bottom of the stairs, people die. How? It's a grenade sink. This is where grenades land, and the cadre have a lot of grenades. You're staging your stack, somebody upstairs lobs a frag. Clunk and boom—you're all eating a shrapnel sandwich.

Get off the landings, don't get stuck in the middle.

Brace my back against the wall to my right, hunker down, cover the angle with the Mark 23. Two-handed stance, isosceles. It's a switchback. Fifteen feet to the first landing, switch, then up to the second floor. Look up and back—there's a wall above and behind me. A banister to my left leads to the first landing, then another banister continues up the next flight.

The banisters are fine. I can see between the balusters—the posts. The walls are bad news. People forget bullets go through wood. In Afghanistan, thick mud and rock walls provided cover. American and European buildings use wood. You can't see through wooden walls, but you sure as shit can get shot through them.

I climb the steps with deliberation, clearing as I go. It is so easy to trip when you're clearing a staircase. When I reach the middle of the staircase, I get antsy. The middle of any of these is a bad place to be. At the bottom, you can duck to one side. In the middle, you got no place to go.

Powell short-stocks his M4, glues himself to my ass. Any closer, we'd be married. Fucking stairs. Move faster, get off the X. The Mark 23 is a handgun, not a two-hand gun. I hold it in my right hand, brace myself against the banister with my left, lean forward, clear higher.

Move, move, move. I'm on the landing. Another great place to eat a frag. In this case, I can kick it past Powell and down the first flight of stairs. Now I can see straight to the second floor. Open doorway, dark room beyond. Move, move, move. Don't get stuck in the middle. Top of the stairs is the second-floor landing. It's a landing, but it's like a room

—blind spots left and right. I can hear Powell breathing behind me, keying off my moves. I step onto the second floor. Dig left, get out of the way. Powell digs right.

Breathe. We clear the room in front of us. The windows open onto the park below. The burning houses, the murder and rape. Flames lick the sky. I turn away from the scene, and we clear the rest of the second floor.

Wolfe's wife is nowhere to be found.

Powell and I stand in the second-floor corridor, away from the lighted windows.

"Alive or dead, she must be out there," Powell says.

"Along with three American engineers. We're not going to find anyone in that mess."

"Where are the cadre? Where are the Umbali? They're not out *there*."

I take a deep breath. "The Umbali are Tombaye's JV team. The real question is, where are the cadre? They had targets in French Village. The pilots, the most senior diplomats. Looks like he's run the table, so he's redeploying his cadre."

"He'll hold key locations. Which ones?"

"His main force will be in St. Croix. It's the seat of government. He'll hold the mine because it's the economic heart of the country. He'll guard the approaches to French Village with a minimum of force. Then he'll blockade all the routes in and out. The highway, east and west. The Arbois International Airport. Maybe the COBRA airstrip, but I don't think so."

"Why not?"

"He's killed the pilots."

"Fair enough."

I squeeze the bridge of my nose. "We *are* running out of options."

"We have two," Powell says.

"Yes. We can go into the bush right now, or we can try for that flight that arrives at 2300 hours."

"Except Tombaye's probably holding the Arbois airport."

I shove the Mark 23 under my waistband, heft the AK-74. "We don't know that for sure. It's worth a try."

"Let's get going."

We hurry down the stairs, rifles ready. Go out the front door and find the fires have spread from the southern crescent to the east. That's the direction the wind is blowing. Before long, Wolfe's house will be consumed. Convection from the fires is creating its own wind that fans the flames ever higher.

The scene in the park is medieval. The townspeople have repressed their anger and hatred all their lives. They won't spend it all in one night. They are out of control, each atrocity worse than the last.

Still, no cadre. No Umbali.

"This way," Powell says.

Together, we dart between Wolfe's house and the two-story next door. Find ourselves at the edge of the north slope that leads straight down the hill. I scan the different levels. There are narrow footpaths to follow, and gentle switch-backs. To my surprise, several levels below, I recognize the bungalow that Enwright and I had been assigned.

In the distance, St. Croix's Vieux Carré is in flames, but the fire seems to have spared the southern section. That means the fires in the American consulate and French embassy have spread north.

"I know where Tombaye's cadre are," I say.

"Where?"

"St. Croix, fighting fires. Tombaye never wanted to burn down the city. The townspeople did that. They lit the consulate and the French embassy. Out of control, the fire threatened the Hôtel de Ville and the Presidential Palace. The townspeople have swarmed up the hill and the Umbali aren't interested in fighting fires. Tombaye's using his cadre to build firebreaks."

"Looks like the whole town could burn down."

"Then we're in luck," I say.

"How do you figure that?"

"Tombaye's got limited resources, remember? He just might have left the Arbois airport uncovered."

Powell and I wind our way down the hill. French Village is a nightmare I want to forget.

9

SATURDAY, 1950 HRS, ST. CROIX – GUEST BUNGALOW

Did we really leave this bungalow just two hours ago? I feel like a lifetime has passed, but there it is. The open door, the two Umbali dead on the hill between us and the tree line.

"Wait one," I say.

Powell stops, turns back to me. "What's up?"

I lead the way into the living room. Flies are buzzing around four dead Umbali. Clumps of the green insects cover the pools of congealed blood. They explode into flight as we enter. Two of the giants lie outside the kitchen, and one at the side window. The last lies crumpled with his legs on the shattered coffee table, his torso half-slumped on the sofa.

The dead Umbali's hand is still closed around the haft of my Cold Steel OSS. He'd jerked it from his neck before I shot him. I take the weapon and wipe the blade on his pants leg. Rigor hasn't set in yet, another reminder that not a lot of time has passed.

"Nice blade," Powell says. "Let's go."

I lift my jeans leg, slide the Cold Steel back into its

sheath, haft-down. Velcro it in place. "Plane doesn't get in till 2300. We have a few minutes."

Go to Enwright's bedroom door, drag a wing chair back to the living room. I sit down, motion Powell to take a seat on the sofa next to the dead Umbali.

"Oh, great. What do you want to do next? Sit these dead dudes around the table...like we have an audience? Breed, you're cracking up."

"No, everything has been going too fast. We haven't stopped to think in two hours."

"That's the way it is when a few hundred of these guys are trying to kill you."

Powell picks up Enwright's laptop, examines the Umbali lance stuck through its keyboard, tosses it aside. The SEAL grunts and sits next to the dead Umbali. Pats the corpse's bald head and looks at me. "Okay, what's to it?"

For the first time in two hours, we appraise each other. Here we are, two operators. Professionals talking shop.

"Do you believe Wolfe didn't know Tombaye was back in Wambesa?" I ask.

That was one of the worms wriggling in my brain. Before I boarded my plane, Stein told me straight up that Tombaye was in-country. Wolfe and Bernard acted like talk of his return was idle gossip. Stein knew because the State Department had told her. Wolfe was the senior State Department official in Wambesa.

"I have every reason to believe him," Powell says. "Don't you?"

"No. Tell me *why* you believe him."

"Tell me why *you* don't."

"You first."

One professional to another, Powell tells me.

THE PREVIOUS MONTH, the consulate's mailbox received an email from the State Department. Drue Powell opened the secure envelope and decrypted the message. Printed it out and read it again. It was an alert, but the wording was vague.

Attention:
Consul General, Wambesa
Head of Security, Wambesa

Be advised intel suggests Marien Tombaye may return Wambesa. Intentions unclear. Take all necessary precautions.

After six months in Wambesa, Powell knew the country reasonably well. He'd heard the stories of Marien Tombaye. The locals took Tombaye seriously, the French less so. To the locals, Tombaye was a hero who had left home to fight for Boko Haram and al-Qaeda. They thought of Tombaye as a legend. The French thought him a rabble-rouser they'd run out of the country on a rail.

Powell got up and crossed the hall into Oren Wolfe's office. The consul general was sitting in his leather recliner, enjoying the cold air that blasted from the air conditioner. Mounted in his office window, little paper ribbons were fluttering from its grille.

The consul general was surfing the web. That's what he did most days. Powell didn't hold it against him. Time had no meaning in Wambesa. Every morning, one woke up to another in an endless string of days. In a place like St. Croix, one felt immortal.

"Take a look at this." Powell handed Wolfe the message.

"I'm amazed they remember we're here."

Wolfe took the sheet of paper and squinted at it. "Not very helpful, is it? What do they mean by taking all necessary precautions? Do you know what this is, Drue?"

"What is it, sir?"

"This is what we call a cover-your-ass message. They don't know what Tombaye is up to. They don't know where he is, what he's doing, or where he's going. On the off chance he does come to Wambesa, they want to be able to say they let us know."

Powell had survived five deployments in Afghanistan and three in Iraq. He told himself that if there was any doubt, there was no doubt. The message was vague, but it was a step-change from yesterday. Powell took it seriously.

"Let's count the US citizens in the country," Wolfe said. "Review the emergency action plan."

"Yes, sir."

Wolfe completed the necessary precautions before lunch. He and Powell checked the list of US citizens. It was a short list. Wolfe and his wife, Powell, Troy and Carol Grady, three mining engineers living in French Village.

The emergency action plan was simple. In the event of a national emergency like an earthquake or violent riots, all US citizens would be contacted and asked to gather at a marshalling point. They would be transported to the French army barracks for protection until the situation was resolved.

An evacuation could be ordered by the State Department in DC, or by the consul general on-site. American citizens could not be forced to leave. It was assumed that the situation would have deteriorated to the point they would be desperate to leave.

US African Command, AFRICOM, was responsible for providing security and transportation in that event. The evacuation would be organized by AFRICOM's headquarters at Kelly Barracks in Stuttgart, Germany. AFRICOM would provide resources and assistance as quickly as possible. If absolutely necessary, the consul general could charter whatever mode of transportation was available to execute the evacuation.

There weren't many routes out of Wambesa. Because the country was landlocked, evacuation was possible only by land or air. That meant chartering a plane, bus, or train. The key was to get all the Americans to meet at the consulate first.

"Is a warning in order, sir?" Powell asked. "In fact, there are so few people on the list that I can visit and warn them in person."

Wolfe stroked his chin. "I don't think we're at that stage yet, Drue. If we receive confirmation that Tombaye is in-country, a warning would be appropriate. Not before."

The consul general's decision sounded reasonable. In fact it was consistent with the consulate's escalation procedures. The problem was, Powell never considered procedures to be a substitute for judgment. That was why you needed human beings in the decision loop. But Wolfe was *that* human being and the senior official on the ground. Powell didn't agree with the decision, but Wolfe was in charge. Powell remained silent.

Job done, Wolfe asked Powell to put the documents back into the office safe. The consul general then returned to his web surfing.

Powell did not consider his job done.

Ever since he was a kid, Drue Powell wanted to be a Navy SEAL. His brother had brought some DVDs home, and they'd watched a movie about the unit. It was so cool he immediately became obsessed with joining. He spent every waking hour running, swimming, and studying martial arts. He worked summers lifeguarding. He didn't learn to swim until he was fifteen, but once the SEAL bug bit him, he turned half fish.

Right after graduation, he went into the navy and BUD/S, the basic SEAL qualification program. Hell Week gave a man a thousand reasons to quit, but Powell never did. Quitting was inconceivable. Quitters set their helmet down, rang the bell, and slunk off in shame. Powell resolved to die first. He had wanted to become a SEAL for so long, he had no other options. Every man who quit improved his odds. It paid to be a winner.

Later, after Seal Qualification Training, he was given his trident, the insignia that proclaimed to the world that he *was* a Navy SEAL. He joined a platoon and learned that not every mission was like the movie. SEALs *did* get to do the things you saw in the movie, especially in training, but not all at once. That was okay by him. He was where he wanted to be, doing what he wanted to do. He was living his best life.

Powell saw a lot of action in Afghanistan. He was selected for SEAL Team Six. Like the army's Combat Applications Group, it was a secretive unit. They called them DEVGRU and Delta Force. The names didn't matter, they changed regularly. Civilians were *supposed* to be confused by the names. The units weren't supposed to exist. Commandos who talked about their missions, or even their association with the units, were ostracized.

Breed and Powell were cut from the same cloth. Let's not sugarcoat it—SEALs and Delta Force are "direct action" units. Their job is to kill people. Rescue hostages, kill terrorists. Powell became very good at his job.

But the war wound down. The guys in the head shed said they were "experiencing a reduced operational tempo." That meant missions became fewer. Powell left the service and took lucrative work as a contractor working for PMCs and the CIA's Ground Branch. A few years down the road, he was ready for time off. He took a job with the State Department—Head of Security for the consulate in Wambesa. He figured he'd do the job for a while until he figured out his next move.

Powell never lost the qualities that made him a good SEAL. He stayed fit, and he kept his skills sharp.

You're not here to survive, you're here to take charge.
Stay low, go fast. Kill first, die last.
One shot, one kill. No luck, all skill.

The SEALs had an aphorism for everything. There was one for brushing your teeth.

Powell went back to his office and turned off his computer. Then he walked to the front door. He stopped at the reception desk. Margot was there, with her usual bright smile. "I'll be gone the rest of the afternoon, Margot. If the consul general needs me, he should call."

He stepped outside and closed the door behind him. Greeted Edouard, the uniformed security guard. The tiny US consulate didn't rate a Marine detachment. If trouble came to visit, Powell and Edouard were all there were to stop it. And Edouard wasn't going to stop much.

"Quiet morning, Edouard?"

"Very quiet, Drue."

The two men stood together for a moment and watched the bustle of the Vieux Carré. Officials walking to and from the Hôtel de Ville and the Presidential Palace. Businessmen going to work in their offices around the square, or stepping outside to the cantinas for a cold soft drink.

Everything looked normal. Powell offered Edouard a cigarette. The guard gratefully accepted, and Powell lit it for him.

The message was disturbing.

Marien Tombaye may return Wambesa. Intentions unclear. Take all necessary precautions.

Powell lit a cigarette for himself. Got into the consulate Impala. He drove to his bungalow on the hill, navigating the narrow roads carefully. Avoided pedestrians, because in Wambesa, the most common means of transportation was walking. The next most common means were bicycle and scooter.

French Village was one of the nicest places he'd ever lived overseas. It was like a middle-class suburb with nice houses, tidy lawns, and children riding bicycles on the street. His bungalow had two bedrooms and a big sitting room. It would be considered nice in an army town like Fort Bragg, San Antonio or El Paso. Compared to hovels in Afghanistan or Iraq, it was luxurious.

He went to his bedroom and opened the closet. Moved pairs of dress shoes and trainers out of the way, then pried up two floorboards. The space underneath was cement, lined with a plastic tarp. He pulled out a long wooden box and laid it on his bed.

The lid of the box was fastened with a sturdy hasp and padlock. Powell took a key from his pocket and removed the lock. Inside the box was an M4 carbine and seven thirty-round magazines of 5.56mm ammunition. He checked the weapon, loaded it, and slid it into a black canvas carrying bag. From a drawer in his wardrobe, he took a load-bearing vest, velcroed the magazines onto it, and folded it into the same bag as the rifle.

Powell covered up the hidden cache and carried the rifle out to the consulate Impala. Locked it in the trunk.

Lunchtime. The Head of Security drove to the La Salle and sat down for a beer and a western-style ham and cheese sandwich. Opened a conversation with Charles, the bartender. Old Charles, fluent in three African languages, English, French and German. Rijk Bröer sat in his usual corner, nursing a whisky.

"What's happening, Charles?"

"Another day, Mr. Powell. Same as always."

"The mine is expanding again. Flying more engineers into the country."

"I heard that, sir. Good news. More work, more money."

"Have they come into town?"

"Not yet, but soon. They'll want to get comfortable first."

"Let me know when they do."

"I suppose you'll see them yourself, sir. But of course I will."

Bröer looked up and lifted his drink in a mock toast. "Taking an interest in the town, Powell?"

"Why not, Bröer? I live here."

Heat rushed to Powell's scalp. The old man chuckled and downed his drink.

Powell got into the car and drove out to Machweo. At the turnoff, he headed south. It was a warm, sunny day, and he was amazed by the beauty of the landscape. Mount Wambesa was lush and green. He could see the low spur that pushed northwest from the mountain toward St. Croix. The houses of French Village shone bright in the sun.

The structures of the Gradys' ranch blended into the tree line. Scallops of the forest had been cleared, and four large villas had been built with mock-thatch roofs. One of them was two stories and could be leased by a single family. The other three were quad structures, with four suites each. The main building, with its attached garage, was in the center, with two villas on either side. It was two stories, with a bar and restaurant on the ground floor, and a forty-meter pool in the back. The Gradys lived upstairs. Grady had diverted flow from the Lokola River. That diversion ensured ample water for the pool and the rest of the ranch's needs.

Powell parked in the driveway in front of the main building. Troy Grady stepped onto the porch to meet him. Big and brawny with fiery red hair, Grady would have done well playing a Viking, wielding a Nordic axe.

"What brings you out here, Powell?"

"Just a friendly call. Wanted to see how you folks are doing. Bringing in paying customers yet?"

"We've started advertising. All the units are ready, our chef will arrive next month, and we have pre-bookings. Come on in for a drink."

Grady pushed open the front door. It was finely hewn native teak. The Viking led Powell into the cool interior.

The main house was luxurious. There was a grand staircase that led to the living quarters on the second floor. A wide sitting room that connected to a dining room every bit as big, and a kitchen behind. Sliding glass doors opened to a patio, pool deck, and the swimming pool itself. A long bar extended half the length of the sitting room on one side and separated it from the patio. With the glass doors open, the bar would serve both.

Two white roan antelope skulls were mounted on a hardwood shield on the sitting room wall. The shield was trimmed with dark wood on a polished tan surface. The horns, from mature males, were curved like scimitars, thirty inches long.

"Did you bag those yourself?" Powell asked.

"Yes. I have more, from Tanzania and South Africa. I'm not sure I should display them, because those animals aren't indigenous to Wambesa."

"I think you should." Powell could only imagine the hunting Grady had done south of the equator. "They'll make good conversation pieces."

The furniture was deep and comfortable. Carved African Khaya, a kind of indigenous mahogany. The cushions and armrests were soft, dark leather, with shiny brass studs. Powell inhaled the rich scent of fine leather. It was clear Grady had spared no expense.

"Let's sit at the bar," Grady said. "Pick your poison."

"Bourbon and branch."

Grady led the SEAL to the bar. Poured them both Bourbon and branch water.

"Everything quiet?" Powell asked.

"What do you mean?"

"You guys are off by yourselves out here. At least until you start getting guests. Have you had any trouble from people on their way to and from the airport?"

"Not at all. Carol drives out to the airport from time to time to buy fresh produce from the vendors. I go to tank up the trucks. We're five miles out of the way here. Nobody comes up from the highway. We have noticed the odd Umbali watching from the tree line, but they leave us alone."

Powell studied a savanna buffalo skull mounted on a shield over the bar. The animal had been a giant. The buffalo's horns bowed gracefully downward on either side, then curved sharply up and back, toward the head, like majestic black hooks.

"You mean those hunters? The hill people?"

"That's right," Grady said. "Big guys, built like they drive iron all day. Bald. Some of them have ritual scars cut into their faces. Marks of seniority. They carry machetes and hunting lances. I reckon they've tracked game into the forest south of here. Come to the edge of the tree line out of curiosity."

Umbali were hill people. It was unusual to see them in the lowlands. "Have they ever come onto the ranch land? Gotten in among the houses?"

"No. I think they're happy to leave us alone so long as we leave them alone. If there's trouble, Santos and I both know how to shoot."

Grady nodded to a tall gun cabinet at the end of the bar. There were double-barreled and bolt-action hunting rifles. Twelve-gauge shotguns. The cabinet was locked. Drawers below provided storage for boxes of ammunition.

"If there's trouble, you know who to call."

"Not the police." Grady's laugh came from deep in his belly, but nothing in the big man's frame shook. The Viking was solid muscle. "I'll take care of it myself."

Powell knew what Grady meant. The Wambesa police did not inspire confidence. Security had to be bought. Men had to be hired and trained. The mine had the luxury of the French army and enough money to hire a security force.

"If there's trouble," Powell said, "call me."

The men finished their drinks, and Powell drove back to the city. He was comfortable that Grady could take care of himself. The only thing that bothered him was Machweo's isolation.

Powell wouldn't find the engineers at French Village. They'd be out at the COBRA mill. He drove back to the consulate. Later in the afternoon, he worked out. For the next four weeks, he would carry his rifle into the house and sleep with it by his bed. Carry it out to the car and take it to work. He kept his ear to the ground.

There was no hard evidence that Marien Tombaye had returned to Wambesa. One day, Wolfe asked Bernard and Laurent straight up if they had heard anything. Both men loosened their collars, both men said no. Tombaye's return was nothing more than a rumor.

Two days ago, Wolfe called Powell into his office.

"These rumors of Tombaye's return have made it back to Paris," the consul general said.

"How?"

"Who knows? Engineers and managers fly back and forth. People gossip at the water coolers. The point is, COBRA head office is concerned, Thierry Laurent and Marcel Bernard have assured them nothing is amiss, but the COBRA board is not satisfied."

"It's their job to worry," Powell said. "I get it."

"They've hired a private military company to do an evaluation of security at the mine. Evaluate conditions in the country."

Powell said, "That's sensible. Which PMC? I know all the best ones."

"Long Rifle Consultants. They're sending someone called Breed."

"Good company, solid. I know Breed by reputation. Strong operator."

"What's he like?"

Powell searched his memory. Breed had begun as a Green Beret, a Special Forces weapons and intelligence sergeant. Later, he was selected for Delta Force—Combat Applications Group. At the time of his discharge, he had been a Special Forces warrant officer.

Breed was a legend. In Afghanistan he and his team had executed long-range, deep-penetration patrols into the Hindu Kush. They'd trekked along mountain ranges that followed the Kagur Valley through Kunar, Nuristan and Badakhshan. Some said his team had penetrated as far as Tajikistan and China through the Wakhan Corridor. They'd mapped Taliban caravan routes and supply bases. He had been involved in direct operations as an assaulter and sniper.

Breed's military career came to an end when he shot Afghan women who were flaying American prisoners alive. First, he shot one of the prisoners to put him out of his misery. Then he killed the women. Nobody wanted the embarrassment of an Article 32 investigation and a court-martial. Breed's resignation and early retirement was expedited.

Anyone else might have disappeared under a cloud. Breed continued to work as a contractor for PMCs. He took on personal protection assignments. He took contracts for the CIA's Ground Branch. The operations were classified.

"He is a *very* heavy dude," Powell concluded.

"Well, he's arriving tomorrow morning, and he'll be carrying a weapon in his checked baggage. The PMC wants us to smooth his way through customs. You know what I mean."

"I know what you mean."

Powell hesitated at the door. Turned to Wolfe. "I haven't seen any further messages about Marien Tombaye. Have you?"

The consul general shook his head. "No. Not a word."

"Do you think we should issue a warning? Data points are adding up."

Wolfe thought about the escalation procedure.

"No. I don't think we're there yet."

"I SAW THE MESSAGE MYSELF," Powell says. "The consul general didn't take it seriously at first, but over the last couple of weeks, he's gotten worried. Everybody's felt the tension, but no hard data points until today."

"I have a friend in the Company," I tell him. "Told me before I came, there was no question Tombaye was in-country."

"So either Wolfe lied to me about not receiving another message, or..."

"Or State didn't tell its own consul general the whole story."

Powell takes a deep breath, looks at the carnage of the living room. "What does this mean for us?"

"We need to get out of the country. We keep an eye on Wolfe."

"Roger that."

"I trust my friend one hundred percent," I tell him. "Something is rotten in the State Department."

10

SATURDAY, 2000 HRS, ST. CROIX – COLUMN

Together, we make our way down the hill, return to the Impala. The consul general gets out of the car, hurries to meet us.

Wolfe's face expresses his anguish. "Where's my wife?"

Powell breaks the news to the consul general. "We couldn't find her. Don't know if she's alive or dead. The pilots—we know they're dead."

"Get out of the car." I open the driver's door and wave Enwright out.

My AK-74's stock is sturdier than Powell's M4. The M4 is a good rifle, but, in my humble view, a lot was sacrificed to give it a modern design. I could just about live with the telescoping stock, but drew the line when they eliminated the bayonet. The AK-74, on the other hand, has a *great* bayonet.

I smash the front window of the Impala. Knock all the plexiglass out of the frame. "Brush that crap off the seats," I tell Enwright.

Go around to the back, do the same with the rear window.

"What did you do that for?" Enwright asks.

"We're going to have to fight our way out of this country," I tell her. "Now we have clear fields of fire. One rifle in front, another in back."

"If we're going to try for Arbois, we should avoid the highway," Powell says.

"Is that possible?"

"Not all the way, but for most of it. I know some roads."

I check my watch. "Can we make it?"

"I think so."

An engine growls, and Powell jerks his head to one side. Several hundred yards west, vehicles are approaching from the direction of the slum. They're running with their headlights off. "Son of a bitch."

We crouch and raise our rifles. The vehicles have rounded a turn and approach head-on.

"Five-ton truck and a minibus," Powell says.

"Why would Tombaye's men run dark?" I ask. "By now they own the place."

"You think they're French?"

"We're missing five bodies," I say. "Cover us."

I get to my feet and take Enwright by the hand. Her palm is damp. I pull her onto the road, walk toward the oncoming vehicles. If they don't stop, I'll push her into the bush, jump after her.

"Are you crazy?" Enwright walks with me in the middle of the road.

Cadre wouldn't be driving with their lights out. If I'm right, these are the remnants of the French detachment on the hill. Civilians running from the massacre.

The five-ton truck's lights come on. Blinding bright.

When the French see a white man and woman on the road, they'll assume we're friendly. I hope.

With my right hand, I raise the AK-74 over my head, raise Enwright's hand in my left. "You're crazy." Enwright's voice is a hiss. "If we ever get out of this alive..."

The five-ton stops. The door opens, and a figure gets out.

"*Identifiez-vous.*"

"We're American."

"Breed, is that you?"

I know that voice. It's Lieutenant Sauve. "Yes. Powell is in the brush. He's coming out."

Powell steps onto the road.

"Kill those lights," I tell Sauve.

"*Étienez les lumière*," Sauve says to the man at the wheel.

The man douses the five-ton's headlights. We walk toward the French.

"How many men do you have here?" I ask.

"Myself and five soldiers," Sauve says. "There are civilians as well."

Without asking, I walk past Sauve to the back of the truck and look inside. There, I see four French soldiers in woodland camouflage, carrying 416s. None look wounded.

Behind the soldiers are a dozen civilians. Men, women, and children. The children are teenagers. A boy and girl, maybe thirteen years old. An older girl of sixteen. There are wounded.

My heart skips a beat. Cecile is on one knee, bandaging a woman's arm and arranging a sling. She looks up. For a second, our eyes lock in recognition. She's startled too. Glad to see me, yet overwhelmed by the stress of circumstances. She turns back to her work.

"How many wounded?" I ask.

"Four," Cecile says. "One of them badly."

I turn away from the five-ton and go to the minibus. It's a white Citroën. The driver is an old man in a short-sleeved black shirt and clerical collar. He wears a straw hat with a wide brim. Stares at me through sharp eyes set in a gaunt face. His pointed jaw is covered with white stubble. He's a village priest. I can see him sitting at a café in rural France, bitching.

"Who are you?" the man asks.

"I'm Breed. Who are *you*?"

"Father Ducasse. What are Americans doing in Wambesa?"

"We've been sent here for our sins," I tell him. "What have you got in there?"

"Women and children from the hospice," he says.

"How many?" I strain to see past him to the seats in the back. Six children and two young women stare at me, faces thin, eyes wide as saucers. The children are boys and girls. The youngest is a four-year-old boy. The others' ages fall between nine and thirteen. The women look like they are nineteen or twenty. All look like they are of mixed ethnicity. "Are any of them injured?"

"Eight, no injuries. One of them is pregnant."

Sauve has followed me. I turn to him. "What happened? Who's on your tail?"

"The enemy attacked from the northeast and overran my unit. We took what civilians we could in the truck and withdrew to the west. We encountered the doctor and these civilians as they were leaving the mission."

"Is anyone after you?" I step around the lieutenant and examine the tailgate of the five-ton. No bullet holes. Sauve's uniform is spotless, as are the uniforms of the soldiers in the back.

Powell joins us. "Truck's in good shape," he says. "Full tank of gas. The troopers have 416s and two hundred and ten rounds each."

"That's their basic load."

The SEAL's expression is grim. "I don't think their weapons have been fired."

Rage swells in me. It's obvious Sauve left his men. The chief sergeant led the defense at the top of the northeast road. Sauve hung back with five men. The cadre and Umbali overran the sergeant and drove civilians from the center toward the west. Before the cadre reached him, Sauve piled into his truck and fled. I'm surprised he bothered to take any civilians with him.

More damning, Sauve got his truck down the hill without encountering cadre. Why not? The reason is straightforward. Sauve bolted before the cadre dug their foxholes.

"Later," I tell Powell. Turn to Sauve. "Pull these vehicles off the road. Hide them in the bush behind our car. Right now."

Sauve gives me a blank look.

"*Now*, Lieutenant. Move."

When the five-ton and the minibus have been concealed, I shuffle the passengers. I pull the soldiers out of the five-ton and climb in with Cecile.

It's a wonder that circumstances have thrown us together like this. Once again, I'm struck by her beauty. She's wearing jeans, flat shoes and a loose white shirt. Her wavy hair, unbound, falls loose and curls about her shoulders.

"Are the wounded better off in this truck or the minibus?" I ask.

Cecile looks up from her work. "I can take better care of them here."

"Show me their injuries."

"These two men and the woman have cuts all over their arms. The woman has been slashed, and her arm must not be moved. I have sewn it up and done my best to immobilize it."

The woman, in her fifties, is whimpering with pain. She belongs in a hospital. Cecile may have performed minor surgery and first aid, but infection can set in quickly. All of these wounds could be gangrenous before we reach modern medicine.

"You have morphine?"

"Yes. All the morphine I had at the clinic. And all the antibiotics, packed in ice. They will go bad once the ice melts."

"Those are defensive wounds," I say. "These people are lucky to have escaped."

"This man has been stabbed in the belly," she says. "He needs surgery."

The middle-aged Frenchman is lying on his back on the cargo bed, a jacket rolled up under his head. His eyes are closed, and he's groaning. Cecile has bandaged his wound as best she can with torn clothing.

I've seen enough battlefield injuries to have an idea which casualties can be saved. This man has a chance if we get him to surgery within an hour. No problem if we had a surgical facility in-country and a medevac helo.

"Can you do it?" I ask Cecile.

Cecile shakes her head. "I am not a surgeon, and there are no facilities."

The man's as good as dead. I move on to the next. "The pregnant woman. Is she better off with you here or in the minivan?"

"The minivan," Cecile says without hesitation. "But if she has issues, you must call me."

"Alright," I say. "There's a plane flying into Arbois International Airport in a few hours. We're going to try to reach it. Can you translate for me?"

"Of course. I'm finished here for the moment."

I jump from the back of the truck and help Cecile down. She puts her hands on my shoulders, and I hold her by the hips. The sensation of touch is electric, a promise of what might be. She steps from the tailgate, and I lower her to the tarmac.

Sauve's men are young, but one or two are older than he is. I study their features, their chevrons. One is a sergeant, another a corporal. The sergeant is a squad leader, the corporal a fire team leader. Both men have at least as much experience as Sauve, if not more. I doubt the lieutenant's cowardice extends to his men.

"Come with me," I say. Cecile translates.

The minivan has a sliding side door. I pull the handle and drag it open.

"What are you doing, man?" Ducasse is outraged. "Leave those children alone!"

"I'm not hurting anyone, Father. We have to get ready to move."

Two of the children, I send to the five-ton. That leaves six, including the pregnant girl, to occupy the most comfortable seats. I go to the back and smash the rear window of the minibus. Ducasse protests, but Cecile puts her hand on his arm. Reassures him.

The rear seats fold back to make space in the cargo bed. I put the sergeant and the corporal into the minivan with their rifles pointed to the rear.

I take Cecile aside. "What happened back there?"

"We heard the shooting on the hill," Cecile says. "Shooting in St. Croix. Shooting everywhere. Then we saw flames. I went to Father Ducasse and told him we should go to the Marawi border. We put everyone in the minibus with as much food, clothing and medicine as we could carry."

"How did you run into the army?"

"We came upon them right away. Or they came upon us. We left the mission and encountered them on the road. They made us stop. The lieutenant told us to follow him. A few minutes later, we saw you."

"But you were heading east. Marawi is west."

Cecile looks miserable. "The lieutenant told us to follow him. I thought he was taking us to the army barracks."

"No. The army are all dead except for these men," I tell her. "The lieutenant doesn't know what he's doing."

"Should we try for Marawi, then?"

"I don't think so. You had the right idea. We have to leave the country, but Tombaye will block the highway in both directions. Had you driven west, I'm sure you would have been stopped. You would have had to find a way to cross on foot. Probably through the bush."

Cecile's forehead furrows. "Then it's true. Marien has returned."

"Yes. He's been back for several weeks, and he brought armed cadre with him. He's forged an alliance of some sort with the Umbali. They have killed all the French in St. Croix and all the French in the Village."

"Did they kill Bröer?"

"He was alive when we left him. Seemed certain Tombaye would leave him alone."

"Marien has no war with Bröer."

"Most of the killing is not being done by Tombaye's cadre. Nor by the Umbali. The townspeople have gone crazy. I don't think even Tombaye can control them."

"That is what centuries of oppression do," Cecile says. She points in the direction of the slum to the west. "Those people, who work the mines, are afraid now. They do not know what is happening. We are fortunate they have not lost their heads."

"They've been beaten down, haven't they? It's the townspeople who want to supplant the French."

"You may be right."

"We have to go. Get in the truck."

Cecile climbs into the five-ton. One of the French soldiers, a kid not yet twenty, extends a hand and pulls her aboard.

I walk forward, find Sauve next to the truck's cab.

"We'll travel in column," I tell him. "Lights out. The consulate car first, then your truck. Minivan brings up the rear."

Powell, Cecile and Wolfe are standing by the Impala.

"Our options are closing down fast," Powell says.

"I know."

Wolfe frowns. "Why is that?"

Powell shrugs. "The four of us could have made a go of it in the bush. There's no way to take all those civilians along. We have to fly or drive out."

"You said we could reach Arbois without using the highway."

"Yes," Powell says, "but we have to get past the crossroads."

"I don't think Tombaye will guard the crossroads. Like I said, he's got most of his cadre fighting fires in St. Croix. He'll have another unit at the mine."

"He's got three hundred Umbali."

"We can't do anything about them," I say. "Tombaye's using them as blunt instruments. We'll have to deal with the Umbali as and when."

"What if we do run into them at the crossroads?" Enwright asks.

It's a fair question. Hope for the best, plan for the worst.

"We drive straight through," I tell her. "I'll shoot from the front passenger seat. Powell, you shoot through the front windshield while sitting between us in the back. Full auto, rock and roll."

Powell chuckles. "You know we're not running suppressed? I'll blast your eardrums out."

"It beats getting dead."

"We should pick up Troy Grady," Wolfe says.

Powell takes out his phone, dials Grady, holds the handset to his ear. After a moment, he shakes his head, disconnects the call. "Grady's still not picking up."

The man with the ranch. Poor bastard will never see a dime from that investment. If he's still alive.

"How far out of the way is he?"

"Five miles southwest of the airport," Powell says. "I reckon we've got time."

"Okay, we'll give it a try. But no promises. Let's move out."

Our little group piles into the Impala. Before I get in, I signal Sauve's driver to follow.

ONE BY ONE, our vehicles pull onto the road. I lay the AK-74 on the dashboard within easy reach. Take out my phone and punch Stein's speed dial.

"What's happening, Breed?"

I don't think Stein's stepped away from her laptop and phone since the last time we spoke.

"Doors are closing on us, Stein. Tombaye's taken the seat of government in St. Croix. COBRA has a Dash-8 at the company's private airstrip. We went up to French Village to look for the COBRA pilots, but Tombaye's cadre got there first and killed them. Worse, the townspeople have gone nuts and murdered all the French they could get their hands on. We've hooked up with a handful of French army and twenty or so refugees."

"What are the refugees like?"

"A doctor, a priest, a pregnant woman, and four wounded. A bunch of others. One of the wounded is not going to make it without surgery and advanced medicine."

"I still can't get a rescue force to you before midday. And it *has* to be covert. Things are getting complicated."

"How complicated is sending in the 75th Ranger Regiment? Hell, we can take back the country."

"Very complicated. Tombaye has secured the Presidential Palace, the city hall, and the radio and television stations. He gave a television address. His men have seized control of the government and liberated the country from French colonial oppression. All the French troops who resisted have been killed, and all foreign assets have been nationalized. That means COBRA. President Mumbaye has been deposed and is being held prisoner. If any attempt is made to enter the country, he'll be killed."

"There's a flight scheduled to land at Arbois International at 2300 hours. We're going to try for it."

"We're diverting that flight."

A giant hand squeezes my guts. "Stein, you can't do that. It's our only way out."

"Tombaye said he's sealed the country. Nothing gets in or out."

"He's bluffing. He's resource-constrained. No more than fifty cadre, maybe three hundred Umbali. The townspeople damn near burned down St. Croix, and he's had to pull in most of his cadre to fight the fires. Otherwise that TV station would have been toast."

"We can't take the chance, Breed. Why should we put an airplane full of people into a country that's already on fire? Give Tombaye more hostages and a PR victory?"

"Have you contacted the airport?"

"Yes. The tower says everything is normal."

"So let the plane land."

"You know as well as I do that air controller could have a gun to his head."

"Stein, let me go in there and determine who owns the airport. If Tombaye has it, I'll wave you off. You've got my word."

"Wait one." Stein puts me on hold.

Enwright and I exchange glances.

Stein comes back to the phone. "Breed?"

"I'm here."

"The plane is going to attempt a landing on schedule.

Unless I hear from you that the airport is clear, I *will* wave it off myself."

STEIN DISCONNECTS THE CALL, and I exhale through puffed cheeks. Enwright, Powell and Wolfe heard most of the conversation. They're silent. We all know the odds are against us. The only good news is...*if* that controller is speaking with a gun to his head, Tombaye hasn't cratered the runway.

I'm happy to sit in silence as we make our way toward the crossroads. We're surrounded by flames. Apart from the Presidential Palace and Hôtel de Ville, the center of St. Croix is an inferno. French Village is on fire, and so are the vehicles at the crossroads.

Columns of smoke pour from the burning buildings. The columns spread out into low clouds that blot out the stars. The clouds are colored by flames that lick their bellies. The clouds are the color of blood.

11

SATURDAY, 2030 HRS - MACHWEO

From a quarter of a mile away, the burning tank destroyer lights up the sky. There were four trucks. Now I see three. The five-ton at the rear of the column burns fiercely. The truck in front of it is missing. The other two are still there.

"The cadre took one serviceable truck," I say. "Wait here. I'm going forward on foot. Come when I signal."

Powell and I dismount the Impala. He stands beside the car as I move forward.

We're approaching from St. Croix, so the French vehicles are pointed in our direction. I walk slowly, careful to stay out of the ditch. The ambush is fresh in my mind. The French infantry were slaughtered by antipersonnel mines.

My eyes search the grass and shrubs on both sides of the road. No sign of cadre, no sign of Umbali.

The bodies standing in the tank turret have been crisped. They've been turned into comic Halloween caricatures. Black posts of carbonized flesh and white teeth. The bodies of the men in the cab of the last truck are obscured by flames. The drivers of the other two five-tons are slumped over the steering wheels. The men in the passenger seats are hanging out of the cabs. All have been riddled with bullets.

The hood of the truck immediately behind the tank destroyer has been propped open. The cadre thought it might be drivable. Tried to fix the engine and gave up. Those diesel engines are tough. I doubt AK-74 fire could have done much damage, but it would have been hard to conduct repairs in the dark.

No bodies on the road. The men all took cover behind the trucks and in the adjacent ditch. A hundred yards to my right is the low rise from which Tombaye mounted his ambush.

I approach with the AK-74 at my hip. There's frenetic movement among the dark shapes lying in the ditch. Rats scurry in all directions. A low growl. Demonic eyes flash in the glittering firelight. Hyenas tear at the flesh of the dead French soldiers, ripping away mouthfuls of raw meat. The rib cage of the first body has been exposed, and the animals tug at internal organs. Jackals circle, looking for opportunities to grab their share of the feast. The larger hyenas growl and snap, defending their prize.

The Umbali made it easy for the scavengers. Razor-sharp machetes lopped off arms and legs, quartered corpses. The hyenas enjoy their pick of the torsos. The jackals make off with severed limbs.

I'm tempted to fire a shot to frighten off the animals. Decide against it. A shot would be a useless gesture and might alert cadre at the COBRA mine.

The air is thick with the nauseating odor of burning

flesh. Next to the second truck in the column, I recognize the pungent smell of diesel. The fuel tank's been riddled, and a lake has spread across the road.

I'm standing in it.

Diesel has a higher flash point than gasoline. Less combustible. I step out of the lake and walk past the vehicle.

There are no weapons lying about. I look inside the cargo beds of the trucks. The soldiers killed by the first bursts of fire are slumped on the fold-down troop seats or sprawled on the floor. Rats explode from the bodies and scurry past me on their way out. No larger scavengers in the trucks. The hyenas and jackals are occupied with the meals served in the ditch.

The cadre gathered weapons and ammunition. Loaded them into the truck they took. Probably went to the army barracks for unguarded vehicles.

I continue along the road until I've traversed the length of the column. Stand by the flames consuming the last truck, turn and wave to Powell. He gets back into the Impala, and Enwright guides the car forward to pick me up.

"Reckon they've got cadre at the mine," I say. "Probably took out Sauve's last two squads. Let's get out of here."

Our convoy continues past the crossroads. The French soldiers in our little band stare at the carnage as they pass. Welcome to war.

A short distance farther along the highway, Powell directs us to take a turnoff. Enwright pulls onto a side road that runs south-by-east. The farther we get from St. Croix, the easier it becomes to drive by moonlight. We drive at a moderate speed, with a separation of fifty yards between vehicles.

To a night-adapted eye, moonlight can be a blessing or a curse. On patrol or on the road, it can be bright enough to light your way. Crossing a wide, open space, it can light you up like targets in a shooting gallery.

"Roads like this aren't bad," Powell says. "There are some out-of-the-way tracks that run through the bush. They're not paved, they're always wet and can be muddy all year round. I've seen eight-wheel-drive trucks bog down."

"We can't afford to get bogged down," I say.

"Don't worry, we won't. Tombaye won't have enough cadre to cover all the secondary roads. If he's going to plug a hole, he'll plug the highway."

The trip to Machweo takes an hour. That's twice as long on the side roads than a straight drive along the highway. I don't mind. With so many civilians in our party, I want to avoid contact.

We bump onto the main road, and Powell tells Enwright to turn south. "Ten minutes," he says, "and we're there."

Enwright leads the column along the narrow road. The dark mass of Mount Wambesa rears up ahead of us. The forest stretches like a broad black belt at its base. The terrain is flat on either side of our path, broken only by distinctive umbrella-shaped acacia trees.

I tap my finger gently against the AK-74's receiver. Glance back to make sure the five-ton and the minibus are maintaining separation. The French driver knows what he's doing, but I'm not sure about Father Ducasse.

I'm half expecting to see lighted ranch buildings. If the buildings are lit, it could mean the Gradys have been given no hint of danger. That could be a good thing. If the buildings are dark, it could mean they've been spooked.

Machweo is dark. I tell Enwright to slow down.

Powell leans forward, between me and Enwright. Strains his eyes to study the ranch.

"See anything unusual?" I ask.

"There should be more lights."

"I thought so."

The buildings are arranged the way Powell described them to me. A big, two-story ranch house in the middle, flanked by four large villas—two on either side. They've been built on plots carved from the forest. Between the house and the first villa on the right is a low garage, wide enough for four vehicles. The garage has been built as an extension of the main house.

"Stop here," I say. "Powell, watch the tree line. They turned the lights out for a reason."

We pull up about a hundred yards from the ranch. I get out and advance with my AK-74 at low ready. Scan the tree line, the dark spaces between the villas. I don't see anything, but it could be another ambush. Cadre or Umbali would have faded away at our approach.

Machweo lies in a different world from that of St. Croix and French Village. It's quiet except for the muted cries of birds in the forest. The birds are reassuring. I've learned that in the bush, the absence of sound signals the approach of men. Birds and animals flee when disturbed. They leave an ominous silence.

Sniff the air. It's hot, but not as dusty as it is during the day. Nothing. Downwind, under the right conditions, you can smell the enemy at two hundred yards. The Umbali have a distinctive body odor. That mix of rancid sweat and sweet nut-oil I first encountered in the bungalow. Again, outside the La Salle. The air is still. If the Umbali are in the forest, there is no breeze to carry their scent to me.

There's a wide porch with comfortable rockers. The front door opens a crack, and a rifle barrel pokes out. It's pointed straight at my chest.

"Who are you?" A man's voice, low and rough as gravel.

"I'm Breed. We're from the consulate."

"Where's Powell?"

"Back at the car."

The door opens another inch. A tough, bearded face looks through the crack. Checks out Powell's figure standing next to the Impala, M4 at low ready.

"A car and two trucks from the consulate?"

"Marien Tombaye is back. He's got a cadre of guerillas and three hundred Umbali. They've killed all the French. We're gathering Americans and any survivors."

"Looking to save your skin, eh?"

"It covers my body."

The man makes a decision. "Get in here and make it fast."

I signal Powell. He posts Enwright at the driver's door and jogs forward.

"Grady, we've been trying to phone you," Powell says.

"Lost my phone last week. Don't you have Carol's number?"

The consulate only had one number for the Gradys. If anything can go wrong, it will.

Grady swings the front door open. Powell and I step onto the porch and duck inside.

We find ourselves in a rustic sitting room lit by a single table lamp. Seventy-five feet long and thirty feet wide, the room is big enough for a small hotel. Furnished with comfortable sofas, easy chairs, and coffee tables. The lamp isn't bright enough to push the shadows back further than a small circle close to the front door.

My eyes take in the shuttered windows, the long bar, the hunting trophies, and the sliding glass doors. The doors open to a pool deck half the length of a football field. That's an obvious vulnerability. I would have lit the pool deck and turned out all the interior lights.

Grady, a bear of a man with fiery red hair, wears a white shirt open at the collar. The sleeves are rolled up to expose brawny forearms. He's carrying a Winchester Model 70 in .375 H&H Magnum. Across his shoulder, he's slung a haversack of spare ammunition.

Standing at the bar is a dark-haired man with a pointed chin and a face shaped like a shovel. He's carrying a .460 Weatherby Magnum and a haversack like Grady's. The man's covering the long glass door.

Those are hunting rifles. The Holland & Holland was introduced in 1912. Over a hundred years, it's been proven the most versatile and effective dangerous game cartridge in Africa. Compared to the sniper calibers I use, it packs colossal punch under three hundred yards. Professional African hunters don't like to shoot farther than that.

There's a middle-aged woman standing behind Grady. Colored blond hair, dressed in a cowboy shirt, bolo tie and blue jeans. In her hand is a Glock G40, 10mm Long-Slide. She's carrying it with elbow bent, muzzle pointed at the ceiling.

"This is my wife, Carol," Grady says. "The guy with the Weatherby is my foreman, Santos."

"You expecting rhinos or elephants?" I ask.

"Umbali," Grady says. "Along the tree line. Big as rhinos."

"How many?"

"A dozen at least, maybe more."

"Okay, make your way back to the vehicles," I tell him. "There's room in the five-ton."

Grady looks around at the magnificent sitting room, the high ceilings, the long bar. "Every penny I have has been sunk into this place."

He hasn't seen what Powell and I saw in French Village. "Is it worth your life? Let's get going."

"Who put *you* in charge?"

"That's the way it is. Now move—or we'll leave you."

Grady hesitates. "I have my own truck in the garage."

"No time. You'll be exposed if you try to reach it. Let's back out of here in a tight group. Make like a hedgehog."

Grady nods to his wife. "You first."

Dark figures rush at the sliding glass door. Smash it with the butts of their lances. Santos raises his rifle, and the big Weatherby crashes. The heavy-caliber round, big as a man's thumb, punches an Umbali in the chest and puts him down. Santos racks his bolt and extracts the spent shell casing.

Umbali fight their way through the shattered glass door. Grady levels his Winchester and fires as Santos chambers another round. The shot cuts an attacker down in mid-stride. The Umbali falls to one knee. Hurls his lance from the kneeling position.

There's a whack. The lance penetrates Santos's sternum and exits his back. The exit wound is two inches off-center—behind his heart. He drops his rifle and crumples.

Two more Umbali rush into the room. I raise my AK-74 and fire two quick, three-round bursts. Both score hits —tight groups, center mass. Grady points his Winchester at the man who speared Santos and shoots him in the face. The H&H slug blows the Umbali's head into a canoe. A gory mass of bone and shredded meat between two ears.

"Get to the truck," I tell them. "Powell and I will cover."

Grady racks his bolt and chambers another round. His hunting rifle packs a powerful punch, but it's slow. In a situation like this, give me an assault rifle and a thirty-round mag any day.

We back out of the sitting room. The Gradys run for the vehicles, Powell and I cover their withdrawal. Powell covers right, I cover left. More Umbali attack from the sides. Two are already behind us, going after the Gradys.

Carol Grady stops, turns, and fires four times, two-handed. The Glock 10mm will stop a bear, and she knows how to use it. The rounds go into the Umbali's stomach. He jerks with every impact, tumbles headlong into the dirt. Grimacing with pain, he struggles back to his feet, draws his machete. She fires four more times. Twice into his chest, twice into his face.

Another Umbali tries to thrust his lance into Grady, but the big man knocks it aside with the butt of his Winchester. Reverses the rifle and smashes the butt into the Umbali's mouth. The Umbali falls on his back. Carol Grady shoots him three times in the chest.

That's more proof that, in this kind of fight, a semiautomatic weapon beats a bolt-action rifle. That first Umbali Carol Grady shot absorbed eight 10mm rounds. The last two in the face killed him. Gut shots don't count. The best way to stop an Umbali is to put his lights out.

Two Umbali charge Powell. One hurls his lance from twenty feet away. The spear misses Powell's head by inches. Misses *me* by two feet. Powell blasts the pair on full automatic. Short bursts, to keep his weapon controllable. The Umbali sprawl in the gravel.

Yet another Umbali comes at me. I raise the AK-74 and shoot him in the face.

Umbali charge from the tree line toward our column. A number emerge from the shadows between the Machweo villas to the right. The two French soldiers from the five-ton are on the ground next to the tailgate. One kneeling, one standing, they fire free-hand into the charging Umbali. They're raw recruits, young boys. It may be the first time they've fired their weapons in anger.

Dark figures tumble like tenpins. Struggle to their feet, keep coming. The French drop their mags, reload, slap their bolt releases. Continue firing. The two French soldiers in the minivan drop the tailgate and climb out to help.

Willing hands pull the Gradys into the five-ton. Enwright has the Impala's engine running, and Powell jumps into the back seat. I jump into the front.

Another Umbali hurls himself at the vehicle. I aim my rifle through the gaping space that used to be the Impala's windshield and shoot him as he tries to scramble across the hood. Fire three rounds into his upper torso. He jerks, drops his lance. Grabs the dashboard with his left hand, reaches for his machete with his right. I'm staring at a leering face. Pale scars arch across his dark, shiny cheeks. His eyes glitter, his teeth shine white in a feral rictus. He's going to pull the machete and come across the dashboard to get us.

The Umbali on the hood is so close I have to lean back and short-stock the AK-74. I still can't bring the muzzle to bear. Claw for my Mark 23. The Umbali swings his machete at me, tries to get it through the opening of the windshield. I raise my left arm to ward it off. The blade strikes sparks from the frame before entering the driver's compartment. Enwright shrieks, dodges to one side. The blade, slowed by the impact with the roof, gashes my forearm.

Powell pushes the barrel of his M4 into the space between me and Enwright. Shoots the Umbali in the face. A tight group of three rounds between his eyes. The gunshots feel like an ice pick stabbed into my left ear.

"Go," I tell Enwright. "Go."

Enwright steps on the gas, and the Impala leaps forward. The acceleration slams me into my seat. Off-balance, Powell tumbles backward. Enwright stamps on the brakes and the car lurches to a stop. I'm thrown against the dashboard, and Powell slams into the backs of our seats. The Umbali sprawled on our hood slides off and disappears from view. Enwright steps on the gas, and the Impala bounces over his body.

I cast a sidelong look at Enwright. Tonight, with this car, she's crushed two Umbali. Hasn't had to draw her pistol once.

"Which way?" Enwright asks.

"U-turn," Powell tells her. "Back to the highway."

Enwright turns sharply, throwing up a dust cloud. I look over my shoulder. The army driver is following her. The five-ton sways on its suspension. Father Ducasse has trouble, but manages the maneuver. The French soldiers are back in his cargo bed, firing at Umbali through the shattered rear window.

We're all getting bounced off the walls. I hope the pregnant woman is okay.

Our little column speeds down the road. I look in the passenger's rearview mirror, get half the picture. Twist in my seat, look past Powell and Wolfe. The Umbali are falling behind. There were more of them than we expected.

"Powell. Did you see any cadre?"

"Negative."

"Tombaye's using the Umbali to fill gaps in his coverage. Arbois could be a hornets' nest."

"Then why are we going there?"

"Because we're running out of options."

12

SATURDAY, 2145 HRS - ARBOIS INTERNATIONAL AIRPORT

The international airport wears a halo of white light. We can see the low terminal building, the lighted tower, and the maintenance hangars. The structures are too far away to make out any detail. I'll have to get a lot closer to the runway to learn what I need to learn.

We've concealed our convoy in the forest, a quarter of a mile away. I want to give the group time to rest.

"Getting close is going to be a bitch," Powell says.

"I'll go alone," I tell him. "If it's all clear, I'll signal you."

"And if it goes tits up?"

"Then I'll be dead, and you're in command."

Like most airports, Arbois has been constructed on a plot of flat ground. It's all knee-high grass and scrub sprinkled with acacia. Difficult to get close, but not impossible. The only issue is vulnerability. That expanse of flat ground is a kill zone. If I'm trapped out there, I'll find little cover.

I go back to the improvised camp. We've posted French soldiers at four points of the compass. Cecile and Ducasse are tending the wounded. Enwright is speaking with Sauve, practicing her French. Sauve looks as clean and sharp as he did this morning when we met at the mine. Not a trace of five-o'clock shadow, not even peach fuzz.

I walk to the pair, nod to Enwright, and address the lieutenant.

"We need to talk," I tell him.

Sauve looks nervous. I guide him outside the perimeter, deeper into the trees. When I'm sure no one can hear us, I stop.

"Let's have this out," I tell him.

The lieutenant can't meet my eyes. He says nothing.

"Where were you going when we ran into you?"

"What do you mean?"

"I mean, where were you going? You were leading thirty people somewhere. Where were you taking them?"

"I was taking them back to the camp." The boy's voice trembles.

"In the middle of a firefight. You ran out on your sergeant," I tell him. "You're a coward. Your men know it. They're not looking to you for leadership."

"That's a lie."

I fight the urge to slap him.

"Neither you, nor your men, fired your weapons at the Village. You got into the truck and ran as fast as you could. Tonight, at the ranch, *you* didn't fire your weapon. You sat in the truck, shaking."

I want to grab the boy.

"Look at me, Sauve."

The lieutenant slowly raises his eyes.

"Next time there's killing I want done, you'll do it. Otherwise, I'll kill you myself. Understand?"

Eyes wet, the boy mumbles something unintelligible.

"Don't say anything. Just fucking do it."

I walk back to the vehicles, pass Powell and Enwright on the way. Enwright looks puzzled, Powell calm and composed. He knows what went down. Everybody's got a story, and we don't need to hear Sauve's.

The side door of the minivan is open, and Father Ducasse is rationing water to the women and children in the back. There's no drinking water or food in the five-ton. Only Cecile and Ducasse, from the mission, had time to provision themselves.

"How are they, Father?"

"They're alright for now, you miserable heathen."

"How would you know?"

"I have eyes. You and that other one." Ducasse jerks his chin toward Powell. "You're both up to your necks in blood."

"The blood of the Godless, some would say."

"There's no difference between you and Umbali."

"One difference, Father. Your flock sleeps soundly only because heathen like us protect it." As soon as I've spoken the words, I regret them. "How's the pregnant woman?"

"She is fine, as far as I can tell. No thanks to you."

"Father, any time you want, you can take her to Tombaye and the Umbali."

Ducasse grunts. "You know Marien is insane, don't you?"

The priest hands me a bottle of water, a peace offering. I take it and drink. "No, I didn't know that. All his moves have seemed rational to me."

Ducasse looks away. "He wears the mask of sanity."

"How do you know?"

"It's not my place to say. Ask Cecile."

I jerk at the mention of Cecile. Hope my reaction wasn't noticeable. "What's Cecile got to do with it?"

Ducasse shakes his head. "I've said too much. Leave us."

I hand the water back to the priest. "There are twenty people in the five-ton and four in the car," I tell him. "Work out a water ration. Share it around."

I go to the five-ton. The French soldiers are on guard duty, the Gradys are sitting together by the tailgate. Grady's holding his rifle, butt on the flatbed, barrel and action between his knees.

"Do you really think this is going to work, Breed?" Grady asks.

"We'll find out," I say. "No plan survives contact. We have to improvise as we go along."

I look at the twelve other refugees. The children are in the best condition. Huddled in a corner of the cargo bed, they're speaking together. Two of the wounded are sitting on fold-down troop seats, leaning back against the canvas rain cover. They're stoically bearing their pain. The old lady with the sling is doing the same, but her face is screwed up with misery. The morphine is at the limit of its efficacy.

The man with the stomach wound is on his back, silent. That's not good. Cecile takes a syrette from her sack and gives the old woman another dose of morphine. When she sees me, she closes the flap on her bag and comes to the tailgate.

"How are they?"

"The three are not too bad," Cecile says. "The old woman is better than she looks. People deal with pain differently, some better than others. So far, no infection has set in."

"What about the belly wound?"

"He's gone. There was nothing I could do for him." Cecile points to my arm. "Breed, you've been cut."

I hadn't noticed. The heat of battle floods your system with adrenaline and endorphins. "It's nothing."

Cecile climbs over the tailgate and jumps down. "Let me see it."

"Alright. Just a minute." I lower myself to the ground. "Sauve, get over here."

When the lieutenant presents himself, I say, "The man with the belly wound is dead. You and your driver take him into the bush where the others can't see. Dig a grave. Collect his identification and say a few words."

Ducasse, standing next to the minivan, overhears me. "I will perform that service."

"No, Father. You're needed here. Distribute the water rations."

Sauve goes to fetch his driver and a trenching tool.

I call after him. "Lieutenant."

Sauve stops, turns.

"When you've covered him up, piss on the earth."

The lieutenant hesitates. "Yes, sir."

"Breed." Ducasse's voice is hard-edged with anger. "You *cannot* desecrate a grave."

"It keeps the animals from digging it up," I tell him. "Either we desecrate the grave, or the scavengers will."

Tired, I turn my back on the priest. His eyes burn into me as I step around the corner of the truck with Cecile. Sit with my back to one of the five-ton's big rear wheels. Cecile kneels next to me and takes bottles of water and alcohol from her bag. Takes my hand, stretches my arm out. Her fingers are cool against my skin. I set the AK-74 on the ground and push up my sleeve.

"You'll get a nice scar from this," Cecile says. She scrubs

away the congealed blood, reveals a wound four inches long. Scrubs the wound clean, sets to work stitching it up.

I allow myself to relax, watch Cecile work on my arm.

"I owe you an apology," she says. "There has been no opportunity to deliver it."

"It's not necessary. Everyone was a little heated."

"Except you."

"I saw Charles use the telephone. Had no idea who he was calling."

"I've known Bröer since I was a child," Cecile says. "He's gotten worse. I don't think he has long."

"What's his story?"

Cecile looks thoughtful. Finishes stitching my arm, dresses the wound. She disinfects her instruments, then puts them away in her bag. Finally, she takes a syringe and draws a dose of tetanus vaccine.

I push up my sleeve for the shot, and she studies the black-and-white tattoo of the American flag on my arm. "Why is it the wrong way around?" Cecile asks.

Women always ask that. The field of stars faces front, ahead of the stripes. During the Civil War, the flag-bearer led the charge, and wind blew the flag backward. The flag would appear this way to anyone viewing the attack. If the flag-bearer was killed, another man would pick up the flag and take his place.

"When we're safe, I'll tell you."

An enigmatic smile. "Is that a promise?"

"Yes. Now tell me about Bröer."

Cecile jabs the needle into my shoulder.

"Ouch."

"Big baby." She's teasing me. A glimpse of the playful

child who grew up in the streets of St. Croix, did her homework for lessons at the mission school.

I wait patiently. Give Cecile time to collect her thoughts, decide how much she wants to tell me. When she's finished pumping in the vaccine, she withdraws the needle and brushes my arm with an alcohol swab.

"He's South African," she says. "A mercenary and a pilot. Fought in South Africa, Angola, Rhodesia, Mozambique. Many places I don't know. He liked to come to Wambesa between jobs. Saved his money so he could buy his own airplane and start a cargo business."

"Was he successful?"

"Yes, for a time. He flew cargoes everywhere. A number of his routes involved flights from Morocco to Spain. One day, he found his most lucrative client was using him to fly loads of hashish. He wanted no part of it and quit."

"Gangsters don't like you to quit."

"No. They killed his copilot, burned his plane, and beat him to within an inch of his life. He was a broken man when he returned to St. Croix. His left knee is unstable. His right elbow will not fully extend. Today, he's in constant pain. That is one reason he drinks so much."

"Were you operating the clinic at the time?"

"Yes. I earned my medical degree in Paris. I returned to Wambesa the year before."

"Why did you come back?"

"I love Africa. I love my country. I want to do good."

I roll my sleeve down. "I don't think Bröer cares if he lives or dies."

"His mission in life is to drink himself to death."

"And yours is to save him?"

Cecile shakes her head sadly. "I'm not naïve, Breed. I cannot save everyone. I help who I can."

I remember what Ducasse told me about Tombaye. The priest made it sound like a sensitive topic, so I choose my words carefully. "Father Ducasse tells me Tombaye is disturbed."

Surprised, Cecile looks me in the eye. "Is that what he said?"

"That's *all* he said. I didn't believe him, and he said you might be able to convince me."

"Why should I convince you? Why do you care?"

"Tombaye has been responsible for the deaths of hundreds. Before the night is over, we could be among his victims. I need to know all I can."

"You want to know your enemy."

"Of course."

Cecile sighs, gathers her thoughts. "Alright. Marien and I grew up together. I was an orphan, brought up at Father Ducasse's mission. Marien was a boy from St. Croix. Muslim, as most of the people are in Wambesa. However, his parents wanted him educated in western subjects, as well as the Quran. We both went to the mission school."

"Were you friends?"

"You could say that. We were both good students and were sent to Paris to study. The Church sent me on a scholarship. I studied medicine, he studied history. He finished his studies before I did and came home. When I returned, I found he had been arrested for activism. Marien is a nationalist. He wanted the people of Wambesa to assume more responsibility in the administration of government. He wanted Wambesa to retain a greater share of the profits from the sale of our resources."

"Most of those debates were held after World War II."

"Yes, but as you know, many countries were granted *faux* independence. The old powers retained a great deal of influence, if not outright control. In any case, the French considered Marien a terrorist."

"Of course, he was nothing of the sort."

"Not at all. But the label was convenient for the French. Marien was taken to the army barracks and held for two years. They tortured him. When they released him, he was not the same. He was quiet. Uncommunicative. After a few weeks, he made his way across the border to Marawi."

"We know he joined Boko Haram. Became an Islamic fighter."

"Yes. Marien has a will of iron. He succeeds at whatever he puts his mind to. The French found him dangerous because people followed him. There was talk all over town. Marien was fighting in Mali. No, he was in Algeria. No, Marien was fighting in Libya. In Syria. He became a legend."

"That means he's a committed fighter. That doesn't mean he's crazy."

"Breed, Marien hates like you have never seen a man hate. What the townspeople did at French Village was done because he permitted it. He *knew* what they would do, and he stepped aside."

Torture can bend a man's mind. Operators like Powell and myself are prepared for it. That's what SERE school—Survival, Escape, Resistance and Evasion—was all about. But one important lesson is that everybody breaks.

I touch Cecile's upper arm, stroke her gently, lower my hand. "We have to get out."

"You didn't expect to have to carry us, did you?"

"No, but..."

"But?"

I feel lost in Cecile's eyes. "But anyone as beautiful as you has to be saved."

Embarrassed, yet pleased, Cecile lowers her eyes. When she raises them, she says, "Breed, you say the most outrageous things."

"What's worse, I mean them."

We stare at each other for what feels like forever. Cecile leans forward and puts her hand flat on my chest. Kisses me softly on the lips and leans back. Without another word, she gets to her feet and walks to the minivan.

Father Ducasse has been watching us.

I'M COVERED in dirt and scrub, crawling toward the airport. My AK-74, ammunition vest and jeans are dark colored. In broad daylight, I'd stand out against the tan soil. At night, I don't need to do much to reduce my profile.

Low grass, scrub, and scattered acacia trees cover the quarter mile of flat ground between the forest and the airfield. Floodlights on the roof of the terminal building cover the strip with a brilliant glare. White light washes over the surrounding ground for a hundred yards.

That's a clear limit to how close I can approach. Did cadre light the place up because they expect infiltration? Maybe it's business as usual when a flight is expected. I advance in a low crawl.

The important thing is to avoid features in the landscape that are obvious hides. If I were standing in the control tower, sweeping binoculars over the surrounding ground, where would I look? The acacias are prominent. I would look there first. Any ditches next to approach roads are next. Look any place a man might hide, especially if he is looking for both cover and concealment. Concealment hides you from view. Cover stops bullets.

I'm gambling that concealment is my best cover. If the enemy can't see me, they can't shoot me. Big gamble. Reconnaissance by fire can be deadly. All the same, I decide to stick to the low scrub in the open field. It's all over the place. If I flatten myself down in that, there's nothing to draw a sentry's eye.

I stop a hundred yards from the tower and lie with my chest on top of the AK-74. The human eye is drawn to straight lines. Anything straight and hard-edged in a natural environment looks man-made. It's a dead giveaway.

Take a breath, study the airport.

Two-story terminal building, three-story control tower. The glassed-in tower is lit from within, but all I see are the shadowy shapes of air controllers. I work my phone out of my pocket. I've dimmed the screen till it's barely visible. Plugged in a single earphone.

I punch Stein's speed dial.

"Breed."

"I have eyes on the airport," I tell her. "Where's the plane?"

"On its way, maneuvering onto its glide slope."

"Are you in contact with the tower?"

"Yes. All in order so far."

My eyes sweep the field. The single runway ends right in front of me, a hundred yards away. Two parallel lines of runway lights extend straight north for two miles. The builders of the airport didn't have to skimp. No shortage of flat land around here. This airport can easily handle Boeing

737s and 787s. The terminal building and tower are on the left, with wheeled boarding stairs.

To the right are hangars and maintenance buildings. I see a parked fuel tanker truck and a fire truck.

Far in the distance, three bright lights in the shape of a triangle flick on. Landing lights. One on each of the wing roots and a third below the nose. The one on the nose appears higher than the other two because the plane is starting to flare.

Stein's voice, tense, crackles in my earphone. "Breed, talk to me."

"Wait, Stein. Wait."

I hear a growl, and the fire truck starts up. Is that business as usual? The truck starts to roll toward the runway. Its lights are off. Surely *that* is not BAU. It pulls up twenty yards from the strip on the east side.

Flick my eyes back to the shadowy figures in the tower. They're acting normal.

The landing lights are getting bigger. The plane is on its glide slope.

Another engine growls to life. From behind the terminal building, a truck rolls into view. With its headlights off, the vehicle looks like a menacing bull.

Shit. It's a military five-ton. The canvas rain cover has been taken down, and two men with rifles are standing on the cargo bed, leaning on the roof of the cab. Cadre.

"Wave them off, Stein. It's a trap."

Stein speaks into another telephone. "Abort landing. Repeat—abort."

The plane continues to descend. The five-ton rolls into position on the west side of the runway, opposite the fire truck.

"The plane's still coming, Stein. Did they acknowledge?"

"Affirmative."

Lower and lower, the plane descends. It's a jetliner. An Airbus or a Boeing with two engines. The landing lights are dazzling. Their glare blots out the cockpit windshield.

Dark sticks of landing gear are visible. My throat clenches.

Cadre are standing on a mat of rolled-up fire hoses in the cargo bed of the fire truck. AK-74s cradled in their arms.

Less than three hundred feet from the surface of the runway, the pilot applies go-around thrust. The plane's engines scream, and the plane rockets toward me. It's no longer descending. Its nose, already flared skyward, pitches up another hair.

The cadre stiffen with shock. Turn to watch the big airliner roar past them and climb away. One man raises his rifle but lowers it without firing.

"Landing aborted, Stein."

"I'm sorry, Breed."

"Exfiling now. Speak later."

I pull the earphone from my ear and roll it up. Squeeze it, and the phone, back into my pocket. Lie still, watch the cadre at the trucks. They're shouting to each other in a language I don't understand. Sounds Arabic. The men in the fire truck jump down and join the other three in the five-ton.

One of them lifts a handheld radio to his ear. He's reporting to HQ.

No sign of Tombaye. He must be at the Hôtel de Ville.

I back away from the airport and crawl to our vehicles. Take my time, move with deliberation. As I withdraw, I review our steadily diminishing options.

THE FACES that greet me span a range from accusation to despair. Grady's voice is truculent. "What happened, Breed?"

"Tombaye had cadre at the airport," I tell them. "At least six men, probably eight. They were waiting to ambush the plane."

"Ambush! What the hell for?"

"Who knows? He's already made his public announcement. There was every reason to expect the plane to be called off. But so long as there was a chance it would land, he wanted to seize it. Impounding an airliner at *his* airport would make another great headline."

"But was he looking for *us*?" Cecile asks.

"I don't think so. Their attention was completely focused on the airplane. They didn't have anyone watching the approach to the airport. I got to within a hundred yards without anyone noticing."

Powell strokes his stubble. "Then it's possible he doesn't know we're out here."

"It's possible, but I wouldn't count on it. He'll have done a body count on the French army, so he knows he's missing six bodies. He wanted to kill Consul General Wolfe and couldn't catch him at the La Salle. He had Umbali covering Machweo, so he knows the Gradys escaped. That tells him he has a band of fugitives loose in Wambesa."

"I reckon he has a couple of other clues," Powell says.

"Yes indeed. If he was out to get Consul General Wolfe, he was certainly out to get *you*. He knows you weren't at the consulate and probably escaped with Wolfe from the La Salle."

"And he sent six Umbali to kill *you*," Powell says. "At the bungalow."

"Exactly. Our friend Tombaye is well informed. He knows you and I are wild cards shuffled into his deck. He wanted to eliminate us early in the game. He has failed so far, but I think he'll keep trying."

Enwright puts her hands on her hips. "Here's a question for you, Breed. *What do we do now?*"

I made the decision while I was crawling back from the runway. "We go with Cecile's idea."

"What is that?" Cecile asks.

"We try for the Lokola border."

13

SATURDAY, 2300 HRS - LOKOLA BORDER

"Lokola's a hot border," Powell says.

"What are they fighting over?"

"Wambesa and Lokola have been fighting over cobalt claims. Neither side has much of an army, but Lokola's brought in Wagner advisers. They've ramped up military spending, bought Russian weapons and hardware."

Wagner PMC is a Russian private military company. Widely misunderstood in the west, even by military officers. The "musicians" aren't mercenaries or contractors in the western sense of the word. Wagners swear allegiance to Mother Russia.

I once gave a lecture on Wagner at one of Stein's symposiums. Top intelligence professionals didn't understand Wagner PMC. Russian law drove the creation of the company. Wagner was created in 2014 during the Ukrainian War in Donbas. The Donbas militia, resisting the Ukrainian army, needed help. Russian law was very specific. The Russian army was not legally permitted to operate *outside* the borders of the Russian Federation. By the same token, private military companies were not allowed to operate *inside* the borders of the Russian Federation.

The Russians, however, are masters at getting around legalities. Russia's highest authority arranged for the creation of Wagner PMC. As a private military company, Wagner *could* legally operate in the Donbas, outside Russia's borders. Wagner's elite first tier of operators were drawn from the 45th Guards Spetsnaz Brigade, based outside Moscow. The VDV airborne unit was Russia's special operations force. It was tasked with conducting reconnaissance and kinetic operations against enemy command and control. Their mandate included the assassination of enemy leaders.

Wagner PMC operated in Donbas, advising and reinforcing the local militia. I encountered them at the Battle of Debaltseve, and they kicked our ass. Years later, they continued to be active during Russia's invasion of Ukraine in 2022. However, a problem arose. Along with other regions, Donbas and Luhansk constitutionally joined the Russian Federation. That meant that, under Russian law, Wagner PMC was no longer legally permitted to operate in the provinces of Donbas and Luhansk. Long story short, Wagner contractors were given a choice—either rejoin the Russian army, or join Wagner operations in Africa. All the Wagner units in Donbas and Luhansk were disbanded.

The bottom line is that Wagner is an unconventional instrument of Russian foreign policy. Russia is using Wagner to expand Russia's footprint in Africa. The great powers are jostling for position. Influence of the old colonial powers is waning, and that of China is waxing. China owns eleven out of fifteen cobalt mines in the Congo. All across the Sahel, countries have experienced coups and forced France to withdraw. Coincidentally, Wagner PMC has shown up in each of those countries to provide military advice and support in counterinsurgency operations.

This military involvement has been coordinated with extensive Russian and Chinese economic initiatives. The old European powers have been sent reeling from the continent. Our own involvement has been minimal. If America doesn't get involved, if we don't get our act together, the west will lose Africa.

It's not too late, but we have to win some hearts and minds.

With Lokola bringing in Wagner PMC, and Tombaye wiping out the French, COBRA's mining interests in Wambesa are up for grabs. Indeed, that might be exactly what Tombaye has in mind.

"I don't think we can make it to Marawi on that highway," I tell Powell. "Do you think different?"

"No. By now, Tombaye will have gotten his firebreaks built. Secured the Presidential Palace and the Hôtel de Ville. That frees up a lot of his cadre."

Exactly what I feared. I look around our little group. "If anyone has ideas, speak up. We need options."

The group is silent.

"Okay," I say. "Let's move out."

POWELL GUIDES our blacked-out column over back roads to get around the airport. I don't want to run into Tombaye's cadre on their way back to St. Croix. The problem is, Tombaye could just as easily send them to the Lokola border.

I confer with Powell, and we decide to get back on the

highway after bypassing the airport. It's a better road, and it will save us time. We'll take the risk of encountering cadre on the road between the airport and the border.

Our column rushes east.

"Slow down," Powell says.

Enwright brakes gently.

"Bridge." Powell points to a structure two hundred yards ahead. "That's the Lokola River."

"Pull over," I tell Enwright.

"What do you think?" Powell asks.

"There's two ways to control a road," I say.

"Yeah. Troops on a roadblock, or land mines."

"We'd have run over land mines long before now," I say, "but they could have mined the bridge. The lead vehicle sets off the mine and takes out the crossing. Stalls the rest of the column."

"Let's check it out."

Powell and I get out of the car and approach the bridge. I allow him to lead, staggered with seven yards separation. Thirty yards from the bridge, he crouches and waves me to the ground.

I fall prone and cover him with my AK-74.

The SEAL advances in a low crouch. When he reaches the bridge, he falls prone and crawls to the riverbank. Swings his legs over the edge and climbs down. From below, he can check the piers and abutments of the structure.

Minutes tick by.

Check my watch. What the fuck is the hold-up? Powell must have found something.

Powell sticks his head above the riverbank. Places his rifle flat on the ground and levers himself up. Waves for me to approach.

When I join him, he speaks in a low voice. "Four concrete pillars," he says, "two to a side. The rest of the structure is timber, built solid. Packages of plastic explosives strapped to one pillar, detonator wires hooked to a pressure plate on the road surface. No booby trap, no secondary charge. I snipped them."

Powell holds something out to me. "Sniff my stinky finger."

"Dude, I hardly know you."

We chuckle together.

I take the puttylike substance from him. Smell it, taste it, spit it out. "Not C-4."

"No," Powell says. "I was a breacher, and I've seen a lot of stuff. It's Russian. Higher velocity than ours, but less stable. There are demolition manuals. Formulas to calculate the ratio of explosive to concrete thickness, so on and so forth. The Russians are very quantitative, they have equations and shit for everything. This guy was following a Russian manual. He was trained that way."

"You ever get the feeling someone keeps pushing you in a certain direction?"

"AK-74s, PKMs, Kornet ATGMs and now Russian plastic?" Powell nods. "Yeah, I know what you mean."

"We're not figuring it out now. Let's go."

"You bring up the column. I'll check the other side, wave you over when it's clear."

"What if there's another pressure plate?" I ask.

"Then you'll have to cross someplace else."

"Be serious."

"Plate's set for a thousand pounds. *This* bony ass won't set it off."

Half expecting to hear an explosion behind me, I walk

back to the column. Traffic on the border highway must have been light tonight. We're lucky another car trying to leave the country didn't set the explosives off.

Nothing, thank God. I signal Sauve to follow us, get into the Impala. Lay my rifle on the dash. I am bone-tired.

"Crank 'er up," I tell Enwright.

THE BORDER FENCE is twelve feet high and topped with barbed wire. There's a big, wood-framed butterfly gate with an administrative building, armed soldiers, and vehicles behind it. Two of the vehicles have their headlights on. They bathe the approach to the gate in white light. The glare silhouettes soldiers at the gate. They stand with their feet apart, rifles at port arms.

Flat ground extends to the left of the highway, forest lies on the right. The forest has been cleared for fifty yards in front of the fence. I find myself wondering how far the fence stretches on either side.

Enwright stops fifty yards short of the gate. Short of the clearing, the edge of the forest on our right. Shallow ditches line both sides of the highway. The ditch on our right lies between our column and the forest.

I turn to Wolfe. "Go to the five-ton. Ask Dr. Abimbola to come forward."

Wolfe gets out of the car, strides the length of our column. Ten yards behind our Impala is the five-ton, with Sauve and his driver in the cab. At the tailgate of the five-ton are the two young soldiers and the Gradys, with Cecile and other civilians in the cargo bed. A further ten yards behind the five-ton is the minivan, driven by Father Ducasse. The children are in the back, with the sergeant and corporal in the cargo bed, rifles pointing to the rear.

"How do you want to play this?" Powell asks.

"I'll go forward and try to get us across. You stay with the column. If anything happens to me, you take command."

"You're depressing."

"Hope for the best, plan for the worst. Those cadre at the airport?"

"What about them?"

"Do you think Tombaye called them back to St. Croix or sent them here?"

Powell doesn't hesitate. "Sent them here. With the Umbali from Machweo."

"That's what I'd do. And I'd take half my cadre from St. Croix and have them cover the highway to Marawi."

Cecile looks into the Impala. "What do you want, Breed?"

"I need someone to translate for me."

I climb out of the car. Walk with Cecile toward the gate. I'm conscious of the cleared zone on either side. We're leaving our column and the forest fifty yards behind.

One of the soldiers yells something. I don't understand the language, but the tone says "Halt!"

"Tell him we want to talk," I say.

Cecile translates my words.

Now that we're closer, I sweep the fence, count the troops and vehicles.

There must be forty or fifty infantry arrayed behind the fence. AK-74 rifles, woodland camouflage BDUs, khaki ammo vests, green berets. Clean and well turned out. Disciplined troops. I notice a dozen are white men. They wear the same uniforms except the whites wear camouflage hats with floppy brims.

Wagners.

The soldiers' vehicles are Toyota Land Cruisers. Two are equipped with 12.7mm Dushka machine guns on pintle mounts. In front of the administration building is a tank. Soviet-era T-62 with a 115mm smoothbore main gun. The coaxial machine gun is a 7.62mm PKT. Another Dushka stands pintle-mounted on the turret.

The administration building has been sandbagged. There are four short, sandbagged barricades, two on either side of the butterfly gate. Land cruisers are parked with their headlights shining through the spaces between the barricades. That places the engine blocks of the vehicles where they can plug the gaps. With the Toyotas in place, the vehicles and sandbags make a bulletproof bulwark. If large numbers of people need to pass, the vehicles can be backed out of the way.

One of the Wagners climbs onto the tank and lays a hand casually on the Dushka.

The sentries swing one wing of the butterfly gate open. Two men step out and approach. A black officer and a Wagner. They stop and face us. The officer says something.

"He asks what we want," Cecile says.

I would have thought the answer was obvious.

"The French in Wambesa have been massacred. We're Americans, fleeing. We have women and children. We seek sanctuary in Lokola."

The officer and Cecile exchange words. The black officer makes a dismissive gesture. He's waving us off.

"He says the border is closed," Cecile says. "He wants us to go away."

I think of the Russian weapons Tombaye's cadre are carrying. If Russia is backing Tombaye's putsch, the Wagners won't be sympathetic. I decide to gamble, address the white soldier in Russian.

"Hello, comrade. Can you help us?"

"How?"

"Does Russia make war on women and children? We have children and a pregnant woman." I'm sure my accent is butchering the Russian language, but I'm getting my meaning across.

"Women and children die in war."

"Women and children can't fight back. Take our women and children."

"The border is closed until the situation is clarified. I would take them if I could, but I cannot."

We sure as hell can't fight our way across the wire. What else can I try?

The Wagner looks past me at our column. "Send your pregnant woman," he says.

I'll take what I can get. Turn to Cecile. "Bring the pregnant woman. Hurry it up."

Cecile runs back to the minivan. Ducasse helps the pregnant girl step from the vehicle and Cecile walks her to the gate.

The Wagner signals one of the sentries to come forward and take the woman.

"Thank you."

From behind our column—the crack of a rifle.

Automatic weapons fire snaps down the length of our column. It's coming from the highway, and the cadre aren't watching their background. They don't care that the border is in front of our convoy and the Lokola army is in the line of fire.

There's shouting and confusion. I'm praying the Wagners and Lokola army don't think we're shooting at them.

Cecile and I are caught in the open. I drag Cecile to the ground and cover her with my body. The Wagner and the Lokola officer run behind the gate. The sentry hurries the pregnant woman through.

"*Ne strelyay!*" the Wagner yells. "Hold your fire!"

Wagners and the Lokola soldiers take cover behind the sandbags and their vehicles. The Wagner on the tank keeps one hand on the Dushka, crouches behind the frying-pan turret.

The French soldiers in the back of Ducasse's minivan are firing. The muzzle flashes of cadre twinkle like fireflies a hundred yards behind them. The cadre have dismounted their vehicle and fanned out on both sides of the highway. They form a "T", allowing all their guns to bear on our column.

"Into the ditch!" I'm waving at Powell. It's really hard to hear anything in a firefight. That's why the Unit went to electronic earpro. Bullets kick up dirt and asphalt around us. Powell waves back. Signals Sauve. Pulls open the doors of the Impala, drags the consul general and Enwright out the side of the vehicle nearest the forest.

Powell shoves Wolfe flat on the ground, urges him into the ditch. Enwright gets the idea, crawls after him.

"Stay flat," I tell Cecile. "Do as I do, follow me."

The vehicles are fifty yards behind us, the ditch twelve

feet to our right. I cradle the AK-74 in my arms and snake my way to the ditch. Tumble into it, drag Cecile in after me. Bullets skip off the surface of the road and whack into the sandbagged Lokola positions. The soldiers are disciplined. They hold their fire—for now.

Our column is not doing nearly so well. Bullets rake the minivan and the five-ton. The cargo truck is protecting the Impala. Powell, Wolfe and Enwright are not taking a lot of fire.

Sauve and his driver jump from the cab of the five-ton and roll into the ditch. The two young soldiers at the tailgate hustle the Gradys and other civilians to cover. Jump in after them. One soldier makes it, the other doesn't. He's hit in the back by AK-74 fire, sprawls on the highway.

Ten yards behind the five-ton, Father Ducasse pushes the children into the ditch with one of the French soldiers. Where's the other one? Probably hit. The metal skin of the minivan offers no cover.

Gasoline, more flammable than diesel, leaks from the minivan's punctured tank. Russian bimetallic ammunition strikes sparks like it's the Fourth of July.

The minivan bursts into flames.

Careful to stay below the lip, I lie flat in the ditch. Twist on my side, look back at Cecile. Signal her to follow me. Chin in the dirt, she nods her head a fraction.

I crawl as fast as I can along the ditch. Fifty yards to reach the Impala, bullets snapping overhead. Wish I had elbow and knee pads. Look back every fifteen feet to make sure Cecile is with me.

Reach Powell, grab him by the shoulder. "You see any Umbali?"

"Yes. They're in the bush behind the cadre."

"They didn't get here on foot."

"Look at the trucks."

A hundred yards past the burning minivan squats the hulking shape of a five-ton truck. Its windshield is orange with the reflection of the flames. Muzzle flashes wink from the rifles of cadre on either side.

Behind the five-ton sits a massive red pumper fire truck. The one from the airport. "Son of a bitch."

We once packed the better part of two platoons into a five-ton. With a bunch more riding on top of that fire truck, we could be facing eight cadre and fifty Umbali.

I pull Cecile and Enwright toward me. "Come with me along the ditch. We'll gather the civilians, the children. Go into the bush, head for Machweo. It's south-by-west, got that? Do you know how to tell which way south-by-west is?"

Enwright gives me a blank look.

"Look for Mount Wambesa. The ranch is five or six miles in that direction." I gesture with a knife-hand. "If in doubt, steer to the right. First you'll cross the Lokola River, then you'll hit the Machweo road. Do you understand?"

Enwright shakes her head. I want to tell her the ranch is next to the fucking Starbucks. I turn to Cecile. "Can you see it, Cecile? Head toward the mountain, keep right. You'll hit Machweo road. Follow the road to the ranch."

"I understand," Cecile says.

"Listen. I'm going to get *Grady* to lead you to Machweo. It could get confusing in the bush. I'm telling you this so that, *if you lose him*, you'll know how to get there on your own."

I tap Enwright, point to Cecile. "If you lose Grady, follow *her*."

We crawl over Powell and Wolfe. Make our way ten yards farther back along the ditch to Sauve and his driver. Both have shouldered their 416s and are firing back at the muzzle flashes. I don't know if they're hitting anything, but suppressive fire is better than nothing. Powell and Wolfe abandon the Impala and join us.

I put my hand on the lieutenant's shoulder, yell into his ear. "Single shots only, save ammo. Hold until I say otherwise."

Scramble over him, turn, pull Cecile and Enwright after me.

The teenagers from the truck are shielding the wounded civilians, holding them below the lip of the ditch. Carol Grady is comforting the old woman who has her arm hung up in a sling. Four other civilians huddle together.

One man sits up and turns to look at me. "Get down!" I motion to him with the flat of my hand.

A bullet, traveling the length of the ditch, hits him in the back and blows straight through. Smashes his right clavicle and spatters us with blood. He's flung forward and falls among the children. Clamps his free hand over the wound. It's not spurting like a fire hose, so the round missed the artery. I tear off his sleeve, tear it in two. Crumple half and plug the small entry wound in his back. Wad up the other half and cram it into the gaping exit wound. I feel bone crunch, and the man screams. I take his bloody hand and plant it on the dressing. "Keep pressure on that." Turn to Cecile. "Stay with me, patch him up later."

The soldier who was shot helping the civilians from the five-ton lies face-up on the tarmac. His dead eyes glitter in the firelight. I reach for one of his arms, drag his body to the lip of the ditch. Arrange the corpse as a sandbag to cover the ditch around the Gradys.

I pull Cecile and Enwright close. Huddle with the Gradys.

"We're pulling out of here," I tell Troy Grady.

"Where are we going?"

"*You* are leading the civilians to Machweo."

"Machweo? That's five miles on foot."

"We can make it." I turn to Enwright. Put my arm around her shoulder, pull her close, yell in her ear. "We have two groups of civilians. This bunch from the five-ton is your responsibility. The ones from the minivan are Cecile's. Each of you keep your groups together."

"Do we go now?" Enwright asks.

"Not all at once. Enwright, you go first with your group. Take Wolfe with you. Crawl into the bush and hide. Grady, you follow. Wait for Cecile to join you with her group, then all of you head out together."

Enwright goes to work, gathers the children and other civilians. I tap Cecile's shoulder. "Come on."

We crawl another ten yards. Bullets lash the bush to our left. We find Ducasse and the young woman sheltering the four children from the minivan. If only the Wagner had taken the kids, too. He wasn't supposed to take anyone. By taking the pregnant woman, he saved two lives in one package. In war, one encounters both cruelty and humanity.

At the far end of the group is the sergeant. He's firing at muzzle flashes twinkling in the bush.

The heat from the burning minivan is scorching the right side of my face.

I pull Cecile and Ducasse together. Address Cecile. "This is your group. Take them now. Crawl into the bush. Hook up with Grady and Enwright. You have three weapons.

Enwright and Carol Grady have pistols, Troy Grady has a rifle."

Cecile nods.

"Work with Grady and Enwright," I tell her. "Get everybody to Machweo, we'll meet you there."

"Exactly *what* is in Machweo, Breed?" Ducasse asks.

"No time to explain. Just follow Cecile and Grady. *Get there.*"

Cecile leads Ducasse and the children into the bush. I glance back along the ditch. Sauve, his driver, and Powell are all firing. They're covering the withdrawal of Grady and Enwright. The civilians from the five-ton have already disappeared into the forest.

I lie next to the sergeant. Count the muzzle flashes. Eight cadre. To my right, I see the corporal lying on the highway. He was killed climbing out of the minivan.

"Fall back," I tell the sergeant.

I don't know if he speaks English, but he knows what I want. Body language and vocal tonality are wonderful things. Cecile and Ducasse have disappeared into the bush. Powell, Sauve, and the other soldiers are firing on the cadre. The sergeant and I fall back to them.

When I pass the dead soldier from the five-ton, I drag his corpse into the ditch. Pull four magazines from his vest. Crawl back to Powell and hand him the ammunition. "Here. Christmas came early."

The 416s and the M4 take the same magazines, fire the same ammunition. Powell takes the mags from me and crams them into his vest. "Aren't you tempted to charge those motherfuckers?"

"It's going to be a long night. The cadre can afford losses, we can't."

Shadows flit among the trees to our left.

"Umbali," Powell says. "They're flanking us."

I grab Sauve by the arm. "Take your men, fall back to the river. We'll be right behind you."

Sauve needs no urging. He pushes his three men ahead of him. Powell is firing into the bush where he saw the Umbali. As the French plunge into the bush, a round from the cadre hits Sauve's driver in the back, between the shoulder blades. The impact knocks him flat on his face.

The lieutenant drops to one knee, tries to lift the man.

"Leave him," I tell Sauve.

There's no way we can carry critically wounded through the bush.

Our volume of fire has dropped from six rifles to two. The cadre advance, firing.

From the border, a heavy machine gun hammers. The Wagner standing on the tank is firing the Dushka over our heads. The automatic fire is deafening. The cadre's muzzle flashes look like fireflies, but the Dushka's look like lightning bolts. Green tracers stab the dark. The Dushka is the ultimate macho weapon—it takes a Cossack to wrestle it.

Cadre throw themselves to the ground. The Wagners are covering our withdrawal.

"Let's go." I turn away from the firelit highway and plunge into the forest. It's like diving into a black ocean. The vegetation parts, then closes behind me.

I THROW caution to the wind, thrash through the brush. Trip, fall, get up and run farther. The Dushka is still hammering. The cadre are pinned down. They can't chase us along the road before following us into the forest. They have to go the long way around—cross on their bellies and follow the Umbali.

Umbali. The hunters are in their natural element. Powell and I can operate as effectively as they can in the forest, but the civilians and the French soldiers can't. We have to find a way to buy time for the others.

The Lokola River is a natural defensive barrier. I took a long look at it when we drove in from the airport this morning. Powell pointed out that the creeks were dry and the rivers low at this time of year. He was right. The Lokola is fast-moving, but it's shallow. We won't have trouble crossing it.

I catch up to Sauve. The boy is sucking wind.

"We have to buy time for the civilians," I say. "We'll try to hold them off at the river."

Sauve, drenched in sweat, nods once.

Powell jogs at my shoulder, one step behind. "When we get to the river," I tell him, "I'll hold on this bank. You cross over with Sauve's men and set up a base of fire. Cover my crossing. We'll make a stand there."

Standard bounding tactics. A plan is forming in my mind. The civilians are fleeing south-by-west. Once across the river, we'll hold the cadre and Umbali for as long as we can, then run south parallel to the river. With luck, that'll draw our pursuers away from the slower group of civilians.

With a start, I find myself in the open. The banks of the river are relatively clear for a few feet on either side. The scene is lit by moonlight—the rocky riverbed, the rushing water, the brooding forest.

One of Sauve's men is already splashing to the other side. Powell picks his way down the rocky bank into the riverbed.

Sauve and another of his men are a few feet ahead of me, looking for a place to cross.

There's a blur of movement to my right. A hideous shadow detaches itself from the forest. An Umbali. White teeth flashing in a savage grin, he hurls his lance. Sauve's soldier is staring at the hunter, paralyzed with fear.

The lance penetrates the boy's chest with a sickening wet thwack. I fire into the Umbali's face. The Umbali and the French soldier go down at the same time. The boy drops his rifle. Arms spread, he falls on his back with a stunned expression.

More dark shapes thrash through the vegetation. I tear a Russian lemonka grenade from my vest and pull the pin. Loose the arming lever, let it cook for two seconds, hurl it into the bush.

The blast hurls a body from the forest and onto the riverbank. Grenade fragments shred flesh and foliage. A cloud of dark smoke rolls from the forest. The sharp smell of cordite mingles with the odor of vegetation. The hunters have been silent through every attack. For the first time, I hear Umbali scream.

Sauve fires into the twitching form of the Umbali rolling on the ground. I raise my AK-74 and fire into the bush.

Powell splashes across the river.

Lance raised, another Umbali bursts from the forest to my right. I smash him in the mouth with the butt of the AK-74. He goes down. I step on the wrist of his lance hand and bring the butt of the rifle down on his face. Crush his cheeks flat to the level of his ears.

Yet another Umbali charges from my left. Sauve fires and cuts him down.

Tear my last lemonka from the vest. Pull the pin, cook it and throw.

Another blast. More screams from Umbali cut down by shrapnel.

There's the crack of rifle fire and muzzle flashes in the bush. The cadre have caught up to us. Sauve cuts loose on full automatic. Empties a magazine, reloads, slaps the bolt release. Bullets snap around us. My AK-74 clacks empty. I lever a fresh banana magazine into the well.

Powell reaches the other side. Seeks cover behind a tree, readies his M4.

"Go across," Sauve says. "I will follow."

I turn and pick my way down the rocky riverbank. There's just enough moonlight to see. Twisting an ankle now would be fatal. Behind me, Sauve continues firing on full automatic. I splash into the river. Crossing demands caution —mossy rocks lie invisible beneath the rushing water. Hip-deep in the middle, I slip and fall on my face. Water closes over me. Surprised how cool it is! Soaked, I struggle to my feet, spit and keep going. Bullets whine off wet stones on the opposite bank, throw up little spouts around me.

Powell and the French soldier are firing over my head, semiauto. The soldier who was killed by the lance was a boy. The soldier with Powell must be the sergeant, a squad leader. They're aiming at Umbali and the muzzle flashes of cadre on the bank behind me. I become conscious of yelling.

I half-turn. Sauve is on one knee on the other bank, emptying magazine after magazine into the forest. Full auto, that's what the 416 was designed for. Defiant, he's shouting at the Umbali.

I trip, fall. Watch a bullet clip Sauve and spin him around. He struggles back to his knees, continues to fire. I get up, reach the other side. Scramble over the rocks to reach Powell and the sergeant.

Gasping, I reach the tree line twenty feet to Powell's right. I throw myself prone behind a fallen tree trunk. Brace the AK-74 against it, open the bolt, drain the barrel. Blink sweat and river water out of my eyes, release the bolt. Fire on Umbali attacking the lieutenant.

Sauve's 416 locks empty. The Umbali fall upon him. I shoot one, Powell another. A third thrusts with his lance and sticks Sauve in the belly. The lieutenant drops his rifle and claws at his attacker. Powell and I shoot the Umbali at the same time. Sauve slumps forward on his knees, his body impaled on the lance.

Powell is on my left, the sergeant on my right. We're firing on semiauto, picking our shots. Muzzle flashes wink from the forest. Umbali gather on the opposite side, and we fire into them. Right away, they spread out on both sides of the bank, make their way onto the riverbed, and start to run across.

I focus on the Umbali, make every shot count. Single shots, aimed fire. They have to descend into the riverbed, splash across, then climb to the riverbank. That gives us the advantages of cover, concealment, and an elevated position.

An Umbali clambers over the rocks, charges toward me. I've always preferred the AK's iron sight picture to that of an M4. I lay it on his face and squeeze the trigger. Twenty yards away, his head jerks, and a grisly black fan blossoms in the air behind him. *Hit.*

Umbali run across the riverbed, climb toward the bank on our left. Range easily forty yards. A target travelling *across* your sight picture is moving faster than a target coming straight at you. I lead one of the Umbali and pull the trigger.

Watch the bullet splash against rocks behind him—a white puff off black stone. *Miss.* Adjust lead, fire again. The round blows off his left arm and goes into his chest, spinning him in mid-stride. *Hit.*

We can't hold them. They are so dispersed it is impossible to kill enough to keep them from reaching our side of the river.

"Run south," I yell to the sergeant and Powell. "Break contact."

The sergeant gets up and starts running. I give him a minute, then signal Powell I'm leaving.

"Go," Powell says.

I run after the sergeant. Powell alternates his fire between the Umbali crossing the river and the cadre on the opposite bank. When the cadre realize there's only one rifle firing, they venture forward.

When the cadre start to scramble down the riverbank, Powell tears a grenade from his vest. Pulls the pin and hurls it with all his strength. Without waiting for the grenade to land, he turns and follows me.

There's a sharp explosion, the sound of the grenade exploding on the riverbed.

Behind me, I hear Powell yell, "Suck on that!"

14

SUNDAY, 0030 HRS - MACHWEO

I want the Umbali, and the cadre following them, to think we're going to cross back over the Lokola River. Make another try for the border. That will throw them off the trail of the civilians, who are fleeing to Machweo.

We've been running south for half an hour. Powell and I can sustain this pace for another hour, but the sergeant is sucking wind. I stop, wait for Powell and the sergeant to catch me. We're standing together on a patch of rocks. "This is it," I tell them. "Watch what I do. We're going to throw them a curve."

The riverbank is a few yards away. I climb down to the riverbed, then step over the rocks until I reach a sandy surface that slopes gently to the water. I stride to the running stream and step in. Stop.

Then I backtrack. Walk backward in my own steps, careful to put my weight on my heels. When I reach the rocks where Powell and the sergeant are standing, I stop. "Powell first," I say. "Take your time. If you smudge a step, you'll spoil it. The Umbali are trackers."

Powell follows my example, walking close to my path, offset by a short distance. Tries to make it look natural. When he returns, I'm satisfied. Nod to the sergeant, hold my breath as he copies our moves. We can only try this once. If we blow it, the Umbali will figure out what we've tried to do.

The sergeant returns, and I allow myself to exhale. His effort will pass muster. "We're not yet done. Follow me. Exactly."

I advance along the riverbank, walking on the rocks, leaving no tracks. Finally, I fade into the woods. I turn to Powell and the sergeant. Point to the forest floor where I am going to step. I turn sharply west, walking on brush and deadwood. Careful not to leave signs for a hunter's eye to detect.

This anti-tracking tactic has worked for me in the past. I've circled behind stalkers and sniped them. This time, there are far too many Umbali and cadre to take on. All I want to do is break west while the Umbali follow the river south. They'll waste time looking for signs of us stepping out of the water.

I pick up the pace, forging south-by-west. The landmarks I pointed out to Cecile and Enwright were the most in-your-face guides I could think of. In fact, the subtle gradation of terrain provides a natural compass. Arid scrub borders the Sahel. It shades into savanna, then forest, and finally rainforest the farther one travels south. I'm sure that to locals like Grady direction-finding based on their surroundings has become second nature.

When we hit the Machweo road, I breathe a sigh of relief. Look north in the direction of the highway, half expecting to see a five-ton of cadre roaring toward us. Nothing. I step back into the bush where we can find concealment. Then I set off toward the lodge.

"Think we lost them?" Powell asks.

"They aren't on top of us," I say, "but they won't be fooled long. With any luck, that move bought us an hour. The Umbali won't be used to head fakes. Sooner or later, they'll figure out they've been had. Then they'll double back. Hopefully, they'll still think we are trying to cross the border."

"That assumes they've given up on the civilians."

"True enough. It assumes they put more value on our armed element. They'll figure they can pick off the civilians at will."

The dark buildings of Machweo are barely discernible against the black of the forest. I signal Powell and the sergeant to fan out.

We step across the carnage we left in the driveway. Was it only three hours ago?

Tracks in the gravel mark where our vehicles made hard turns to escape. The crushed body of the Umbali run over by Enwright. More dead Umbali killed in front of the ranch house and the villas.

No sign of the civilians. I walk to the ranch house and the garage. There are two big garage doors that roll up. Handles on the bottom, but likely equipped with automatic door openers.

"Wait here," I say.

I go inside, look for an interior entrance to the garage. Find it next to a utility closet behind the pantry. Feel around for the switch, flick on the lights. As expected, the door opener switches are an inch to the right.

Sweep the interior. There's a huge Mercedes All-Terrain Unimog with an extended cab and a flat cargo bed with fold-down rails. Unimogs, ubiquitous in Africa, were once a favorite of the Rhodesian SAS and Selous Scouts. Next to it is an old Land Rover Santana with an open cargo bed and a big spare tire mounted on its hood.

There are two bright green all-terrain vehicles, too small to be useful.

In a space all its own, a 1938 Brough Superior SS100 motorcycle. It's a beauty, and if I could ride it out of the country alone, I would. Troy Grady, if he's still around, would certainly object.

I turn the lights off and thumb the door switches. There's a rattle, and the electric winches roll the doors open. They retract into the ceiling to reveal Powell and the sergeant looking in on me.

"Let's check the gas," I say. "Do you think he stores gas at the ranch?"

"That Unimog is a diesel," Powell says. "The Land Rover, too. Grady tops up at the airport. He should have some spare jerry cans around."

"Breed."

A woman's voice. It's Enwright, standing at the door.

"You made it."

"Grady led us right to the ranch," she says. "We thought we'd be sitting ducks in here, so everybody is waiting in the bush."

"Bring them in."

Enwright goes off to collect our civilians. I tell the sergeant to go up the road a hundred yards and keep watch for trucks arriving from the highway. I start the clock in my mind. Give us one hour on the Umbali. Every minute we sit, we lose time.

Our refugees struggle in. Twenty-three men, women and

children. Grady is carrying the four-year-old on his shoulders. The little boy looks asleep. Carol Grady is carrying her husband's Winchester. Everyone looks exhausted, and who wouldn't be? They've hiked five or six miles as the crow flies. The wounded are the worst off. Cecile will tell me if the four with defensive wounds look worse than they are. The man who was shot in the shoulder shuffles like an automaton.

My eyes search the group, evaluating their capability, their mental and physical resources. There's Cecile, tired and drawn. The strongest among the bunch are Cecile, Enwright, the Gradys, Wolfe and Ducasse. The young woman from the hospice is doing well, as are the children. The teenagers are tired, but their youth makes them a resilient bunch.

Ducasse strides toward me. "Alright, Breed. Here we are. Why?"

I tilt my head toward the garage.

"We couldn't take our vehicles from the border," I tell him. "Here are new ones."

Grady lowers the little boy from his shoulders. The boy wakes up, and Grady lets his wife hold him. "You've got my trucks if they'll help, Breed. But where do you want to take us? Another crack at the border?"

"The Umbali will track us," Ducasse says. "They'll follow us into Lokola, kill us there. They're hunters. They don't recognize borders."

Powell joins us. "The tanks are full," he says, "and I've found jerry cans of spare fuel."

"In a minute, I'm going to find out what the rest of the world knows," I tell them. "Here's my thinking. Tombaye knows we're out here, and he wants us. He's got a good idea where we've been, and he's going to try to guess where we're going. I think he's betting we go south, through the bush, and try for the Lokola border again."

Grady crosses his arms. "*You* want to take us someplace else."

"He won't expect us to head back to St. Croix."

Powell groans. "What the fuck is in St. Croix?"

I meet the eyes of each person in the front rank, end with Powell.

"A pilot."

Cecile stiffens. "No."

I lift an eyebrow. "Bröer and that Dash-8 are our only chance."

She bows her head, nibbles her thumbnail.

Ducasse plants his hands on his hips, stares at me like he's at a loss for words.

Powell looks skeptical. "Breed, if he's still alive, Bröer will be fucking comatose."

"Bröer *was* a soldier *and* a pilot. Somewhere inside that shell is a man who can fly us out of here."

"How do we get there?" Powell shifts his weight, adjusts his rifle on its sling. "By now, Tombaye will have cadre patrolling the highway in both directions. Umbali beating the bush for us. And he'll be giving the Wambesa police a 'you're either with me or against me' speech. Shooting dissenters."

"You're right on all counts," I say. "We won't take the highway. We'll take the railroad."

Grady's face breaks into a grin. "By God, I would *never* have thought of that."

"COBRA transports its processed concentrate by rail. The railroad runs east-west to both coasts. I understand they always have locomotives at their processing mill. Concentrate gets shipped out of either coast depending on its final destination."

"You want to take the trucks cross-country to the COBRA plant," Grady says.

"Yes. We have twenty-six people and two vehicles. Work out who goes where. Cecile decides where to put the wounded."

"What if we can't get a train to run?" Wolfe asks.

"Then we'll drive west alongside the railroad tracks. Same thing if there's no locomotive."

Wolfe looks defeated. "I hope you know how to drive a train."

Grady laughs. "If it's there, I'll figure it out. That's a promise."

I STEP OUTSIDE of the garage and walk to the ranch house. Go inside and collapse into a leather easy chair. From the shadows, the empty-eyed skulls of hunting trophies scowl at me. Some kind of antelope on the wall, mounted on a hardwood shield with crossed spears. A massive savannah buffalo skull above the bar, horns six feet across.

Creepy.

Damn, this leather smells good. Soft as butter. I sit in the dark and pull my phone from my pocket. Close my eyes and punch Stein's speed dial.

"Breed, where have you been?"

"We tried Lokola and couldn't get across the border. The cadre and Umbali caught up and we took contact. Lost five French army KIA and one civilian wounded. Lost our vehicles and escaped through the bush. There are twenty-six of us looking for a way out."

"I still can't get help to you until midday. In fact, it's getting more difficult."

"Why?"

"The French want to go in and take Wambesa back."

"Great. Have them rescue us right now."

"Commando Jaubert is good to go, but they need a security force to support them. They can't project power without us. State is not inclined to supply airlift for that purpose. We want the French to negotiate with Tombaye."

"I bet that's going over well."

The French commandos are the equivalent of our Navy SEALs. They specialize in direct action and hostage rescue. The problem is, in a situation like this, they need to know *where* to strike, and they need a larger force of more conventional troops to secure the perimeter for their commandos.

"France refuses to negotiate now that French blood has been spilled. They want Tombaye's head on a pike."

"I have sympathy for that."

"In any case, if we send a rescue force in to get you while denying support to the French, they will not be happy."

"Didn't you say, 'Fuck the French'?"

"Yes, that's why I'm putting together a rescue force anyway. Can you dig in and hold until tomorrow morning?"

"Stein, I reckon the Umbali are less than an hour behind us. We have to move. If we dig in, we'll be overrun."

It's axiomatic. If you're under attack and you stay in one place, you die. You have to keep moving. It's certainly true in Wambesa.

Another thought comes to me. "By the way, we ran into Wagners at the Lokola border."

"Not a surprise. Wagner is active throughout the Sahel, and they're expanding their footprint."

"They were in an advisory capacity, but have a high degree of control. When we took contact, they helped us out."

"How?"

"Covering fire that helped us break contact."

"Unusual."

"I thought so. Stein, we've found more evidence that Tombaye is financed by Russia. The cadre mined a bridge. The explosives were Russian. The technique used to set up the trap was Russian."

"Why would the Wagner at the border help you?"

I exhale. "Exactly. It could be he was the idiot who didn't get the memo. Somehow, I don't think so."

"Will there be an international incident?"

"Not a chance. The cadre came up behind us on the highway and opened fire with the Russians in our background. Just saying—I see things that don't compute."

"It's probably nothing."

"My head hurts," I tell her. "Okay, I have to go herd the flock."

"The flock?"

I get up and stretch. "Yeah, a lot of them are kids from a Catholic mission in town. The local padre has been busting my balls. Talk to you later."

POWELL AND GRADY have worked out the distribution of passengers in the two trucks. Enwright, Cecile, Powell, Wolfe and I will ride in the extended cab of the Unimog ATV. Thirteen civilians, including the children and wounded, will ride on the cargo bed. The Gradys will drive the Land Rover, and six civilians will ride in the back.

The stars, scattered across the vast dome of the clear African sky, wink down at us.

"Let's mount up," I tell Powell.

"Breed," Cecile says, "I need to speak with you."

She leads me outside.

"What is it, Cecile?"

"Breed, you'll be asking everything from a broken man."

Cecile's eyes are wet. I take her by the shoulders. "Cecile, why are you protective of him?"

"Because..." Cecile shakes her head and looks away.

"There's a kernel of dignity in Bröer worth saving," I tell her. "I think you see it. You either believe in him, or you don't."

GRADY LEADS the way in the Land Rover. Following neither road nor map, he sets off across the Wambesa countryside. Riding in the Unimog, we maintain a respectable distance to avoid his dust plume. Both trucks have high clearance, and we roar across the scrubland.

It's not hard to follow his thinking. The rail line runs east-west, parallel to the highway. The COBRA mill is adjacent to the railroad to facilitate loading. We want to avoid the highway and the road that connects the mill to the mine. The logical approach is to skirt the forest behind Machweo, then head south till we hit the railway. From there, we turn west and follow the tracks until we reach the mill.

"You think Umbali will spot our dust plumes?" I ask Powell.

From a distance, moonlight reflecting off a dust plume would make us stand out.

"No, the moon is setting. Anyway, it's a chance we have to take."

"There's the railway," Enwright says.

The railway is on a low ridge running parallel to the tree line. That ridge is an embankment that slopes gently down to the plain of scrubland. I scan the tracks with an infantryman's eye. If the cadre and Umbali attack from the north, I'll take us onto the tracks. Compared to the flat scrubland, the railroad is an elevated position. From there, we can make an attacking force pay dearly. Break contact and run north to the forest.

Grady arrives at the foot of the embankment, spins the wheel, and roars west. I check my watch. The COBRA mill isn't far away. It's already visible in the distance. A sprawl of long processing buildings, warehouses and loading bays.

There, next to the tracks, is the rail yard I'm looking for. Sidings and a switching yard for engines and flatcars. There's a locomotive, conveniently pointed west. There are flatcars already coupled to it, though I can't tell how many. To the right are the loading bay and processing plant. The mill is filled with heavy machinery. Huge slabs of metal, wheels and gears are visible through open gates in the walls.

Grady and Powell park between the buildings and the tracks. This way, our vehicles can't be seen from the approach road. We pile out, and I summon the French sergeant. Touch Cecile on the shoulder.

"Tell him to stand watch on the far side of the mill," I say. "Warn us if anyone approaches from the highway."

Cecile translates for me.

Rifles slung, Grady and Powell join us. I address Grady. "You sound like you know engines."

"I'm good with my hands, Breed. Do a lot of maintenance myself. Anything that needs to run."

"Alright, can you make that engine run? It looks like it's pointed in the right direction."

"I'll make it run."

I turn to Powell. "Why don't we get the civilians piling anything that looks like cover onto that flatcar? Sandbags may be too much to ask for, but let's see what we can find."

Powell grins. "I'll get Enwright to help. It'll keep this bunch from moping."

"I only wish we had a couple of those Dushkas from the border."

Eyebrows knit, Cecile steps up to the Unimog, pulls her medical bag from the back seat of the cab. "All the antibiotics and morphine we have left are in this bag," she says. "We lost all the rest at the border. Our wounded will be at mortal risk by the end of the day."

"Do what you can."

"I have been, Breed. If your plan doesn't work, we must consider other options."

My jaw tightens. "Like what?"

"Surrender."

15

SUNDAY, 0130 HRS, COBRA – THE MILL

Father Ducasse jumps from the cargo bed of the Unimog and strides toward me. "Breed, I want a word with you."

"That's good, Father. I want a word with *you*."

I walk into the big loading bay. The walls are constructed from sheets of corrugated iron. Piled against one wall are hundreds of white canvas bags stacked halfway to the ceiling. Each bag has been stitched with a set of canvas straps to make them easier to carry. When stacked one on top of the other, the straps are folded or crushed flat.

Sling my rifle, pick up one of the bags. It's heavy, well over a hundred pounds. I put the bag down, look around.

"Breed, those people are exhausted."

"We all are, Father."

The opposite wall is stacked with metal drums. Almost all the drums are painted bluish gray. A small number are painted bright yellow. In the middle of the floor are two forklifts and a pile of pallets.

I walk to the loading bay doors and wave to Powell.

"What's up?"

With a sweep of my arm, I indicate the canvas sacks. "I found our sandbags."

"What's in them?"

"Cobalt, I reckon. Each one is about a hundred pounds. Stack them two high around the flatcar, we got us an armored train."

Powell jerks his chin toward the drums. "What's in those?"

"Am I an expert? More cobalt, I guess. COBRA's customers might have different requirements for packaging."

"I'll get on it."

I make a circle of the room, examining the drums. Then I go into the machinery space. It's dark. Light from the open loading bay doors isn't enough to penetrate the gloom. I cast my phone's flashlight beam around the room. It's filled with huge iron machines.

The big Caterpillar trucks run ore to the mill, where it is loaded onto conveyor belts. The conveyors carry the ore to chutes and pour the rock into massive crushers. When they are in operation, the din in the mill must be deafening.

Ducasse follows me into the next building. My flashlight reveals massive vats where the crushed ore is treated with chemicals. I know nothing of the mining process. Only that the output ends up in the sacks and drums in the loading bay.

"Breed, you're obsessed."

"With living? I plead guilty."

"This is a sport to you. A blood sport."

I poke around the vats. The containers are taller than I am. I point my flashlight at the ceiling. There's a catwalk that overlooks the room, pipes that run chemicals into the vats from above, drain them from below.

A ladder leads up to the catwalk. I climb halfway, shine my light downward. The vats are filled with a vile slurry of chemicals and crushed rock. The edges are encrusted with a gray powdery substance. I sniff the air, recoil from the acrid odor.

The process must use chemicals to extract product from the crushed ore. Separates the valuable minerals and discards the rest with effluent. It wouldn't do to fall in. I climb back down.

"Let's get out of here. I don't think breathing this air is very healthy."

I turn off my flashlight, squeeze the phone into my pocket next to the spare Mark 23 magazine. Lead Ducasse back into the machinery room.

"Are you even listening to me?"

"Of course."

"You're infected with the sin of pride, Breed. You against Tombaye. Do you really care about the rest of us?"

I sigh, unsling my rifle, and use the back of my hand to rub sweat from my eyes. "If I didn't, Father, Powell and I would be in the bush and long gone. We'd leave you to the tender mercies of the Umbali. We could slip through the border and be on either coast in a week."

There's a metal staircase that leads to an overhead catwalk. It's dimly lit by the open loading bay doors. Every surface in the place is covered with a thin layer of rock dust. I stoop, blow some off a couple of steps, and sit down. Set the AK-74 across my knees and look at the priest.

The feel of the metal in my hands is comforting, the

smell of the gun oil familiar. A fine weapon. More reliable than the damaged humans one regularly encounters.

"What do *you* want to do, Father? Rely on Tombaye's mercy, his love of humanity, to keep him from killing you? You didn't see what was done in French Village. You'll be lucky if all they do is kill you."

Ducasse stares at me. A vein in his forehead throbs. I'm tempted to count his heartbeats, time his heart rate. Something to do.

"You strike me as a responsible, rational man, Father."

"I do not require your flattery."

"It's not flattery. I'm trying to figure you out."

Ducasse says nothing.

"You're not shy, so if you had a plan, you'd speak up. We'd all listen. You *don't* know a better way out of here. You're *not* busting Powell's balls. Why don't you like me, Father? I'm deeply hurt."

"Cecile is a good girl, Breed. She is not for you."

I check my watch.

"The clock is ticking, Father. We've gained another half an hour on the Umbali. Unless they've been picked up by trucks from St. Croix. If they have, all bets are off. I reckon Grady and Powell will have the train ready to leave soon. I need you to tell me what I need to know, right now."

"What are you talking about?"

"You're protective of Cecile, Father. You think I'm no good for her. Cecile, on the other hand, is protective of Bröer. Now... Bröer seems to think Tombaye will kill everybody else and let *him* drink himself to death. You see what I mean?"

Ducasse uses both hands to brush back his hair. Stares at the ceiling as though appealing to God. I press my attack.

"Wambesa, a tiny country in the middle of Africa. St.

Croix, a tiny town in a tiny country in the middle of Africa. And in St. Croix, we have the village priest, the village doctor, the village drunk and the village revolutionary."

"Damn you, Breed."

"Bröer is the only person who can get us out of here, Father. Tell me the story of St. Croix."

Ducasse tells me.

THIRTY YEARS AGO, Father Ducasse was an idealistic young priest. Wambesa was the last place a priest wanted to be assigned, but Ducasse was keen to make a difference. He worked tirelessly and built the mission.

Ducasse worked with the aid agencies and recruited a teacher for the school. He arranged for aid workers to help him manage a home for foundlings. Most of the orphans he took in were mixed race. In Wambesa, mixed-race children were usually abandoned to die. Neither parent wanted them.

One night, there was a knock on the door of the rectory. Ducasse opened the door to Rijk Bröer. He had met the man once or twice, but did not know him well. The priest had heard stories from diplomats and mine employees. Ducasse said mass for the French and Catholic locals. His proselytizing met with modest success. The local imams tolerated him because his flock was such a minor component of the population.

Father Ducasse would stop for meals and drinks at the La Salle. From the French managers and engineers, he heard about the dashing South African mercenary. Just thirty years old, Bröer was another Mike Hoare, and a pilot in the bargain. Handsome, with long, wavy hair. He would have been dangerous among the young wives of the expatriate French. Ducasse expected trouble, but he heard no complaints from the men, and no confessions from the women.

Rijk Bröer wasn't about to foul the community in which he lived while he was not flying and killing. He satisfied his sexual appetite with prostitutes in St. Croix. Later, he had taken one of them as a mistress. Once, at the market, Ducasse had seen him with his woman. She was beautiful, almost as tall as Bröer.

Ducasse ushered Bröer into the sitting room, asked him to sit down. The priest eyed the large picnic hamper the pilot carried. He knew what was coming.

"To what do we owe this unexpected visit, Mr. Bröer?"

"This is difficult for me, Father." Bröer sat on the sofa, the hamper on the table between them. "I'm not good with words, so I shall be straightforward."

"Please."

"Adele has left me and our little girl. There is no one to care for her when I am away."

"May I see?"

Bröer nodded his permission.

Ducasse leaned forward, peeled away the soft flannel cloth that covered the hamper. Inside was a beautiful baby girl. Her dusky features marked her as mixed race. She was asleep, but Ducasse could see the girl looked healthy. There was a plastic bottle of formula next to her, with a rubber teat.

"Her name is Cecile." Bröer pleaded with his eyes. "Will you take her?"

The priest was not about to refuse. When he arrived in St. Croix, Ducasse had been appalled by the treatment of mixed-race foundlings. The expatriate French, often married, simply abandoned the mother and baby outright. The child was worse than an inconvenience. It was a mark of shame. The mothers could not support themselves *and* the baby. The rates of infanticide and abandonment among the mixed-race population were one hundred percent.

One couldn't condone the practice, but one could understand it. A local woman, pregnant from a Frenchman, was abandoned by her man. She could not work or support herself while nursing a baby, so she rid herself of it. No longer nursing, she became attractive enough to work, and soon became pregnant again. The whole process fed a vicious circle.

The only saving grace, if such it could be called, was that the expatriate population was small enough that few such foundlings found their way to his door.

"Understand," Bröer said, "I love her. I would care for her myself if not for the nature of my work."

"You do not have to explain."

Bröer ignored him. "I will send money. I have heard stories of not enough formula, not enough medicine. Whatever Cecile needs, she will have. You will see to it, yes?"

"I promise."

"I will visit when I am not working," Bröer said. "You and I will arrange for me to meet her, though she must not know I am her father. That would lead to difficulty."

Ducasse saw what Bröer meant. As Cecile grew up, she would become naturally curious about her father. If she knew him and knew about his work and long absences, it would create an unsustainable situation.

Bröer plowed his hands through his long, wavy hair. Brushed it back. Then he leaned forward and kissed the baby on her forehead.

"I will go now," he said. "I have your word."

Solemnly, the two men shook hands. Ducasse led Bröer to the door and watched the unlikely Valjean walk away into the night.

DUCASSE AND BRÖER had been the same age when the mercenary brought Cecile to the mission. In a way, they grew up together, and Ducasse became Cecile's second father. He baptized her under her mother's name, Abimbola. Cecile grew up to be a beautiful young girl. Both her parents were attractive. Bröer was handsome and masculine, Adele long-limbed and fine-boned.

It was natural to be protective of Cecile. The girl was mischievous and fun-loving. Diligent and studious, she was easily the best student at the mission school.

One day, a teenaged Cecile came to see Ducasse.

"Can we speak, Father?"

"Of course."

Cecile had grown up to be a forthright young woman. Ducasse did not know if she had acquired that trait from her father. The priest had arranged for her to meet Bröer "accidentally" on several occasions, and the encounters had gone well. Once, at a football match sponsored by COBRA. The French present had been cold to Cecile, but not too rude. Again, at the La Salle, where Ducasse met Bröer for a drink. The priest called Cecile to drive the minibus to the hotel. Had her take him back to the mission because the day was too hot to walk. Bröer joked with the girl, and they chatted until it was time for Ducasse and Cecile to leave.

So it went. Over the years, father and daughter came to know each other, without the girl learning the truth.

Hands flat on her thighs, Cecile said, "I have met a man I want to have sex with."

Ducasse reeled. He shouldn't have been surprised. A beautiful young girl, an avid reader. She wasn't ignorant of sex or birth control. She knew men were attracted to her, and it was natural she felt the same. He was surprised she hadn't confessed the usual litany of impure thoughts in the sanctity of the confessional.

"Do you love this man?"

"I think so, Father. But I am too young to marry, so what I feel must be a sin."

"It is, and it is good you understand."

"I understand, and it troubles me. I want to use birth control."

Ducasse swallowed. Kneaded the back of his neck, which had grown stiff. "God will understand. Confess your sins, and be prepared to pay a heavy penance."

Cecile left with a spring in her step. Ducasse poured himself three fingers of whisky. Drank it in one gulp.

The priest had given Cecile the same advice he would have given any other girl in her situation. He would have given that advice no matter who the man was. In this case, he was sure he knew.

Cecile was the best student at the mission school. The second best was a passionate young man named Marien Tombaye.

MARIEN TOMBAYE'S parents were shopkeepers in St. Croix. They were Muslim, but not considered to be devout. They struggled mightily to run a successful business. They were ambitious for Marien and wanted him to become proficient in western subjects. For that reason, they sent him to the mission school.

The boy was intelligent and quick-witted. Like Cecile, he learned to speak English and French. He excelled in history and mathematics. The boy's single-minded intensity made Ducasse uncomfortable. Perhaps it was because the boy took his parents' ambition so seriously. He resented the privilege enjoyed by the French, as well as their unconcealed racism. In that resentment, his parents encouraged him. He did not conceal his contempt for Ducasse.

It was natural that Cecile and Marien would grow close. In any class of fifty students, it was easy to see who would make a mark. They enjoyed challenging each other. More importantly, Cecile's playfulness lightened Marien's intensity.

When Cecile confessed that she was having sex with Marien Tombaye, Ducasse routinely absolved her. But he was not happy.

DUCASSE KNEW Bröer had retired from mercenary work. He had taken his savings and bought an airplane. It was a US Air Force surplus C-118 Liftmaster. The plane was perfect for Bröer's purpose because it was already configured to haul cargo. The Liftmaster was the Air Force version of the Douglas DC-6, a reliable long-range commercial transport.

The plane was a gamble, because it cost more to operate

than a twin engine, like a C-47. But it could carry more cargo over longer distances. Bröer had contacts all over Africa and southern Europe. He made the business pay.

When Cecile was accepted to study in France, Ducasse told Bröer. The priest was worried the mercenary would not be able to afford an expensive Parisian education.

"It will require a great deal of money."

Father Ducasse and Rijk Bröer faced each other over whiskies in the rectory sitting room. The priest pushed a piece of paper over to the mercenary. On it was an itemized list of expenses and a bottom-line figure. The costs required to subsidize Cecile's education in Paris.

"I've done my best to reduce her expenses to the minimum," Ducasse said. "I've given her a small allowance, which you can adjust as you see fit. Of course, if she takes part-time work, she can supplement that."

The cost was considerably more than the amount the pilot was already providing.

"I will provide the money," Bröer said.

Cecile went to France. She promised Ducasse she would become a doctor. Return to Wambesa to build a clinic at his mission. He told her to study hard and remember to enjoy *La Ville Lumière*.

Marien Tombaye was also accepted to study in Paris. His parents funded his education at a less expensive, less prestigious institution than Cecile's.

Before she left, Cecile confided her plans to Ducasse. Marien was studying history and would return to Wambesa five years before Cecile. This was because Cecile intended to study medicine, and her program was much longer. When she returned, Cecile and Marien intended to marry.

Ducasse was horrified. Devout Islamists only permitted

Muslim men to marry non-Muslim women if the women converted to Islam. They did not permit Muslim women to marry non-Muslim men. This ensured the continued growth of the faith.

Cecile assured Father Ducasse that she was not converting to Islam. Marien was not a devout Muslim. They would have a civil marriage and a church marriage. The church marriage would be held under Father Ducasse's supervision. If he required Marien to convert to Catholicism, Marien would do so.

One day, Ducasse sat with Marien in the rectory. The priest faced a young black man, clean and neat, wearing a white dress shirt, dark pants, and dress shoes. His round, metal-framed glasses gave him a studious appearance.

"Do you love Cecile?" Ducasse asked Marien.

"We love each other very much, Father."

"Are you willing to become a Catholic to marry her?"

"I will do anything you ask."

Ducasse didn't like the way Marien gave his assurance. It wasn't that the priest doubted the boy's word. It was the ease with which Marien gave it. Ducasse got the sense that Marien Tombaye was single-minded in the pursuit of his objectives. It didn't matter if he wanted a higher education or the hand of his true love in marriage. Marien would compromise to get it. Ducasse wanted to see true commitment to the faith.

Ducasse trusted Cecile, but he didn't like Marien Tombaye one bit.

MARIEN CAME BACK from Paris a fiery young man. He had gone to Europe already well-read. In Paris, he engaged in the lifestyle of an ambitious student who had his whole life ahead of him. He went to bars and coffee houses, engaged in spirited debate, and met anti-neocolonial populists. Of course, their interests were focused on Francophone Africa.

The organizations Marien engaged with railed against "la Francafríque." They were driven to build a grassroots platform to mobilize demonstrations across Francophone west Africa. They used the apparent success of a military coup in Mali to highlight the failures of what they called "*faux* democracy." They suggested another way, heavily implying a reliance on military or authoritarian rule. The new political structures were a merger of nationalist militaries and pan-African populists.

Needless to say, this sentiment, combined with the success of nationalist coups in Burkina Faso, Guinea, and Niger, curdled the blood of the French. It was not an understatement to say that France was sliding off Africa's table. As one country after another fell, the French became more desperate.

When he returned to Wambesa, Marien threw himself into his work. It took him years to build relationships among the middle class in St. Croix. Eventually, he was able to organize anti-French demonstrations. He held the first at the Vieux Carré. It was an experiment. He held another one the following year, double the size. The year after that, he held one at the COBRA mine.

The demonstration Marien organized at the mine terrified the French. The unrest spread to thousands of mine workers. COBRA's security force almost lost control. The

French army was mobilized but, by a miracle, did not need to be called into action.

That was when the French arrested Marien. Neither his parents nor Ducasse were able to visit him. To the world outside, he had disappeared.

At the La Salle, Ducasse spoke to Remy Bernard.

"Can you arrange for me to see him?" Ducasse asked.

"It is not my affair," the ambassador told him. "This is between our security services and the local authorities. Understand—these terrorists are active throughout the Sahel. They are supported by our enemies. You should not get involved."

When Marien's friends were released, they refused to speak of Marien or of their treatment at the barracks. Each had been held in isolation.

Ducasse had tried to help because he knew how much Marien meant to Cecile. But he'd seen the protests and riots. The conversation with Remy Bernard convinced him that Marien was trouble.

Father Ducasse gave up.

MARIEN WAS STILL in prison when Cecile returned from Paris. She'd received a medical diploma from the prestigious Pierre and Marie Curie University. She and Marien had continued their relationship in Paris, but she did not enjoy his anti-colonial friends. When he graduated and returned to Wambesa, she occupied herself with her studies and her own friends.

When Marien stopped responding to emails, she called Father Ducasse. He told her what had happened. She knew about Marien's activities, but his arrest surprised her. Had he really gone that far? Apparently so.

Cecile was determined to wait for Marien's release. She found employment with an aid agency, organized her clinic, and rented a house in St. Croix. Ducasse was happy that she loved her work. But he knew that Marien's imprisonment broke her heart.

When Marien was finally released, he went to live with his parents. Cecile waited for several days, then went to see him. She was shocked and hurt when his parents turned her away.

Cecile went to Father Ducasse. "He won't see me, Father. His parents are upset that I went to visit."

"Give Marien time," Ducasse advised her. "It's been difficult. He'll come to you when he's ready."

One day, Marien came to the rectory and asked to see Ducasse. The priest was shocked by Marien's appearance.

The young man had aged ten years in two. He was stooped and emaciated. His eyes were fevered.

"I need your help, Father."

"What is it, Marien? What's wrong?"

"I am told Cecile operates a medical clinic at the mission."

"Yes, she does."

Marien sat down without asking. His hands trembled, and his eyes glassed over. Ducasse went to him and put his hand on the man's shoulder. Found it bony beneath the cotton shirt. "Marien, what's wrong?"

"I need antibiotics," Marien said. "Please tell Cecile I have an infection. I need medicine."

"I will call her. She has been desperate to see you. Why did you not contact her?"

"No. I cannot see Cecile. Ask her for the medication, and I will treat myself."

Ducasse went to Cecile's house. "Marien is here," he told her. "He's very sick, but all he will say is that he has an infection."

"If his condition is *that* serious, he could die," Cecile said. "Infections are a serious matter."

"He's close to death," Ducasse told her.

"I won't prescribe medication without seeing him," Cecile said. "That's all there is to it. There's no hospital in Wambesa, do you understand? There's a limit to what I can do."

She packed her medical bag. Together, they drove to the mission.

Marien was unconscious on the sofa.

"*Mon dieu.*" Cecile rushed to Marien, rolled him onto his back. She took his temperature and his blood pressure. "Can we put him on a bed?"

"Yes. Use mine."

Together, Ducasse and Cecile carried Marien to the priest's room and laid him on the bed. Ducasse was shocked—the young man was light as straw. Marien had always been thin, and he had lost weight while in custody.

They took off his shoes and socks, then his shirt. Cecile gasped. Marien's chest was covered with scars. Raised white ridges against his black skin. Most ran horizontally, but they crisscrossed each other. He had been whipped repeatedly on his chest. Everywhere on his torso were circular and rectangular scars. The circular marks were burns from cigars and cigarettes. The rectangular ones were from heated irons.

"Oh," Cecile gasped. "What have they done to you?"

Ducasse undid Marien's belt and pulled off his trousers and underwear at the same time. "Dear God."

Marien's entire male apparatus was gone. Below his flat belly, he looked like a woman. His parts had been replaced by a grotesque wound closed with bootlaces. The smell of body odor forced Cecile and Ducasse to back up a step.

To Ducasse's surprise, Cecile remained professional. "He hasn't washed in weeks," she said. "The wound is infected, but I don't think it is gangrenous. Help me."

They went to work. Ducasse had never been more proud of Cecile than he was that night. She gave Marien an injection of antibiotics. Noted the dose and time in a notebook. Then, with Ducasse's assistance, she painstakingly cleaned and closed Marien's wounds. The job took hours.

Finally, they went into the sitting room.

"I'll give him a course of antibiotics," Cecile said. She was speaking half to herself. "I must stay here to monitor his progress."

"Does he need a hospital?"

"In an ideal world, yes. This is not an ideal world. In the time it took us to transport him, the infection would progress. He might not survive."

Cecile stared at the wall. Then she held her head in her hands and wept.

FOR WEEKS, Father Ducasse and Cecile tended Marien. She administered the full course of antibiotics. The infection subsided, and he recovered strength. He had been tortured for most of the two years he had been in captivity. Shortly before his release, the French emasculated him.

Marien would not speak to Cecile. When he first regained consciousness, he said to her, "I cannot be with you."

Ducasse advised Cecile not to press him. He needed time to adjust to the horrible mental and physical shock of what had been done to him. She agreed to confine her support to professional medical care.

"Let him come to you," Ducasse advised.

When Cecile was not there, Ducasse sat with Marien. He did not press the man to speak.

"They will pay," Marien said at last.

Ducasse looked up. "Vengeance belongs to the lord."

"He can have the French when I have finished with them."

Marien said nothing further.

Marien healed and grew stronger. He remained at the rectory and asked Ducasse to visit his parents. Cecile went back to work in the clinic and visited Marien once a week.

As the days passed, Cecile noticed that Marien was becoming colder to her. When he spoke, he would be curt, even rude.

"I feel as though he is punishing me," Cecile told Ducasse. "It's worse all the time."

Ducasse suspected that he knew what was happening to Marien's feelings. He did not want to voice his thoughts to Cecile.

When Marien had regained his strength, Cecile stopped visiting. She asked Father Ducasse to report his condition to her. Ducasse moved Marien to a spare room in the rectory.

One day, Ducasse went to check on Marien and found the room empty.

Marien Tombaye had left Wambesa.

CECILE THREW herself into her work, but Ducasse felt like something inside her had died. She was a young woman with a bright future ahead of her. The horror of what had been done to Marien had killed something in her spirit.

Ducasse tried to convince himself that love could be reawakened in Cecile. If only a spark could be found to set it alight.

I SUSPECTED a relationship between Cecile and Tombaye. She told me they grew up together. She, Ducasse and Bröer referred to him as "Marien" while everyone else referred to him as "Tombaye." It took me a while to switch on, but the familiarity was right in my face the whole time.

Ducasse told me half the story. Cecile told me Bröer had been duped into flying drugs into Spain. But the pieces didn't fit. I wanted to know everything.

"Now tell me about Bröer."

16

SUNDAY, 0200 HRS, COBRA – THE MILL

Father Ducasse stares at me out of the gloom. Half of his face is lit dimly from the open loading bay. The other half lies in deep shadow. I watch a bead of sweat roll down the side of his face, fall from his jaw to his shoulder. Tombaye's story was difficult for him to tell. Now he tells me Bröer's story.

"Is Marien still in prison?" Bröer asked.

Ducasse was seated with the pilot in the rectory. It was six months after Marien Tombaye was arrested, A year before Cecile was scheduled to return from Paris. It was true Marien was being held at the army barracks, but everyone spoke of him as being in prison.

"Yes," Ducasse said. "They won't let me see him."

"Perhaps it's just as well," Bröer said.

The priest felt both offended and guilty at the same time. Offended because he sensed an undercurrent of racism in the South African's words. Bröer never said anything overtly racist, but Ducasse sensed that the pilot didn't consider Cecile black. She was mixed race, but he considered her white. He wanted a white lover for his daughter.

Ducasse felt guilty because he had never liked Marien. Thought he was wrong for Cecile. The priest had been uncomfortable telling Bröer about Marien and Cecile's relationship. But Bröer was her father, he was entitled to know. Ducasse had struggled for months thinking about how he would break the news. Had it been any other boy from the school, he wouldn't have been so troubled.

In the end, Ducasse fortified himself with liquid courage and told Bröer. He did it face-to-face, as it had to be done. Bröer took the news well, though he was not happy for Cecile. He had been hoping she would meet someone in Paris. A medical student perhaps.

Now, they sat drinking whisky, calmly discussing Marien Tombaye's incarceration without charge or trial. Ducasse got the distinct impression Bröer would be happy if Marien disappeared forever. Ducasse couldn't blame him.

"This is her last year in school, isn't it?" Bröer asked.

"Yes, it is. I have forwarded the tuition on your behalf."

"Thank you. Disburse six months of incidentals every four weeks. I will return with money for the final six months."

"You have been working hard, Rijk."

"Not for much longer. Next year, I will fly my last special cargo to Spain."

Bröer never told Ducasse exactly what he was doing, but it wasn't hard for the priest to figure out. The pilot was flying cargoes of hashish and other drugs from Morocco to Spain.

Ferrying drugs was the only way he could afford Cecile's tuition and expenses in Paris.

"When Cecile returns, she plans to operate a clinic at the mission," Ducasse told him. "I have arranged for sponsorship with the aid agencies. They will subsidize her salary. She will be able to support herself."

"Excellent." Bröer beamed. "You know, Father, in some ways you and I are Cecile's parents."

They lifted their whisky glasses and toasted each other.

THE FOLLOWING YEAR, Cecile returned from Paris and began her new life. Marien was still in prison. Bröer sent Ducasse a substantial sum of money from his last cargo. This was to support Cecile until she organized employment and lodgings. She did that in short order, and there was money left over.

Life in St. Croix looked peaceful, but an infection was festering beneath the surface. One afternoon, Ducasse went to the La Salle for a drink and found Bröer sitting at his customary table.

"Bröer!" Ducasse extended his hand to greet his friend. "When did you arrive?"

The pilot rose to take the proffered hand. In the space of a heartbeat, he collapsed like an empty suit of clothes. Fell straight down, left arm reaching for the tabletop. A futile effort to support his weight. Tipped the table. Glass and bottle of whisky slid off the table, fell to the floorboards. The whisky from the glass splashed across the room, and Bröer went down on top of the spill.

"Good heavens." Ducasse rushed to Bröer's side. The

priest took the pilot by his right arm and elbow, tried to help the pilot to his feet. The man's left leg refused to provide support, and his right arm appeared to lock at an unnatural angle. "Are you alright?"

"I'm fine," Bröer said. "I'm sorry, Father. This is so embarrassing."

Charles, the bartender, hurried forward. Took Bröer's left arm and got a shoulder under it. That gave the pilot the support his left leg denied him. Between them, Ducasse and Charles helped Bröer back to his seat.

"I'm sorry, Charles." Bröer couldn't apologize enough. "I'll pay for everything."

"Don't worry, sir. These things happen." Charles set the empty glass back on the table. The whisky bottle had been down by two-thirds when it fell. Rolled seven feet across the floor without spilling a drop. Charles picked it up, squinted at its contents, refilled Bröer's glass. "Too good to waste."

Ducasse sat across from Bröer at the table. "What happened, Rijk?"

"Left knee's good for nothing," Bröer said. "Unless I'm careful to align thigh and shin perfectly, it won't take my weight. Goes out at the most inconvenient times."

Charles brought a mop from a closet behind the bar and set to work cleaning the floor.

"How were you injured?"

"I'm being rude," Bröer said. "Charles, please, a glass for Father."

Charles put the mop and bucket away, brought a clean whisky glass for Ducasse. Bröer poured the priest three fingers.

"Thank you," Ducasse said.

"An accident." Bröer's brow creased with pain. Not physical pain. A memory worse than physical pain. The powerful association of events with both physical *and* psychic pain.

"No, that's a lie. *Not* an accident."

"What, then?"

Bröer reached for a cane. The cane hung by its curved handle from the top rail of a straight-backed chair. "I don't like to use it," he said, "but it helps. I can put my weight on it while aligning my parts."

Charles busied himself at the end of the bar, left the two men to speak.

"Rijk." Ducasse spoke with a gentle tone. "Tell me what happened."

Bröer lifted his face. He'd aged ten years in the nine months since Ducasse had last seen him. The priest could see that the man's face was lined with pain, his eyes glistened with a thin film of mist, and his long gray hair was uncombed.

"I suppose I have to tell you," Bröer said. "I came to see you, after all."

"Tell me."

Bröer drained his glass with a single gulp. Poured himself another. "My partners considered themselves to be my employers," Bröer said. "They took exception to my leaving our arrangement."

"Surely you were free to retire."

"I finished my last flight, went to their office to collect my payment. It was a bodega outside Cadiz. They handed me a nice, fat envelope. Provided me with details of the next shipment. I told them I was retiring. They said that wouldn't be possible. When I tried to leave, one of them pulled a gun on me—a foolish display. I took it away from him and left."

Bröer drank half the glass of whisky.

Ducasse frowned. "So, you left, with your money."

"I knew there would be trouble. I took the money and the pistol. I called my copilot, Emil. Told him to meet me at the airplane. Warned him there might be trouble, and that we were leaving right away. Went to my hotel, packed my things, drove to the airport. It was late by the time I arrived. The plane was parked on the tarmac. The hangar was dark. Emil's Peugeot was parked outside the hangar."

"Where was he?"

"I wasn't sure. We were going to fly to Morocco. He could have been checking the airplane, or in the hangar. I called his name. There was no answer. I had the pistol in my belt, under my jacket. I put my hand on it, walked toward the plane."

"By then, you suspected something was wrong."

"Yes, but I was not certain. I called his name again, and this time he answered. 'Rijk,' he said. His voice was muffled, came from inside the hangar. I took the safety off the pistol, held it low at my leg, walked to the hangar, pushed open the service door. Inside, there were two light planes. One in the center, another at the far end. I saw Emil with two of my partner's men. They were standing next to the airplane in the center. His hands were bound behind his back, and they were holding him by the arms. He broke free and ran toward the plane at the back of the hangar."

"Did he think to get away with his hands bound?"

"I'm sure he panicked. I think he was looking for a place to hide. I raised the pistol, but before I could fire, someone hit me from behind. The man who hit me must have been standing to one side of the door when I entered. I dropped my pistol and fell. As I hit the ground, I heard the sound of a shotgun and saw the blast strike Emil in the back. It flung him against the airplane's wing, and the impact spun him around. I heard another shotgun blast, saw it open up his chest and knock him down. I lost consciousness."

"They killed him."

"Yes. When I regained consciousness, I found they had dragged me outside. My partner was there, looking down at me. They took the envelope of money. Then my partner said he was not going to kill me. No, he would make an example of me. They crushed my left knee with the butt of the shotgun. The pain was so intense I almost lost consciousness a second time. Then they held my right arm straight out and crushed my elbow. That time, I did lose consciousness."

Bröer finished the glass of whisky, poured himself another. Ducasse said nothing, allowed the pilot to continue his story.

"When I regained consciousness, they were gone. My airplane and the hangar were in flames. My copilot's body burned inside the hangar."

"Surely the police investigated?"

"I was not helpful to the police," Bröer said. "Understand how that would have been as harmful to me as to my partner. There was no evidence of contraband in the wreckage of my airplane or the hangar. As far as they were concerned, it was a random act of violence. An interrupted robbery gone wrong."

"How much hospital treatment did you receive?"

"Enough to learn that my left knee and right elbow will never regain full functionality. I will never regain a full range of movement in my right arm. My left knee will never carry my weight without some kind of support. I can walk short distances without a cane. If my thigh and calf become misaligned, I fall. I am partially crippled, capable only of limited function. I can drive a car so long as it has an automatic transmission. And I can fly an airplane."

"I'm very sorry to hear this, Rijk."

Bröer had related the destruction of his lifetime's work. With a mighty effort, he summoned his courage. It was a strong performance, but Ducasse was not convinced. Bröer had had everything taken from him at an advanced age. Starting over would be difficult for a man without such handicaps.

"I'm healing, Father. I've taken a room upstairs, as I usually do when I'm in town. However, I need money. Everything I had was tied up in that airplane and Cecile's education. Do you have anything left of the last money I sent you?"

Ducasse brightened. "A fair bit, actually. I can let you have it tomorrow."

"Excellent, excellent. I expect to find work soon."

They relaxed to finish their drinks. Bröer asked about Cecile and Marien. He was relieved that Marien was still out of the picture.

"Do you think he'll ever get out, Father?"

"I don't know," Ducasse said. "They've released all of his confederates. All of them were tortured. Some think the authorities are trying to come up with a way to kill him."

"I hope we never see him again."

"I cannot allow myself such thoughts, Rijk." Ducasse got to his feet. "I'll find a way for you to see Cecile tomorrow. Why don't you come by the clinic and ask her to examine your leg and arm?"

"That's an idea," Bröer said. "I'll stay here and have another one."

No one descends into alcoholism overnight. For most alcoholics, the descent is a long process of corruption. Some never hit rock bottom, but hover and drift in the murky liquid a short distance above.

Bröer's descent took a long time. He took several contracts that year. These brought him money, but the work was short-lived. His disability prevented him from taking mercenary work. In any case, he was too old.

He was still able to fly, but he had no airplane. He collected flying hours from charter carriers in Kenya and the Gold Coast. This kind of work was necessarily irregular. He would return to Wambesa between jobs. He stayed at the La Salle and drank.

That was another thing about drunks. They all tried to control their descent to the bottom. At least, at the beginning. Bröer tried to discipline himself. For a long time, he never drank before noon. Instead, he slept later and later in the mornings until he was rising well after eleven o'clock.

Bröer's brunch consisted of some toast and four doubles of whisky. With guests who drifted in and out of the La Salle, he consumed a few more ounces in the afternoons. Ducasse thought he did it because the physical pain never left him. In any case, if he didn't go out, Bröer's body and mind were numb by three o'clock.

The mercenary was happiest when he was with Cecile. He took to visiting the mission regularly. When he was with Ducasse, he controlled his drinking. He wanted to be on his best behavior when Cecile came in from the clinic to join them for tea or a midafternoon snack. Dinners were a rare treat.

One day, Cecile gave Bröer a present. It was a flexible knee brace constructed of nylon, plastic and aluminum. It was sturdy and could be fastened about his calf and thigh with Velcro straps. By using the knee brace, Bröer could avoid using the cane.

Those were happy times, and they didn't happen often enough for Ducasse. The time came when Bröer could no longer afford to room at the La Salle. He continued to drink at the hotel, but took an apartment in the low-rent part of town. All the while, he drew down his savings.

Stories circulated in town about the South African mercenary who had fallen on hard times.

Push came to shove when the money ran out. Bröer had arguments with his landlady. Sold his watch. He tried to find work. The flying contracts, which had become infrequent, became impossible to get.

Bröer went to Ducasse.

"I need a place to stay, Father. Until I get another contract."

Ducasse was in a difficult position. By then, he considered Bröer a friend, but he could not permit the man to live at the rectory indefinitely. Especially because Bröer had no money and his drinking was becoming a problem.

Cecile had to be told.

DUCASSE AND CECILE sat together in her office. It was at the back of the clinic, a small wooden structure built next to the mission. Every piece of medical equipment was kept neatly in its place. The thermometer, blood pressure monitor, weighing scale, autoclave and minor surgery kit. The walls were decorated with medical posters and charts. They sat on two straight-backed chairs kitty-corner to each other next to her kneehole desk.

"Why didn't you tell me before?" Eyes wide, Cecile held her hands flat on her desktop.

"It was his wish, and there was no reason to tell you. Everything was going as well as one might have hoped for. It was not easy."

"I should have known." Cecile shook her head. "I thought you were just good friends, but he's been so nice."

"Bröer made sure you wanted for nothing," Ducasse said. "He financed your education. To earn the money, he flew drugs to Spain. He would not have done so otherwise. When you graduated, he tried to quit. The gangsters killed his copilot and burned his plane. Beat him, shattered his knee and elbow. He came back a cripple."

Ducasse thought for a moment.

"Never tell anyone that Bröer *knew* he was transporting drugs. He found out by *accident*. As far as you are concerned, the money for your education came from a scholarship. Your reputation must not be tainted. The less people know of your past, and Bröer's, the better."

"And *your* past," Cecile said.

"Yes, if you like. *My* past as well."

Cecile was silent for a long time. At last, she said, "I have two fathers now."

That afternoon, Ducasse walked Cecile back to the rectory. Bröer was in the guest room. Ducasse left them together and walked to the La Salle for a drink.

Bröer moved into Cecile's house, where she supported him as he sank deeper into his addiction. They argued about his drinking, but she could not cast him out. She loved him too much.

Gossip spread through the black community of St. Croix that their mixed-race doctor was the daughter of the South African mercenary pilot. That she had taken the drunk to live with her because he had been cast out of the mission.

The blacks in St. Croix knew, but the French seemed unaware. If they knew, they never brought it up around Ducasse. He decided that they thought Bröer continued to live at a boardinghouse in St. Croix.

That was when Marien was released from the barracks.

Ducasse assumed Marien learned from his parents that Bröer was Cecile's father. Their whole world in St. Croix had been turned upside down.

After Marien revealed his disability and left the country, Ducasse struggled to understand. He concluded that the French could not think of a clean way to kill him. They decided, instead, to mutilate and release him. Threatened to kill him if he ever caused trouble again.

In the pilot's lucid moments, Ducasse and Bröer discussed Marien. They concluded that his mind had been twisted by his ordeal. He had come to hate Cecile because he could no longer be whole for her.

Marien's hatred for the French, however, promised terrible retribution.

Ducasse sighs. "That's all of it, Breed."

I wonder when the priest last went to confession. Priests

do, after all, have their own confessors. Not that Ducasse had sinned. But the secrets of others, particularly those one cares about, can be a burden.

"Thank you, Father."

"You only wanted to know about Cecile."

"Father, it wasn't idle curiosity. This knowledge may help us escape."

17

SUNDAY, 0230 HRS - ST. CROIX

I climb aboard our armored train.
    Grady and Powell did a good job. They worked with the arrangement of flatcars in the yard. We found the locomotive pointed in the right direction, so there was no need for them to use the yard's massive turntable. The turntable is a steel railway bridge mounted in a circular pit. The locomotive sits in the middle of the bridge, which is rotated either manually or by external power. COBRA uses the turntable to point the locomotive east or west along the track as required.

The locomotive stands at the easternmost end of the train. It will push, rather than pull, the flatcars to St. Croix. It's a massive iron beast, sixty feet long and eighteen feet high. Huge wheels, set in stiffly sprung bogies, flank a huge fuel tank slung beneath the locomotive platform. The iron bull is designed to push and pull five times as many flatcars as we're riding. Loaded with ore and concentrate, all the way across the continent.

The first flatcar sits in front of the locomotive. Under

Powell's direction, hundred-pound sacks of cobalt concentrate have been stacked two-high around the edge of the flatcar. They form a continuous hip-high barricade that the civilians can sit, lie or crouch behind. Our shooters can fire from behind them and cover both sides of the tracks.

The second flatcar is coupled in front of the first. It will lead the train and be the first to set off any mines laid on the tracks. There are no cobalt sacks on this flatcar. We do not want our field of fire obstructed.

The wounded and the rest of the civilians are already aboard, sitting on the armored flatcar's cargo bed. The children seem excited by the prospect of riding the train. They're looking up at the engine, with Troy and Carol Grady standing in the cab, ready to go. Like many young people, the children appear unaffected by desperate situations. Either they lack a full appreciation of the danger, or they are happy to leave the situation to adults.

"Saddle up," I tell Powell. "Let's do a headcount before we leave."

I sling my rifle, climb into the cab with the Gradys. Look down at the armored car. Cecile is tending the wounded. Father Ducasse is staring up at me. Wondering if this miserable heathen can do the impossible.

"We're ready to go," Grady says.

"Wait one." I search for Powell. The SEAL flashes me a thumbs-up. "Okay, let's go."

Grady flips a lever from "idle" to "run" and gives throttle. The locomotive lurches forward against the flatcars. The air is filled with loud clangs as knuckle couplers engage and the rail wheels scream in protest. When they start to turn, the train rolls and picks up speed.

Mount Wambesa blots out the sky to the south. To my

right, I see a pall of smoke hanging over French Village. The flames are dying…the belly of the pall is no longer the red of hell. It's a salmon pink.

Powell stacked sacks of cobalt inside the cab to protect the driver. Grady's Winchester is leaning against them in a corner of the cab. I rest my rifle on top of the barricade and lean against it. "How long before we reach St. Croix?" I ask.

"Half an hour. We'll pass the COBRA airstrip first. It'll be a mile north of the tracks."

"Will we get a look into it?"

"Yes. Wish we had binoculars."

I strain to see ahead in the darkness. The railroad passes through a tunnel blasted into the spur that joins Mount Wambesa to French Village. I mention this to Grady.

"That's right," he says. "I reckon we'll reach it fifteen minutes after the airstrip. We'll stop outside the tunnel entrance. Then you can do whatever you want to find our pilot."

"Outside, huh?"

"Yeah. I'm not keen on getting bottled up inside a tunnel with no place to run. Are you?"

I smile. Troy Grady is developing a tactical brain.

Grady's a good guy. The kind of man who does what needs to be done. He knows what he can do. He knows his limitations. He's accepted that his role is to get me within striking distance of St. Croix. The rest is up to me.

We'll have to circle French Village, approach over the east road. I have no desire to hike through French Village again. Making our way through St. Croix will be bad enough. There are two places to check for Bröer. The La Salle or Cecile's house.

My stomach hollows. What if he's at neither? What if we find him dead? What if we can't find him at all?

I force the fears from my mind.

Powell steps over the coupling and onto the locomotive platform. Climbs the ladder and pulls open the door to the cab.

"Can you imagine," Powell says, "we're coming full circle."

"Only place running gets you is back where you started," I tell him.

Powell laughs. "This time, it'd better get us out of here."

"Over there," Grady says. He points ahead to our right.

A pale white glow lights up the sky. It's the glow of floodlights.

The COBRA airstrip comes into view. It's a far cry from the Arbois International Airport. There's a flat, two-story building that serves as an administrative office. An orange windsock is visible from a mile away. The wind is still blowing to the northeast. The tower is a raised platform on the office building roof.

Unlike the Arbois runway, which runs north-south, the COBRA strip runs east-west and is much shorter. That makes sense—there's nothing but Sahel north of Arbois. The COBRA strip, on the other hand, is constrained by Mount Wambesa to the south and the French Village spur to the west.

The COBRA runway is three thousand feet long. It'll handle a Dash-8. The airplane stands on the runway, a hundred yards from the office building. It's an elegant aircraft, designed in Canada. A sleek, white arrow with a high wing, two turboprops, and a T-tail.

There's an old saying—*If a plane doesn't look right, it won't fly right.*

The Dash-8 looks like it wants to fly.

"Son of a bitch," Powell says.

Armed men in battle fatigues are walking back and forth on the field. Three of them are on the office roof, huddled in a sandbagged position.

"That there's a machine gun," Powell says. "I reckon a PKM."

We can't seem to catch a break. I look onto the armored flatcar. The children are looking toward the airstrip, pointing at the airplane.

The other civilians project despair, with slumped shoulders and blank faces. Father Ducasse stares at me from under the brim of his straw hat. Cecile busies herself with the wounded.

I clench a fist.

Grady turns to me. "What the hell," he says. "Breed, let's drive this big bastard right to the coast."

The red-bearded giant's features are tight with determination.

"It's an option," I tell him. "But if Tombaye's smart enough to guard the highway, he's smart enough to guard the railroad. We don't have it in us to take on his cadre again."

"Then we don't have it in us to take that plane." Powell's eyes narrow. "Breed, you said you could find us a pilot. Can you get us past that machine gun?"

"Let's find our pilot first," I say. "We'll figure something out. Grady, if all else fails, I'll take you up on that ride west."

Grady gives throttle, and the locomotive shoves the flatcars forward.

The armored train rolls on, sweeps past the shoulder of Mount Wambesa, leaves the COBRA strip behind. I check my watch. Fifteen minutes.

"Here you are," Grady says at last. He chops the throttle. Brakes the train. The ridge of the spur looms over us. The opening of the tunnel is a gaping maw.

The civilians get to their feet...those who can. I turn to Powell. "You, me and Cecile. Time to walk in the park."

Powell opens the door to the cab and swings onto the ladder. Climbs down to the tracks.

I turn to the Gradys. "You have a rifle and pistol," I tell them. "Don't leave the cab unattended. If you have to leave the cab for any reason, get the French sergeant to guard it. Be ready to move at a moment's notice."

Shouldering her bag, Cecile climbs down from the armored flatcar. She does not look happy.

"Let's go," I say.

We set off toward French Village. We'll follow the southeast approach from the COBRA plant. When we reach the ring road that circles the hill, we'll turn toward St. Croix. I lead the way, followed by Cecile, and finally by Powell. I look back to ensure they're holding five yards separation.

Lined up at the barricade of cobalt sacks, the civilians watch us go. In the middle of the row, I see a tall figure wearing a straw hat.

Smoke.

Over and above the raw smell of forest vegetation, I smell smoke. It's a sharp and woody odor. The fires of French

Village and St. Croix have spread it over a large swathe of the hill.

We reach the southeast road and move quickly. I'm confident Tombaye will have withdrawn his roadblocks from the hill. There's nothing left in French Village to hold. The homes have been razed to the ground, and the French are all dead.

There's no point holding real estate with no tactical value. For the moment, Tombaye's cadre are better deployed elsewhere.

We reach the ring road and turn right. I forge toward the town. Behind us, Powell pulls rear security.

I reach the turnoff that leads to the crossroads. The place where the army column was ambushed. Another quarter mile, and the going gets more difficult. We've left the shadow of the hill, and we're entering St. Croix. We follow the side streets, edge toward Vieux Carré.

St. Croix has calmed down. Grown quieter. The massacre on the hill is over. There weren't as many French to kill in the square. The bloodthirsty entertainment in the Vieux Carré has been exhausted. Most of the rabid townspeople are on their way home with stolen goods.

Now that we're in the city, I signal Cecile and Powell to close up our separation. Outside town, we kept five yards. Now we move nut-to-butt, house-to-house. From the side streets, we watch townspeople walking on the main thoroughfare.

Townspeople returning from French Village, carrying loot. Literally, *sacks* of loot. Women with bundles slung on their backs. They spread sheets on the ground and threw valuables into piles in the middle. Gathered the corners together and tied the sheets into sacks.

Men are carrying sofas between them.

Some men are trundling wheelbarrows over the cobblestones. The wheelbarrows have been loaded with DVD players, laptops, and other electronic equipment.

We hear the occasional gunshot.

The shots are random. When someone is shooting at you, you know it. There's an *intent* to that kind of gunfire. Deliberate clusters of shots in two- and three-round bursts of aimed fire. The snap of rounds as they pass. Sound is important. You can tell how far away a shooter is by the time between the splash of a bullet and the sound of the shot.

The American consulate is a blackened skeleton. Across the street, the French embassy looks worse. Only a few vertical timbers remain standing on the north side. The walls have fallen in, and nothing else remains of the building's frame.

I wave the others into the shadows. We huddle against a rough wooden wall. Cecile crouches behind me, close enough to touch. She's not happy, knows I'm bringing her along to show the way to her house. If we're lucky, we'll find her father alive.

Cecile trusts me. Like a child, she's doing what I want even though it goes against her own instincts. I'm so conscious of that childlike trust that the awareness hurts. I want to be right. I want to get us out of here. I don't want to betray her.

The walls of the American consulate have fallen in. The timbers and other supports are thick posts of smoking charcoal. Embers glow in the debris.

I snap my fingers to attract Powell's attention. Point at the square.

We can see through the ruins of the consulate, across the

Vieux Carré. To the right, the Presidential Palace. Straight ahead, the Hôtel de Ville. Behind the Hôtel de Ville, the dark skeleton of the television tower.

The American consulate and the French embassy have burned down. All the buildings on the east side of the Vieux Carré are toast. Buildings to the north and east are still pouring flames and smoke into the sky. Tombaye's cadre fought the fires, used the French embassy and the American consulate as firebreaks to protect the Hôtel de Ville and Presidential Palace. It looks like the La Salle should be alright. The wind, blowing toward the northeast, spared buildings to the north and west.

Earlier, I determined that Tombaye was using the Hôtel de Ville as his headquarters. I was right. There are two cadre at the gates of the Presidential Palace and two at the gate of the Hôtel de Ville.

Most striking, a five-ton truck has been parked in the Vieux Carré, in front of the Hôtel de Ville. The cargo bed has been sandbagged, and a crew-served PKM has been positioned to cover the square. There are three cadre in the truck, all on the cargo bed. The PKM requires a crew of two. I'm betting the third man is the driver, lonesome for company.

Crumpled bodies lie scattered across the Vieux Carré. French men and women violated in the most obscene ways. Most are partially clothed, some are naked. The townspeople have tired of their fun.

I get to my feet and signal the others to follow me. Stick to the side streets, make my way to the La Salle.

There's motion ahead of me, a good two hundred yards away. I drop to a crouch, wave the others to get down behind me.

A group of townsmen is moving toward us. I scuttle around the corner, lead the others into a black alley. It's a dark passage between two buildings, not wide enough for two people to pass.

Our positions are reversed. I went in first, so now I'm farthest from the street. Then Cecile, then Powell. We hold our breath. I'm close enough to hug Cecile. Conscious of the satin skin of her shoulder. I sense the depth of her breathing. She turns her head, and her eyes meet mine.

Sensation is heightened by danger. Cecile is feeling what I'm feeling. It's a distraction. For me, it's unprofessional. But I'm still situation-aware. Our positions have reversed, and Powell is point.

I look behind us. The alley is completely black.

The townsmen march by, hurrying to the hill for more loot. Powell and I don't need to exchange a word. He makes sure the group has passed, then assumes point. Leads us toward the La Salle.

The back entrance to the La Salle is exactly as we left it. The three dead Umbali, Remy Bernard's butchered body.

I throw the AK-74 on its sling behind me, draw my Mark 23. Powell switches with Cecile to cover me. I hold my pistol at retracted high ready, push the back door open. Dig the left corner while Powell digs the right. For the second time this evening, we clear the kitchen, then the lobby, then the bar.

There's no one sitting at Bröer's table. A couple of empty whisky bottles are broken on the floor. Otherwise, the townspeople did little damage. The liquor shelves are bare. The La Salle's entire inventory has been looted.

To my left, the windows remain uncovered, and we can see the main street. Half a mile away, the Presidential Palace is well lighted, as is the Hôtel de Ville. The flames are behind us, to the north. I tuck the Mark 23 under my waistband and heft the AK-74.

"Where's your house?" I ask Cecile. "North of here, certainly. East or west?"

"West."

"Good. There's a chance it hasn't burned. Take us there."

"What if Rijk isn't there?"

Cecile's voice is trembling. She's afraid of finding him, and of what he'll be asked to do. Afraid of finding him dead. Afraid of not finding him.

"There's only one way to find out."

We leave the La Salle and continue down the back streets of St. Croix. Again, we take a cautious, deliberate approach. Me in the lead, Cecile behind, and Powell pulling rear security.

Deeper and deeper, we penetrate the rat's nest of streets that form the guts of St. Croix. I continue to lead. Now and then, Cecile holds me and points over my shoulder at the direction to take. The smoke, the flames and the orange sky are well to our right. The farther we go, the more comfortable I am that Cecile's house has been spared.

The question, of course, is whether or not it's been looted. Whether Bröer is there. Everywhere, there's evidence of random, capricious violence. The rebellion didn't stop with the French. When the violence began, it spiraled out of control. Tribal and caste divisions hardened, and they turned on each other. Townspeople who had little turned on those who had more than a little.

"There," Cecile whispers.

Cecile's house sits in the middle of a street of bungalows.

It's quiet, and I don't see signs of violence. A few bungalows are lit from within. The rest are dark. Less adventurous townspeople probably turned their lights off, hoping not to attract attention.

We approach with caution. Cecile gasps, and my stomach clenches.

The front door is ajar.

Again, I put the AK-74 aside and draw the Mark 23. The interior of the bungalow is dark.

Gently, I push the door. It bumps against something—a woman's foot. She's sprawled on the living room floor.

There's a sharp crack. The lightning of a muzzle flash stabs the dark. A bullet splinters the door jamb to my left. I push Cecile down. Wooden walls are not bulletproof.

"Bröer!"

Silence.

"Bröer!"

The voice that reaches from the dark interior shakes. "Who's that?"

"It's Breed. Hold your fire. I have Cecile with me."

"Cecile?"

"Yes. Now safety that weapon and put it down."

"Cecile?"

Cecile calls out to him. "Yes, Rijk. It's me. Do as he says."

"Bröer. Is the weapon down?"

"Yes. Safe and down."

I turn to Powell. He's got his back to us, covering the street with his M4. He nods to me.

Push harder on the door, move the woman's leg out of the way, step inside. I'm still holding the Mark 23 at retracted high ready.

Two bodies on the floor. A man about ten feet into the

sitting room, lying on his back, arms outflung. He's clutching a carving knife in his right hand. Shot twice in the chest, dead eyes staring at the ceiling. The woman is closer to the door, on her face. Lying across the man's left arm. There's an exit wound in her back the size of a shot glass. The left side of her head is bloody.

My eyes search the darkness. Two bedrooms and a kitchen. Both bedroom doors are wide open, interiors black.

"Bröer, where are you?"

The voice comes from the bedroom on the right. "In here. Turn the lights on."

"No," I say. "Come out, keep the gun down."

Bröer shuffles from the bedroom. He's holding a Browning Hi-Power 9mm by his leg. The way I hold my beers on a Friday night. I notice his finger is off the trigger, flat on the right side of the frame. Old habits die hard.

Cecile and Powell join us inside the house. Powell drops to one knee like he's in the bush. Keeps his M4 trained on the front door.

Bröer plunks himself down on the sofa. Sets the Browning on the coffee table.

I push the woman's body over with the toe of my shoe. She's as dead as Kelsey's nuts. One bullet in the chest, center mass. Another blew out her left eye and most of her left temple.

"It's the Nyembos," Cecile says. "They live next door."

"They wanted to help themselves to your things," Bröer says. "The man was happy to stick me. I shot him and kept on shooting."

The South African slumps into the sofa. His head rocks back, and his eyes close.

"Wake up, Bröer." I shake his shoulder. "Sit straight, you've got company."

"You're a good man, Breed. We've known each other less than a day and already we're friends."

"Yes, Bröer. We're friends. Now sit up. Cecile, make some coffee."

With a mighty effort, Bröer straightens. Cecile goes into the kitchen, fills an electric kettle, and plugs it in.

"How's the street?" I ask Powell.

"Clear."

Cecile brings a cup of coffee into the sitting room. Hands it to Bröer on a saucer. I take the Browning, check that it's cocked and locked. Shove it under my waistband at the small of my back.

"I don't want it." Bröer holds the saucer, but doesn't put the coffee down.

"Bröer," I say, "pay attention. You're going to fly us out of here."

"Not a chance of that," Bröer says. "I haven't flown in years."

"But you *can* fly. Those Dash-8 pilots on the hill are dead. You're all we have."

I pull up a chair and sit opposite him. Cecile goes to the sofa next to her father and sits down, hands clasped in her lap.

The sitting room, defiled by the violence that took place, has been decorated with a feminine touch. The sofa and wing chairs are covered by cloth upholstery with floral patterns. Matching cushions. There's a vase of flowers in the center of the coffee table. Photographs are hung on the walls. It's too dark to make out much detail, but a number look like images of Cecile in Paris.

Carefully, leaving nothing out, I tell Bröer what happened since we left him at the La Salle. "All the French in the Village have been massacred," I tell him, "and all the ones around the Vieux Carré. We have twenty-six people, including wounded and children, who are going to be killed if we can't get out."

"I'm not the one to do it." Bröer's voice shakes. "Look at me. I can't even hold a cup of coffee."

It's true. The coffee cup in Bröer's hand is rattling against the saucer.

Am I wrong about Bröer? Is Ducasse? I'm not convinced about the priest's judgment of character. After all, he doesn't like *me*, and what's not to like? From the story Ducasse told me, the South African has not hit rock bottom. Ducasse talked a lot about the pilot exercising a pretense of discipline. Of controlling his rate of descent, if only—

—for Cecile.

I have *one* ace up my sleeve. It's brutal, and the play has to be executed perfectly.

"Please, Father," Cecile says, "you must try. I *know* you can do it."

Bröer puts the cup down on the table. Black coffee sloshes into the saucer.

"Drink it, Bröer."

"No."

"Marien will kill us all," Cecile says.

"No, he won't." Bröer leans back in the chair again. His chin tilts up, and his eyes close.

I gather Bröer's shirtfront in my fist and pull him upright. "You don't think so? You miserable son of a bitch. You know Goddamn well Tombaye hates your daughter. He hates her because he isn't good enough for her anymore. He's nothing.

He's not even a man. He doesn't give a shit about you because you don't give a shit about yourself. Everyone else, he'll kill—*including* Cecile. Is that what you want?"

How will Cecile react? I can beat the shit out of Bröer, but unless she comes down on my side, it won't do any good.

"Rijk, *please*." Cecile gets on her knees beside Bröer. Holds his hands in hers. "He's right. Marien wouldn't even speak to me. I could *feel* his hate."

I let go of Bröer. It's up to Cecile now.

"I love you, Father. If you love me, please try."

Bröer hunches forward and hugs Cecile. At last, he says, "Get off your knees, girl. It's not right."

The old man turns to me. "I'll try, Breed. I might crash us all, but I'll try. Now give me that coffee."

18

SUNDAY, 0330 HRS, ST. CROIX – HÔTEL DE VILLE

"That's great," Powell says. "We have *consensus*. Now how do we get past that machine gun, Breed?"

"Is the street still clear?"

"Yes."

I stick the Mark 23 under my belt and heft the AK-74. "It's pretty straightforward. We take Tombaye hostage and trade him for the airplane."

"You *are* cracking up. You know there are seven cadre and a PKM covering that square?"

I first thought about it while we were running from the cadre and Umbali at the border. Didn't know what would make sense until I had another look at the Vieux Carré. That's why I led the group to the square before going to the La Salle. I needed to check it out.

"I am well aware of that. Our basic assumptions haven't changed—Tombaye has fifty cadre, correct?"

"Give or take, yes."

"I think he's got more than seven men in St. Croix. How

many has he got covering the back of the Hôtel de Ville? The back of the Presidential Palace?"

"Let's say two each."

"How many with him inside the Hôtel de Ville?"

"At least one."

"See what I mean?"

Powell does the arithmetic. "Twelve out of fifty. That's a quarter of his force."

"Exactly. He can't have much more than that here, because he only has thirty-four left. That takes into account the one I killed at the ambush and the three we killed at the roadblock. We don't know how many we killed or wounded at the border."

"So, how does he distribute them?"

"Comes back to what his strong points are. Let's say eight at Arbois airport and eight at the COBRA airstrip. Six at the Lokola border, and six covering Marawi. Four at the mine. That's already thirty-two men. The eight from the Lokola border could be busy hunting for us. I'm going to say he keeps two at the army barracks to secure their armory. That makes thirty-four."

"He's spread thin."

"Yes. Twelve men in St. Croix isn't a lot. Especially if he's expecting the French to mount an operation to take Wambesa back."

"But they've got a PKM."

"True enough, but only two men in the back." I turn to Cecile. "The radio and television station is in the back. What does it look like?"

"I don't go there often. There's a fence, a radio tower, and a building."

"Is the TV station a separate building, or is it connected to the Hôtel de Ville?"

Cecile frowns. "I think it's connected."

I get to my feet. "That's our way into the Hôtel de Ville."

WE STEP over the dead Nyembos on our way out the front door. I feel bad for Cecile. It sucks when your neighbors try to rob and kill you. Worse, when your father has to plug them with his Browning. Soil your living room floor with their blood. Cleanup is a bitch.

Bröer could barely hold a coffee cup steady when we found him. Yet he was good enough to score four hits on two attackers. Drunk and in the dark. Three rounds, center mass. The head shot on the woman might have been a pure fluke. She was on the way down when he sent the fourth round. Bröer must have been something back in the day.

I'd like to get to know the man. Everyone says he's South African. But he fought for Rhodesia. Might have been Selous Scouts or Rhodesian SAS.

The TV station is on the east side of the Hôtel de Ville. If we want to approach it using side streets, we'll have to take care to avoid the swathe of St. Croix that is still on fire. It's also likely there will be more townspeople on that side. Fighting fires, or trying to save their personal belongings.

Cecile leads us back to the La Salle. That way, we bypass the worst of the fire. Once there, I use back streets to approach the Hôtel de Ville from the east side of the square. I take point, Cecile and Bröer follow, and Powell takes the rear.

There isn't much to a TV and radio station, really. There's

a tower to raise the antenna high enough to transmit as far as you want to reach. That depends on the frequency of your transmission, terrain, and weather conditions among other things. The inhabited parts of Wambesa are flat. The mountains and dense forest are well south. Bottom line, it doesn't take much for a signal to reach most of North Africa and beyond.

Once you have an antenna, you need a transmitter. That's where frequency and power come in. High-wattage, hi-frequency radios bounce signals off the ionosphere for intercontinental reach. The Wambesa station won't have that capability. It's probably got moderate juice at lower bands for regional coverage. The transmitter will be housed in a designated room inside the station.

That last piece speaks to a power requirement. The radio station needs a lot of power. It needs to be hooked up to the city mains. This is Africa, and brownouts are common. Auxiliary generators are a must. Those will be in an adjacent building. For safety reasons, fuel will be stored in a third building a good distance away from the main structures.

Not much more to a station. You need a pre-lit stage—a set. Microphones, cameras and assorted gear. Beyond that, a receptionist, office, and toilets. You're good to go. How do I know this? Special Forces are trained to seize TV and radio stations... or wreck them. They are part of a country's command and control.

All in a day's work.

I inch my way along a debris-strewn alley east of the Vieux Carré. I'm followed by Cecile, Bröer and Powell. Streets that were presentable this afternoon have been transformed into a disaster area. I carry the AK-74 at low ready. As far as I'm concerned, there are no friendlies in this town.

There it is. The Hôtel de Ville is a boring colonial structure. Not as impressive as the Presidential Palace or the La Salle. Two stories sitting on a square footprint. A wooden structure built on a stone foundation. It's intact, spared from the fire that consumed the French embassy next door. Saved by the wind that fanned the flames that consumed the French embassy and blew them toward the north side of the square.

Half of the French embassy has been demolished by Tombaye's cadre. Lacking heavy equipment, they blew it up. They'd been liberally supplied with Russian explosives. Detonated a charge on the south side, because the north side was too dangerous to approach. The blast took down half the building and created a firebreak to protect the Hôtel de Ville. That's why a few smoking timbers remain upright on the north side, while the south side has been leveled to the foundation.

Again, I'm impressed by Tombaye's cadre. Powell was right. They had instruction in the use of high-velocity Russian explosives. A number of their men were qualified breachers and engineers. They knew the Russian technical manuals cover to cover.

I'm looking at a single-story structure grafted onto the back of the Hôtel de Ville. Right next to the tower with its antennas. That's the station. The buildings are lit from within. Warm sodium light glows orange from behind the blinds.

The back of the building is protected by a ten-foot wrought-iron fence painted green. It's more decorative than protective. It consists of iron bars shaped like spears. The bars are set about six inches apart, with pointy, leaf-shaped blades. The fence is held together by two horizontal iron rails, one six inches from the top and another six inches from the bottom. The fence is broken only by a hinged gate fastened with a heavy padlock.

Where are the sentries? We're expecting two.

I see one walking inside the perimeter. He's smoking a cigarette, AK-74 slung over his shoulder.

Where would I post sentries? The tower. I raise my eyes, scan each level of the metal gantry from top to bottom. Nothing. That suggests that if we're right about our count, there could be at least two men inside with Tombaye.

I turn to the others. "One sentry in the back," I say. "Powell and I will go over the fence, take him out, and find Tombaye. If all goes well, we'll bring him out the front."

The Browning is heavy at the small of my back. I pull it out, check its condition, and hand it to Bröer. "That weapon is cocked and locked. Take Cecile to the other side of Vieux Carré and wait for us. This will be over in half an hour. If things go wrong, if we're not out by then, make your way back to the train. Grady will try for the Marawi border."

I don't detect trembling in Bröer's hand as he takes the Browning from me. I notice he checks its condition before stuffing it behind his belt. This doesn't tell me much. The real test will come when he sits in that cockpit.

If we get that far.

Bröer and Cecile set off. Another circuitous path to avoid townspeople.

"Where do you think we'll find Tombaye?" I ask Powell. "First floor or second?"

"Second."

"Why?"

"He's the Big Kahuna now. He should have the corner office."

"If that's where his head's at, he'll be at the Presidential Palace. No, I think he's on the first floor. Next to the TV station."

"You're pretty cocky all of a sudden. We don't even have a floor plan."

"No. But the TV station has only one floor to clear. If he's there, job's done. If he's not, we clear the Hôtel de Ville. Ground floor first, then the second. If I'm right, we get him on the ground floor."

"Then we go out the front."

"Yes. But if we find him on the ground floor, you have to pull rear security. Because in that event, we will not have cleared the second."

We've known each other for less than twenty-four hours, but from the beginning, we've thought and acted like a team. Powell's good. We have a shared background, a common frame of reference. We are not perfectly integrated yet, but we are very close.

"That fence is too easy," I say. "But how do we get over it without the sentry noticing?"

Powell's eyes flick over the dystopian ruins of the square. "A diversion."

I examine the shadows. The flames from the north side of the town light up the compound. The spear-shaped bars of the fence cast long shadows against the wall of the station. The south side of the building lies deep in shadow.

We still hear occasional gunshots from the town.

"Can you create a diversion to the north?" I ask. "Gunshots, fairly close. They'll sound louder and closer than those others. If you draw him to that side, I'll go over the south fence."

"It's worth a try."

We check our watches. "Five minutes," I say.

Powell sets off to the north, and I move to the south.

THE MARK 23's suppressor is sitting in my sock drawer back in Falls Church. I should have brought it. Then I could take out the sentry *before* climbing the fence. There are too many scenes in fiction where the commando cuts the sentry's throat, garrotes him, or breaks his neck. Take it from me—the easiest thing to do is go around him. The next easiest is to plug him with a properly suppressed subsonic pistol.

It's not my first choice, but today I'll have to put hands on this man. Use the Cold Steel strapped to my calf.

I crouch in the shadows of the building next to the Hôtel de Ville. The sentry paces back and forth. Stops at the foot of the tower and leans against the gantry. Lights another cigarette.

Check my watch. Four minutes gone.

I pat myself down. The Mark 23 is tucked into my waistband. My ammunition vest is loaded with five spare magazines. I've only finished one with all the shooting today. I rarely, if ever, run full auto. I have used both grenades. Powell has two, taken from the dead cadre at the roadblock. The AK-74 is slung over my shoulder.

Crack. Crack.

Two shots, in rapid succession from the north. Closer than the sporadic firing audible from the town. Ninety percent of the townspeople don't have guns. A few have old pistols, some have shotguns. You can tell when you hear the shots what kind of weapon fired them.

These shots are the distinctive, high-pitched crack of

Powell's M4. If this cadre is as experienced as I think he is, he'll notice. You don't fight American soldiers in the Middle East without learning to recognize the sound of American weapons.

The cadre pushes off from the steel gantry. Drops his cigarette and crushes it out with the toe of his boot. Unslings his AK-74, and goes to the north fence. He carries his weapon at high ready, looks left and right. Gunshots can be deceptive. You have to disregard echoes.

Crack.

Powell knows that too. He fired the third round to make up the cadre's mind. The man's head jerks. He stands at the north fence and searches the town with suspicious eyes.

I run to the south fence. Reach up, grab the top rail with both hands, and haul myself up. Plant one boot between two of the spear points. Lever myself to a standing position at the top of the fence. I could jump down, but that would make too much noise. Instead, I swing my body over the tips of the leaf blades and reverse my grip on the rail. Then I lower myself till I'm hanging by my arms only three feet from the ground.

Let go, flex my knees on landing. Turn and fade into the shadows between the station and the Hôtel de Ville.

I hold my breath. For a long time, the cadre stares into the town. There are more shots. Random, farther away. The crackling of flames.

The man turns away from the north fence, slings his rifle. He's annoyed. Paces alongside the fence, walking slowly from north to south. Powell's shots set him on edge. He doubts himself. He thinks he *might* have been mistaken about the shots, but *knows* he wasn't.

The sentry's not in the ideal frame of mind for liquidation. When you kill a sentry, you want him to be relaxed, lazy, and careless. Not uncomfortable, suspicious and alert. This is what I have to overcome. I reach down and draw my Cold Steel.

When he reaches the south fence, the man stops and looks toward the Presidential Palace. In that instant, he's vulnerable. I could wait for him to turn and pace back to the north side, but he might go back to the tower and have another smoke.

This might be the only chance I get.

I step forward and clamp my left hand over the man's nose and mouth. Take the knife and stab the point into the right side of his neck. Double-edged, the blade slides straight in, behind all the plumbing. The point emerges from the other side, and with one motion, I punch the blade out the front. Great gouts of blood spray from his severed arteries.

The man struggles for fifteen seconds before his brain dies from lack of oxygen. I drag him back into the shadows and sit him on the ground with his back to the wall. I wipe my blade on his shirt and replace the knife in its sheath.

I draw my Mark 23 and go to the north side of the fence. Powell's already climbing over. Together, we approach the back door of the station.

We take positions on either side of the door. I reach forward and test the handle. It's unlocked. I push the door open. Enter the station, pistol at retracted high ready. Dig the left corner. Powell follows close, digs the right. Clear. We're in a wide hall. Two doors on the right. The wall to the left is solid. We need to clear the rooms, one by one. As usual, the hall is a killing zone. The hell of it is, once we start shooting, we'll bring the world down on ourselves. We need to find Tombaye quickly.

Step to the first door and push it open. I clear to the left, Powell clears to the right. The room's empty. It's an office, with six wooden kneehole desks in two columns. We step back into the hall, close the door behind us. Move to the second door.

We take up positions on either side of the second door. Same drill as before, we burst inside. I dig left, Powell right. It's a more confusing environment. We've burst onto a stage set. There are large lights on dollies, one on each side, pointed at a table on a raised dais. There's a chair behind the table. Two other chairs have been pushed up against the far wall. Between the lights is a television camera.

Tombaye was sitting behind that table a few hours ago.

To our left is a glass wall. Behind it, the control room. It's separated from the studio by a glass door. Inside the control room are two wooden doors. One behind the long desk that faces the studio. Another to one side.

I lead the way into the control room. Step to the first wooden door and open it. Inside are racks of electronic equipment and cables. These are the radio and TV transmitters, the cabling that connects to the antenna, power mains, microphones and cameras.

Step to the final door.

Judging by the floor area of the studio, we've covered the station. This door must connect to the ground floor of the Hôtel de Ville.

We take a breath and go through the door. Find a long corridor. At the end is a set of heavy wooden butterfly doors with worked bronze handles. In a flash, I realize that the Vieux Carré is on the other side of those doors.

Halfway down the corridor are two doors, one to the left, and one to the right. They must lead to office spaces. Immediately to my left is a staircase leading to the second floor. Where's Tombaye? Is he on this floor, as I expect, or upstairs as Powell guessed?

Footsteps to my left—a blur of motion. A cadre comes down the stairs and steps into the corridor without looking. We were so silent, he didn't hear us come in. I chop him in the throat with the edge of my left hand. He chokes and falls back against the stairs. I clamp my left hand over his nose and mouth, throw my weight against him, and press the muzzle of the Mark 23 to the side of his chest. Not hard, just enough to make contact. Pull the trigger and fire through his ribs into his heart and lungs. *Pop, pop, pop.*

The .45 ACP is a subsonic round, and the man's body acts like a suppressor. The sound of the discharge is muffled by contact with his torso. Not eliminated, *muffled*. He slumps against the steps.

I back up and extend the pistol to cover the hall. This is a nightmare scenario. I'm expecting cadre to enter from the Vieux Carré at any moment. Powell raises his rifle, covers the butterfly doors.

Two interior doors in the middle of the hall, left and right. Does it matter which I go through first? Fifty-fifty. If I'm right, Tombaye has one man left in the Hôtel de Ville.

I inch along the corridor, conscious of Powell behind me and the butterfly doors in front. My heart pounds like a fist beating against the inside of my chest. Throw myself flat on the floorboards. Give Powell a clear shot at the front entrance. Did anyone hear me shoot the man on the stairs?

Corridors are death traps.

Wooden walls are not bulletproof.

Left or right? I flip a coin in my head and go for the left door. I clutch the Mark 23 in my right hand. Reach up with my left, touch the doorknob.

Somebody on the other side cuts loose with an AK-74 on full auto. The first burst rakes the door at chest height. Two more bursts rake the walls on either side. Proof that all our CQB tactics leave us vulnerable to an automatic weapon inside a room. The shooter empties his magazine.

Splinters rain on me. The 5.45mm rounds penetrate the doors and walls on both sides of the corridor.

I get to one knee and throw my shoulder against the splintered door. Mark 23 extended in both hands, I fall into the room. The cadre is swapping out his mags, and I pound four rounds into his chest. One hits his weapon, and he drops it. The other three go into his sternum and knock him flat. Get to my feet and shoot him twice in the face. The bullets go into his mouth and upper lip, blow the top of his head off.

There's a second man in the room. A Makarov pistol lies on the desk, and he holds a squad radio in his hand. He reaches for the pistol as I cover him with the Mark 23. In that instant, I pray to God he doesn't make me kill him.

"Don't! Don't!" I yell.

A thin black man in battle fatigues. Slowly, he raises his hands.

Blood is roaring in my ears. "Step away from the desk."

There's the crackle of automatic fire from the corridor outside. It's Powell's M4. Cadre, coming through the butterfly doors.

"Breed!"

"Hold the corridor," I shout. "I've got him."

I'm staring into the eyes of Marien Tombaye.

19

SUNDAY, 0400 HRS, COBRA – AIRSTRIP

Powell sprays the front entrance with another burst of fully automatic fire. I hear running footsteps. The SEAL dives into the room. "That corridor's too damn hot," he says.

I know what he means. All the cadre have to do is stick the muzzle of an AK-74 through the butterfly doors, point it in his general direction, and fire without aiming. Move the muzzle in a little circle and hose the corridor down.

Tombaye stares at me through his round, metal-framed glasses. The battle fatigues are incongruous. Even in military garb, he looks like an academic, an intellectual.

"Call your men," I tell Tombaye. "Have them back away from the front doors."

"No."

I muzzle-thump him with the Mark 23, low in his hollow chest, just over the solar plexus. His mouth opens in a silent scream, and his legs give way.

"Tell them, or I'll kill you."

Tombaye reaches for the edge of the desktop. I pick up

the Makarov. He wasn't going for the pistol, just looking for leverage to rise to his feet.

"Then you all die."

The cadre sling a hail of lead across the corridor. Powell sticks the M4 around the corner and blazes away. His bolt locks back. He pulls the magazine free, hammers another home, thumbs the bolt release. "C'mon, Breed. Get it done."

I shove the muzzle of the Mark 23 in Tombaye's face. "You'll die first. Now tell them."

Tombaye groans. Keys his squad radio and speaks into it. Arabic.

Cries from outside the Hôtel de Ville. Orders relayed. The shooting from the butterfly doors stops.

"Very good," I tell him. "Where's President Mumbaye?"

"We captured him trying to flee with his money. He has been executed."

"You told the world he's alive."

"The world will learn the truth when I decide."

Tombaye is a real piece of work. I hold the Mark 23 in my right hand, the Makarov in my left. I heft the pistol, hold it up for Tombaye to view. "Very nice pistol," I say. "Russian. Did you pick it out yourself?"

Tombaye glares at me.

"No operation is *this* perfect," I say. "Do you expect me to believe that *every* piece of equipment you carry is Russian? Is your underwear stamped 'Made In Russia'?"

"Believe what you want."

"Whoever is financing you, it's not Russia. You're a whore, Tombaye."

"Whores also make rules."

I safety the Makarov and stick it in my belt at the small of my back. "Now I'm going to make you an offer you can't refuse."

"You are only buying yourself a little time, Breed."

"So, you know my name."

"Of course."

"You sent Umbali to kill me."

Tombaye grimaces. "I should have sent my cadre."

"Here's the deal. Your life for an airplane. We're flying out of here."

"And who among you will fly it?" Realization dawns on Tombaye's dark features. "Oh. You *are* a fool, Breed."

"Permit us to try. Tell your men we're coming out. If anyone makes a move against us, you die."

Tombaye speaks into his radio. Gives orders in Arabic.

"Speak in English."

"My men will not understand."

Son of a bitch.

I unbuckle the dead cadre's pistol belt, then his garrison belt. I take the thin garrison belt and bind Tombaye's wrists behind his back. I hold him by his left arm and stand behind him with the pistol to his head. Pick up his radio and squeeze it into a cargo pocket on my vest. March him toward the butterfly doors. Powell falls in behind us.

The wooden butterfly doors have been splintered by automatic weapons fire, but they are holding up well. They stand two-thirds open. Through the doors, I can see the five-ton parked in the square. The sandbagged PKM on its cargo deck. I hold Tombaye before me like a shield, conscious of his wiry frame. Push him out onto the front steps of the Hôtel de Ville.

Cadre stand arrayed in a semicircle in the Vieux Carré.

Nine men, drawing down on us with AK-74s. Two men crouch behind the sandbagged machine gun.

"Tell the men on the machine gun to jump down. Leave the weapon where it is."

"How do I know you will release me when you have your airplane?"

"You don't."

"Then I have no reason to comply."

"This might be a concept you're unfamiliar with, Tombaye, but I give you my word. That will have to be good enough for you. Now tell them."

Tombaye barks commands. I'm surprised by the authority in the skinny guy's voice. The cadre on the five-ton leave the PKM, dismount the vehicle.

"Tell them all to back away from the truck and move toward the Presidential Palace."

The cadre grudgingly step away from the entrance to the Hôtel de Ville. They remain arrayed against us, rifles at low ready. They're hardened fighters.

"Powell, get the truck started."

"You got it." Powell jogs to the cab of the five-ton and climbs behind the wheel. Sets the M4 flat on the seat next to him and starts the engine.

Still holding Tombaye in front of me, I edge toward the truck. Cross in front of the blunt hood, move to the passenger side. I lift him into the cab. I'm shocked how light he is. Climb in next to him.

"Drive across to the consulate," I tell Powell.

Powell throws the truck into gear. I hold the Mark 23 to Tombaye's head. Powell steers in a wide semicircle that brings us to a stop in front of the smoking ruins of the consulate. The cadre jog toward us, reform their line.

"Bröer! Cecile!" I yell. "Get in!"

Cecile and Bröer rise from where they were crouching. Hiding behind smoking, black timbers. Next to me, Tombaye sucks a breath when he sees Cecile.

"She's beautiful, isn't she?" I say.

Tombaye looks at me sharply.

Cecile stares through the windshield, her eyes flickering from me to Tombaye and back.

"Get in the truck," I tell Bröer. "Help Cecile onto the cargo bed. Stay behind the sandbags."

An engine growls. Powell jerks his head, pushes the muzzle of his M4 out the driver's window. Holds the weapon one-handed. Cadre in another five-ton roar into the square, stop in front of us. I count eight cadre, including the driver.

"Late to the party." I pull the radio from my pocket, hold it in front of Tombaye's mouth. "You know the drill. Tell them to back that truck out of our way. We're leaving."

Tombaye speaks into the radio. One of the men on the ground, a hard-looking guy with a full beard and no mustache, is carrying a squad radio. He's the guy Tombaye has been talking to. The half-beard yells at the men in the truck. The driver grudgingly makes way.

"They'll follow us," Powell says.

"I know. But we have an insurance policy." I look around to make sure Cecile and Bröer are settled in the cargo bed. "Let's go."

POWELL DRIVES the five-ton toward French Village. When we get to the road at the base of the hill, he turns left and heads for the railroad tracks.

"Switch the headlights on," I tell Powell.

I hold the radio for Tombaye. "Tell your men to keep their headlights off."

The cadre had piled into the second five-ton and were following us. They're waiting for a chance to free their leader. Waiting for us to make a mistake, waiting for him to do something creative. He will not get creative. If he tries, I'll kill him.

I glance at Tombaye. "What's in it for the Umbali?"

The generalissimo flashes a broad grin. "I bought them."

"How?"

"The Umbali know nothing of the modern world. Who is the most intelligent man in such a tribe? The witch doctor. I bought him with a promise of shared power. The Umbali believe in their practice of *muti*. Medicine and witchcraft that sometimes involves murder. The tribe's witch doctor holds more power than the chief. And I have his blessing."

Tombaye is a devil.

Powell pulls off the road and drives over a dirt path to the railroad tracks. Soon, we see the armored flatcar and the bulk of the locomotive.

"Turn off your lights," I tell Powell.

"Stop right there," a voice bellows.

I've come to know that voice. It's Grady, and he's got that big Winchester pointed at us. Somewhere on the flatcar, the sergeant has a 416 pointed in the same direction.

"Grady! It's Breed!"

"What the hell you got there, Breed?"

"A way out. Hold your fire."

I turn to Powell. "I have to keep our friend here. Get down and explain everything to Grady. Load everybody onto the cargo bed."

Powell opens his door and drops to the road. Waves to Grady and jogs over to the locomotive.

I grip the back of Tombaye's neck with my left hand. "Tell your men we're loading our people. Have them back up twenty yards. If they interfere, if any of our people so much as trip and fall, you're a dead man."

One by one, I watch our flock climb down from the armored flatcar and climb into the back of the five-ton. Twenty-six lost souls. A pitiful bunch, shepherded by Father Ducasse, the Gradys, and Enwright. As he passes the passenger window of the cab, Ducasse looks in, stares at Tombaye.

"Let us go, Marien." Ducasse isn't pleading. He's offering Tombaye a deal I can't give him. "Let us go, and God will forgive you."

"I am already damned, Father."

I jerk my chin toward the rear of the five-ton. "Get in back, Father. There's work to be done."

Ducasse leaves us, and I hold up the radio. "Now tell your men to come down from that PKM nest at the airstrip."

Tombaye's eyes meet mine. "This, I will do. But it is the last concession I intend to make."

"We'll see."

Grady completes the loading without incident. Steps around to Powell's window. "We're good to go. Breed, I think we'll pull this off."

"Anything is possible, Grady."

The trucks need to be maneuvered around each other, but we manage to get back on the southeast road. Powell turns his lights on and drives toward the airstrip.

I wish I could feel as optimistic as Grady.

THE COBRA STRIP looks like a football field lit for the big game. The floodlights on the roof of the main building bathe it in white light. The light reflects from dust particles suspended in the air, giving the scene a soft, ethereal quality.

I squint at the sandbagged machine gun nested between the floodlights. The PKM barrel is pointed skyward. The weapon has been abandoned.

Cadre wait for us next to the strip. I count eight men, carrying AK-74s. There would have been two on the PKM and six others. Seventeen in the truck behind us makes a total of twenty-five.

A hundred yards away, parked at the end of the thousand-yard strip, lies freedom. A beautiful, two-toned Dash-8. A white enamel fuselage and a shiny red belly. The wings and tail are also two-toned. White, with red control surfaces. The high wings are set far back on the sleek, pointed airframe. This, and the T-tailed empennage, make the airplane look like an arrow already in flight.

The Dash-8 is clean and spotless. COBRA spares no expense on its equipment.

"Everybody out," I say. "Let's start boarding. Powell, get on the cargo bed. The PKM is yours."

"Roger that."

I haul Tombaye from the cab and stand him up against the right fender. The civilians dismount the truck and gather on the tarmac. Cecile and Enwright take special care of the wounded. Carol Grady helps the man with the shattered clavicle. Powell climbs onto the sandbagged cargo bed and crouches next to the PKM.

Tombaye is staring at Cecile, his gaze inscrutable.

Ducasse is staring at Tombaye with ill-concealed distaste.

The five-ton carrying the seventeen cadre accelerates with a roar. It pulls around and stops in front of the Dash-8. Reflexively, I clench my fist in Tombaye's shirt and slam him against the truck. "What is this?"

"I assume you will take me with you to the airplane. Release me when you are all on board. What is there to keep you from shooting me then? I don't trust your word."

"You're going to have to." I press the muzzle of the Mark 23 against his forehead. "Tell them to move, or I'll kill you now."

"No. Go ahead and kill me. Then we all die."

"Can't you see he's mad," Ducasse says. "He doesn't care if you kill him."

"Nobody wants to die, Father. Especially someone who thinks he's damned."

Bröer is holding Cecile. Faces ashen, they stare at us.

"You offered me a deal," Tombaye says. "My life for an airplane. That is satisfactory, but I wish to amend the agreement."

I want to pull the trigger. Blow this eunuch's brains all over the truck.

"I require collateral," Tombaye says. "One of your people to be held by my men until you are ready to leave. You can have that person back when I am released."

Grady steps forward. "I'll do it, Breed. He's got no reason to hold me after you let him go."

The rancher may be the best man among us. "Alright." I hold up the radio for Tombaye. "Grady will go with your men in their truck. Move all your men to the administration building. When we're ready to roll, I will let you walk to them, and they will let Grady walk to us. You pass each other in the middle."

Tombaye cracks a sly smile. "Breed, you have a deal."

I hold the radio for Tombaye, and he gives instructions in Arabic.

Grady hands the Winchester to his wife and walks to the cadre standing by their five-ton.

"Now get them to move the damn truck."

Tombaye speaks into the squad radio. The half-beard is sitting in the cab of their five-ton, radio to his ear. They pull Grady onto the cargo bed. Throw the truck into reverse and back all the way to the administration building.

I signal Cecile and Bröer. "Get the sergeant to roll the boarding steps to the door. Bröer, crank 'er up. Cecile, you and Enwright get them aboard."

Carol Grady steps to my side. "I'm not leaving without him, Breed."

"We'll get him back."

Tombaye surveys the strip with a critical eye. Calculates his chances.

From the cargo bed of our five-ton, Powell snaps his fingers. "Breed."

I look up. Long rows of Umbali have formed next to the administration building. Bare-chested, pectoral muscles oiled and gleaming. They grip their lances in their right hands with the butts on the ground. Over their shoulders, their machetes are carried in leather scabbards. There are hundreds of them. Perfectly aligned. A military formation.

Powell drums his fingers on the receiver of the PKM.

"Can you control those Umbali?" I ask Tombaye.

"Of course," Tombaye says. "Most of the time."

My eyes sweep the Dash-8. Civilians are shuffling

aboard. The older children are helping the adults. The adults are moving as in a dream.

Bröer's visible in the cockpit, hunched over the controls. He's going through a checklist. Flying one kind of plane doesn't necessarily mean a pilot can fly another. Is there enough commonality between the Dash-8 and the planes Bröer has flown?

I can't do anything about it. You don't go to war with the army you want, you go to war with the army you have. I wanted a pilot, and there he is. Rijk Bröer, a half-crippled, alcoholic former mercenary.

What did I say to Cecile? *You either believe in him, or you don't.*

I focus my attention on what I'm good at.

There's a whine, and the Dash-8's left propeller starts to turn. Slowly at first, then faster. The noise from the left engine rises to a throaty roar, then the right propeller starts to turn. Bröer looks down at the controls, then at each of the spinning props.

Bröer's eyes meet mine, and his face breaks into a grin. He flashes me a thumbs-up.

The civilians have boarded. Carol Grady stands by me, staring across the tarmac. Troy Grady is standing next to the tailgate of the cadre's five-ton. Behind him stands the half-beard, Tombaye's second-in-command.

Cecile stands at the door of the airplane, staring at me and Tombaye. Her hair flutters wild in the prop wash. Tombaye turns his head to look at her. There's a gleam in his eye I don't like.

I want this done.

"Get on the plane," I tell Carol Grady. "There's nothing more you can do here."

The feisty woman drags her gaze away from the figure of her husband. Walks toward the plane. When she reaches the door, Cecile helps her aboard.

That leaves me, Grady, Powell and Tombaye on the tarmac.

Tombaye stares at Cecile.

"I lost her love," he says.

I'm trying to assess the tactical situation. Normally, I'd say this man's emotional state is an annoyance. In this case, it's decisive.

"No," I tell him. "You always had it. You lost the will to *return* it."

Tombaye's face tightens.

"Let's get on with it." I hold the radio out to him. "Tell them to send Grady over."

"Untie my hands."

I loosen the belt that binds Tombaye's wrists. Whip it off. He takes the radio and speaks into it. Hands it back to me.

Half-beard pushes Grady forward.

Tombaye steps away from me.

Bröer tests the rudder and other control surfaces. The Dash-8 looks like a bird wagging its feathers, preparing to fly. The pilot adds power, and the plane starts to strain against its brakes.

Grady and Tombaye walk toward each other.

Powell and I exchange glances.

Three faces in the door. Cecile, Carol Grady, and the French sergeant, his 416 ready.

Tombaye and Grady meet at the center of the tarmac. Tombaye looks back at Cecile, a long, hard stare. His face is a taut mask in the white floodlights.

In that instant, I know what he's going to do. "Son of a bitch."

Marien Tombaye runs. If he can reach the safety of his cadre, they'll be free to block the plane.

"Grady! Run for it!"

I drop to one knee, raise my AK-74. Take a breath, fire three single shots. One hits Tombaye to the left of his spine, spins the scarecrow around. That shot probably blew out his heart. The next two rounds make sure. They punch into his sternum and knock him to the ground. Shining in the floodlights, a gob of bloody phlegm spurts from his mouth.

Grady runs like a bull. The big man is neither fast nor agile.

The cadre start shooting. Their five-ton lurches forward.

Powell gets behind the PKM and tears into the enemy five-ton with aimed machine-gun fire. The front windshield explodes into a spray of shattered glass. The driver jerks, and the truck slews to a stop.

Grady is hit in the leg and goes down. Carol Grady screams.

I throw myself forward, sprint to the wounded man.

Powell traverses the PKM, turns it on the cadre. They dive to the ground or break for cover.

I reach Grady. He stretches an arm out to me. I bend, and he throws it over my shoulder. Help him to his feet. We struggle toward the Dash-8. "Come on, you lazy bastard."

Grady's dragging his left leg. We're ten yards from the plane. Bröer is shouting something, but he's behind the cockpit windshield and I can't hear him. The propellers are spinning up to maximum revolutions. Bullets from the cadre snap past us. Sparks flicker against the Dash-8's fuselage. Powell traverses the PKM, forces the cadre down.

Reach the door. Thrust Grady into the arms of his wife and the French sergeant. They haul him aboard.

From behind me, a roar of sound rises above the Dash-8's turboprops. Powell's PKM chatters continuously. The best way to use a PKM is to fire short bursts, correct your fire, and fire again. Powell's clamped his finger on the trigger. I bring up my AK-74 as I turn.

Umbali are charging the plane. Hundreds of them. Powell rakes them with the PKM. The men in the first rank go down like tenpins. I drop to one knee, flick the AK-74 to full automatic, and open fire.

The PKM's belt runs dry. Powell vaults the side of the five-ton, hits the ground, and sprints for the plane.

Cadre are still firing. Some are careful to avoid hitting Umbali. Others don't care and shoot indiscriminately. As Umbali continue to charge, some are shot from in front and behind.

A bullet slams into Powell's right shoulder blade and explodes from high on his chest. He gasps and tumbles on the tarmac. Struggles to his feet.

"Come on!" I yell.

The sergeant and I continue to fire. Powell hobbles toward us, blood soaking his shirt. He falls against me, and I push him up through the boarding door. Father Ducasse and the sergeant haul him in.

I turn and empty the AK-74's magazine into charging Umbali. They're hurling their lances. Bröer's starting to roll out the aircraft. I lunge for the door. Grasp Cecile's hand. The sergeant grabs me by the back of my ammunition vest. They get me half in the plane. My legs dangle as Bröer races across the runway. Ducasse seizes my left arm and heaves.

The three of them haul me all the way in. I flop onto the floor like a landed fish.

"*Allons-y!*" Ducasse and the sergeant are yelling at Bröer.

I twist on my side. Powell is lying on his back, staring at the ceiling. Cecile is squeezing my hand. "Help Powell," I say. Cecile lets go.

Bröer accelerates to rotation velocity and the Dash-8's nose lifts. I lever myself up on one elbow. Grady and Powell are lying next to each other. Cecile has her medical bag open and is working on them. Grady's leg wound does not look critical. The bullet took a lot of meat off the outside of his thigh, but it missed the femoral artery. The bullet in Powell's back went straight through—I can see the exit wound. No idea what organs it clipped on the way.

The Dash-8 lifts off. There's a mechanical hum as Bröer raises the landing gear.

Cecile is opening Powell's ammunition vest.

"It's a shoulder wound," Cecile says. "The bullet shattered his scapula, deflected upwards, exited his right chest."

"Lungs?"

"Intact."

I get to my feet. Wind is howling through the open door. "Let's get that closed," I tell the sergeant.

Make my way forward to the cockpit. I pass Oren Wolfe, who stares up at me with nothing to say. I've decided he's been an honest idiot. It's not like the State Department sends the cream of their crop to Wambesa.

I open the cockpit door and squeeze in behind the pilot. His face is lit by the glow of the instruments. The sky outside is surprisingly bright, an ocean of stars. Brighter than the dark African landscape below.

"I'm proud of you," I tell Bröer.

"That's a lot, coming from you, mate." Bröer gestures with one hand. "Make yourself comfortable."

I lever myself into the copilot's seat.

"Do you know how to use a radio?" he asks.

"Yes."

"When the time comes, I could use your help."

"Where are we going?"

"We've got the fuel to make Lagos," Bröer says. "Nigeria has a good English history and modern medical facilities. I don't think much of 'la Francafríque' will be stable after what happened today."

"Are you alright?"

"Yes, Breed. I am alright." Bröer turns to me and smiles. "And I have not been alright for a long time."

I close my eyes and lean back in the copilot's seat. For the first time in twelve hours, I allow myself to relax.

20

SUNDAY, 0700 HRS - LAGOS, NIGERIA

I have seen some horrible hospital waiting rooms, particularly in the third world. This hospital in Lagos is very good. I find myself a place to sit. Cecile is speaking with doctors who are working on our wounded. Exhausted and short of sleep, I take out my phone and call Stein.

"Breed." Stein sounds glad to hear from me. "You made it out."

"Yes, we did. Incredibly, we didn't lose any of the civilians."

"How did Tombaye die?"

I lift an eyebrow. "You're very well informed, Stein."

"That's my job. How did he die?"

"He tried to renege on a deal, so I shot him."

"Why did he try to renege?"

"I'm not a mind reader, Stein. Do you want me to guess? Tombaye gave in to *hate*. Killing us all was more important to him than Wambesa."

"That's a lot of hate."

"Tombaye had a lot to hate about. Let's get back to what's really important. State told you Tombaye was dead, didn't they?"

"What if they did?"

"How did *State* know?"

Stein hesitates. "State was contacted by Dawud Haddad. He's Tombaye's second-in-command. He is in conversations with us and the French. He said Tombaye died heroically in combat. Haddad is in command of the Wambesa revolutionary army and will be conducting all negotiations."

"Tombaye died running away. I put three bullets in him."

"He'll remain a hero of the revolution."

"I'm sure they'll erect a fine statue in the Vieux Carré. Stein, the Russians didn't finance Tombaye. Who did?"

"How do *you* know the Russians didn't finance Tombaye?"

"He told me. Not in so many words, but he said enough. And I put a few other data points together."

"Like what?"

"Everything was too perfect. They served it up on a plate —Russian weapons, Russian explosives, Russian techniques. When I broke in on Tombaye, his personal weapon was Russian. You and I both know that's not how a covert operation is run. At the Lokola border, the Wagner officer helped us. He wouldn't have done that if he'd been briefed on a coup. But you provided the most important clue."

"What was that?"

"State told you Tombaye was in Wambesa. The consul general, State's most senior executive in Wambesa, didn't know because they didn't tell *him*."

I count five seconds of silence on the phone.

"Stein, *we* financed Tombaye, didn't we?"

"The *State Department* financed Tombaye. It was *their* operation."

"But *you* sat in on the meetings."

"We're a corporation, Breed. The Company is *always* at the table."

And Stein is a senior executive of the Company.

"How was Tombaye recruited?"

"We have profiles on all the top al-Qaeda fighters. When State decided to put Wambesa in play, they asked the company if we knew anybody they could use. As it happened, Ground Branch knew Tombaye was in Syria. Tombaye and al-Qaeda were fighting to overthrow the Assad regime."

"Of course, that made them our allies." Can't keep the sneer from my voice. I hate the duplicitous nature of Ground Branch operations in the Middle East. Al-Qaeda killed three thousand Americans at the World Trade Center. I will never consider al-Qaeda our ally, no matter how much we share a desire to remove Assad from power.

"We have common interests," Stein says. "Ground Branch introduced the State Department to Tombaye through a double agent by the name of Omar Saleh. From then on, State ran Tombaye. We knew Tombaye was a nationalist. Saleh told Tombaye he would intermediate between Tombaye and the Russians. Russia is active in Syria on the side of Assad. Saleh said Russia would support Tombaye's effort to take over Wambesa."

"Russia, of course, knew nothing about it."

"Nothing at all. Saleh promised Tombaye that Russia would finance his return to Wambesa. Money, weapons, training, everything. It was up to Tombaye to recruit a cadre of fifty men."

"Wasn't Tombaye suspicious?"

"Of course he was suspicious. He was very careful, very discreet. Two things made up his mind. First of all, Tombaye was never devout enough for al-Qaeda. He wasn't a true believer. Second, he wanted to take over Wambesa. He didn't care who supported him so long as he got what he wanted."

"He told me even whores had rules."

"Tombaye was a realist. He suspected the US was providing him with Russian weapons. Didn't care. If we wanted to play games, fine by him. He knew our Kabuki theater was for the benefit of the French. Once he was in power, he would hold a strong hand. Big boys' rules."

Everything makes sense. "So he parted ways with al-Qaeda and quietly left Syria."

"An amicable divorce. Made his way to Algeria and recruited a solid cadre. Many of whom he already knew. Built a training camp, drew up plans. He continued to liaise with Omar Saleh. Ground Branch deposited arms caches in the forest of Mount Wambesa. Explosives, Kornet ATGMs, PKMs. It was all waiting for Tombaye. When he was ready, his cadre infiltrated Wambesa on foot. Melted into the forest."

Stein's describing a textbook covert operation. It all hangs together. "You tried hard to convince me not to go. Thanks for that."

"Yes, I tried. Right up to telling you things I had no business telling you. But one way or another, I was sure you'd make it out."

"Did you know State told Tombaye to kill me and the consul general?"

"No. Their *exact words* were that Americans on the

ground were *expendable*. If Americans on the ground were killed, it would make the Kabuki theater more believable."

"Four Americans are missing—three engineers and Wolfe's wife. All at French Village." I pause to allow my words to sink in. "State's instructions to Tombaye included sending Umbali to kill Americans. He sent Umbali out of their way to kill me, Oren Wolf, and the Gradys. I'm not sure if he had Drue Powell on the list, but I wouldn't be surprised. How did he get my name?"

I'm praying he didn't get it from Stein.

"He got it from COBRA. The French hired Long Rifle, so they knew about you. Powell was consulate staff, so State already knew about him. Powell was good, but you were several cuts above. There was a material risk you'd take a crack at Tombaye. Which you did."

"Flattery will get you nowhere, Stein. Why does Wambesa matter so much to State?"

"The French have been screwing up everywhere. We've been carrying them ever since Dien Bien Phu. Country after country is kicking them out, and the Russians and Chinese are moving in. In Africa, the people *hate* the French. They hate Europeans, period. African politicians are telling European diplomats to fuck off, right to their faces. If this goes on, Africa will become Russian and Chinese."

"What makes us think *we* can do better?"

"We haven't been heavily involved in Africa. If the French get out of the way, we can make a fresh start. We'll reorient our model from aid to investment. Compete directly with the Russians and Chinese."

"That's not the only reason, Stein. There's something else."

"Like what?"

"The COBRA mill was interesting. There were three types of containers in the loading bay. Canvas sacks of cobalt. Gray drums and yellow drums. Ninety percent of the containers were white sacks and gray drums. Equal numbers. Ten percent were in yellow drums. What was in the yellow drums?"

"Does anything get by you?"

"Taking notes is part of my job."

Stein exhales. "Yellowcake, Breed. The yellow drums contain yellowcake."

"What's yellowcake?"

"Crude uranium. Uranium ore is crushed and processed into yellowcake. Yellowcake is then processed into uranium fuel."

The last piece of the puzzle. "Or bombs," I say.

"Much further along the chain. The point is, COBRA's geologists found that Wambesa is rich in uranium. Mount Wambesa is all pitchblende, uranium ore. The whole mountain range covering the southern two-thirds of Wambesa is pitchblende. The drums of yellowcake are test product. COBRA was spinning up to open uranium mining operations."

"Why are we so interested in French uranium?"

Stein allows herself to sound smug. "It's not exactly French anymore, is it?"

"I reckon not."

"Uranium is the future, Breed. Cobalt is the past. World demand for cobalt has been overstated. The projections are all predicated on cobalt's use in batteries. The batteries that go into phones, laptops, and electric vehicles—EVs. But EV demand has been overstated. They don't hold a charge in cold weather. They don't have the range of fossil-fuel cars.

Demand for EVs is falling off. US dealerships can't *give* EVs away. EV demand is only holding up where governments *force* people to buy them. The most economical energy sources remain fossil fuels and uranium. Nuclear power is the cheapest of all.

"The world's largest reserves of uranium are in Kazakhstan. That's in the Russian orbit. We need to control our own reserves. That means Wambesa."

"How do we get in?"

"Wambesa will never accept the French. Dawud Haddad will lead an interim military government."

"Dawud Haddad is not from Wambesa."

"No, he's Algerian. Tombaye's reputation and implicit endorsement will carry him long enough. He will lead an interim military regime and shepherd the country to free elections. We'll deal directly with the new government."

"Which we will control."

"Oh, don't be a cynic. They'll work with us because we'll treat them fairly. We'll pay them hefty royalties. Not like the French, who have exploited them for a hundred and fifty years."

"Stein, if the French had treated them fairly, this massacre would never have happened. The exploitation of the population is beyond belief. The managers of that mine didn't give a shit."

"We'll do better."

"I hope so." I feel tired. Will anything change? "Those royalty dollars need to find their way to the people. Tombaye's cadre killed President Mumbaye while he was running away... with suitcases full of French cash."

"That will be sorted out," Stein says. "I'll make sure State's proposed economic model is reevaluated."

"I thought Wambesa is State's project."

Cecile steps out of the emergency room and walks toward me. She looks exhausted. I'm sure I look worse.

"State botched the operation," Stein says. "I think Wambesa will be taken away from them."

I have a feeling Wambesa's file will land on Stein's desk. She has a reputation for turning things around. "Have you figured out how to win the war in Ukraine?"

"How could I? I've spent the last twenty-four hours working on Wambesa."

Cecile sits next to me. Gives me a wan smile, takes my hand. We lace our fingers together.

"If you can make a difference, time spent on Wambesa is time better spent." I turn my head to meet Cecile's eyes. "I'm going to spend some time here in Lagos."

"What are you going to do in Lagos?" Stein asks.

Cecile lays her head against my shoulder.

THE END

ACKNOWLEDGMENTS

This novel would not have been possible without the support, encouragement, and guidance of my agent, Ivan Mulcahy, of MMB Creative. I would also like to thank my publishers, Brian Lynch and Garret Ryan of Inkubator Books for seeing the novel's potential. The novel benefitted from the feedback of my writing group and Beta readers. Special thanks go to Alice Latchford, of Inkubator Books, for her editorial input and coordination of the editorial process. Thanks also go to Claire Milto of Inkubator Books for her support in the novel's launch.

If you could spend a moment to write an honest review, no matter how short, I would be extremely grateful. They really do help readers discover my books.

Feel free to contact me at cameron.curtis545@gmail.com. I'd love to hear from you.

ALSO BY CAMERON CURTIS

DANGER CLOSE

(Breed Book #1)

OPEN SEASON

(Breed Book #2)

TARGET DECK

(Breed Book #3)

CLOSE QUARTERS

(Breed Book #4)

BROKEN ARROW

(Breed Book #5)

WHITE SPIDER

(Breed Book #6)

BLACK SUN

(Breed Book #7)

HARD CONTACT

(Breed Book #8)

BLOOD SPORT

(Breed Book #9)